CARE *of* WOODEN FLOORS

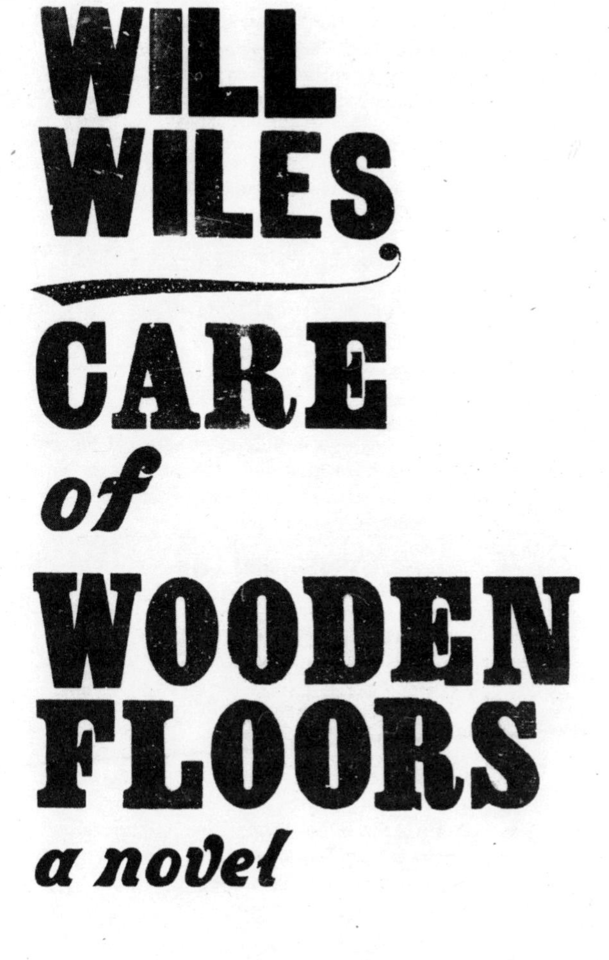

Harper
Press

Harper*Press*
An imprint of HarperCollins*Publishers*
77–85 Fulham Palace Road
Hammersmith, London W6 8JB

www.harpercollins.co.uk

First published by Harper*Press* in 2012
1

A catalogue record for this book
is available from the British Library

HB ISBN 978-0-00-742443-6
TPB ISBN 978-0-00-743126-7

Set in Celeste with Agenda display by
G&M Designs Limited, Raunds, Northamptonshire

Printed and bound in Great Britain by
Clays Ltd, St Ives plc

For Dan Hemingway (1972–1991)

DAY ONE

People are afraid of flying. I've never understood that. It's a most remarkable experience; yes, even in a cramped seat in a noisy compartment on a three-hour budget flight with no food. You are still in the air. You are Above. It is extraordinary in the most direct and apt way; you are outside the ordinary. The ordinary is pushed down, rendered for a score of minutes into a mosaic of green and brown and mercury, and then you're with the clouds.

There has never been a better time to be alive, and that is not simply thanks to penicillin, flush toilets and central heating, it's because now we can look down on the clouds. Clouds are utterly faithful to their promise of ethereal beauty. When I was very young, I imagined clouds to be warm and soft to the touch, because I knew they were water, and so therefore they must be steam because that's what they looked like, and steam was warm. Perfect logic. Of course, they are not warm, but in the air-conditioned cylinder of your midweek commercial flight, they fulfil their old promise because they are awash with sunlight – no matter the daytime weather beneath, the cloud tops must be exposed to the sun, that is their guarantee, that is their tiny miracle.

Renaissance artists must have felt this love of clouds, and appreciation of their natural splendour, and having always felt separated from their true glory were moved to populate them with putti and seraphim; so perfect was their approximation of the wonderfulness of being above cloud level that to be there now is to expect these heavenly denizens to be there with you. But they are not. You are alone above a landscape that is forever changing, forever unique, forever special for you; rolling cirrus meadows and boiling mountaintops across unfathomed distance. You are an explorer and this is your new-found land.

But with all this beauty and isolation there is also an obligation – you must return, you must descend, back to the imperfect.

The landing, airport, passport control, baggage reclaim and taxi are all a compressed wedge of brown neon, sweat and stress in my mind. It was one of those dreadful moments when it occurs that the only things connecting you to who you are, what you are, where you come from, and where you are going, are a little purple-bound book ('Her Britannic Majesty's Secretary of State requests and requires ...') and an address scribbled on a scrap of paper torn from a spiral-bound notepad. The notepad itself is in a holdall that may at some stage, *please* God, appear on a conveyor belt still basically intact. It contains the remaining evidence of Who You Are. Who I am. The address, *unless* it has been incorrectly taken down – was it 70 or 17? – corresponds to an apartment building in a completely unfamiliar foreign city some thirty kilometres from this airport, and the taxi rank is the sinew that links me to it – shelter, a promise of food and comfort – *unless* I am cheated or robbed or murdered, or some baroque combination of those three. These things happen in foreign cities, I had been told, and over the warmth of dinner party conversation I had tried to smile the smile of the seasoned traveller as various lurid myths and truths were recounted. I was no seasoned traveller.

But there were no hitches, and none of the *unless*es happened and the key fitted the lock and I found myself standing at the threshold of Oskar's flat, getting a good look at it for the first time.

> *Thanks so much for this; you're a real friend for helping out. I don't feel comfortable leaving the flat for so long, not with the cats ... you'll like it, it's a nice flat ...*

The flat, 17, was on the second floor of a six-storey, leaden, inter-war, vaguely Moderne block near the city centre, on a street stacked rigid with similarly bulky buildings that was prominent in the mental map of the taxi driver. And it *was* a nice flat.

At university, I remembered, Oskar had travelled under a thundercloud of good taste. Static permanently brewed around him, building readiness to send down a lightning bolt of scornful condemnation in the direction of anything cheap, or badly made, or, sin of sins, vulgar. As the bolt streaked towards its target, his upper lip would pitch into a perfect, practised sneer, a neat capital A for A*ppalling*.

The flat indicated that he had transferred this ideology to his home life here.

A wide hallway stretched from Oskar's front door towards a south-facing living area. The hall was light and airy, with pale wooden floors and icy white walls. Two dark wooden doors were set into the wall to the right, like dominos on a bedspread, one halfway down, and the other near the far end. To the left was evidence of a refurbishment under Oskar's direction: a long glass partition screening a large kitchen and dining area from the hallway. At its end, the hall opened out into the living area, which was demarcated by a single step down. The pale wooden flooring stretched to every corner of the flat, and the glass partition, which I assumed had replaced a non-supporting wall, evenly rinsed the space with the crystalline light entering through the generous south-facing picture windows that took up the far wall of the living space.

Taste and money had met in the crucible of this space and sublimed. The wood, steel and glass were the alchemical solids formed by the reaction.

Closing the front door behind me with a satisfying clunk of weight and security, I walked down the hall. The living room – Area? Space? – centred on a sofa and two armchairs, all boxy black leather and chrome, the design of a dead Swiss architect. The east wall was one large bookcase, mostly filled with books but also seasoned with some *objets*. The kitchen was all aluminium and steel. Everything must have been imported, I thought, considering the home-grown stuff I had seen at the airport. There was a table in the kitchen with three chairs. How often did Oskar entertain? At university, he had been a good but infrequent host. He preferred restaurants that we loan rangers were stretched to afford. The kitchen looked more like a showpiece from a designer's catalogue than a work area. Everything, everywhere, was impeccably tidy. There was a jar of carefully arranged twigs on the kitchen table and another on the glass coffee table, which also sported a hotel-style fan of magazines – *New Yorker, Time, Economist* (more than a month old), *Gramophone.* There were more twigs and a four-day-old *International Herald Tribune* on a small table under the middle of the three picture windows.

In a gesture that was, I suppose, proprietorial, I put my hands on my hips and exhaled, a sigh of relief at arrival and also admiration. It is intensely pleasing when a reality conforms so exactly to expectation, and when a man conforms so exactly to type. This was almost exactly how I had imagined Oskar's apartment to be – it was the obvious habitat for the mind I knew. Multilingual Oskar. Oskar, who appreciated design and modernity and expensive, extravagant simplicity. The apartment's spaces were measured in air miles. Its air had arrived in the bubbles in a thousand crates of San Pellegrino. The beautiful wooden floor didn't have nails, it had a manicure. The only thing missing was a piano.

Had I not already known that Oskar was a musician, it would have been easy to tell from the black-and-white photos tastefully mounted in plain glass frames around the walls: Oskar at the piano, Oskar with baton in hand, a younger Oskar shaking hands with an older man I didn't recognise, Oskar receiving an award, Oskar ... Oskar with me. Four of us, at university, not long before graduation. Thicker, darker hair, no bellies. Another me. I tried to remember the occasion where the photo had been taken. It was gone.

And ... no photos of Oskar's wife. And no piano. No awards. A mystery.

The first door I tried – the one nearest the picture windows – resolved part of this mystery. The flat was in the corner of its building, and the room I entered occupied the corner of the flat. Two more south-facing windows continued the rank started in the main area, and the western wall had one as well, so the light that articulated every corner and dust mote – even the dust motes looked neat, their flight paths as checked and regulated as the red-eye from Tehran coming into LAX – frosted the surface of the grand piano so that the black lacquer was dental-advert white. A piano, in the corner of the corner of the corner, pushed to the outermost reaches of the flat. Any further out, it would be on the pavement by the crossroads outside. Unlike the kitchen, this room had an aura of useful industry. One wall was filled with shelves, and those were stacked with a regimented clutter of box files, CDs, vinyl, cassette tapes, racks of sheet music, framed certificates, (more) photographs, citations, degrees, honours and awards. A life abridged. Under the nearer of the two south-facing windows was a writing desk with its leather-cornered blotter, pots of pens and pencils, and two stacks of paper – one plain, one ruled for musical notation. Next to the desk was a stack hi-fi that looked like the product of an abandoned Scandinavian space programme.

While here, in this open-ended episode of enforced idleness, I wanted to write. In London I had been helplessly, prowlingly blocked, and the four magnolia walls of my Clapham basement flat had shut me up. Without those walls, what could stop me? Could a full book be turned out in the three-weeks-to-a-month I expected to be here? Perhaps the breakthrough would stay with me when I returned. If I could write anywhere, I figured, it would be here. Stewing in London, I often fantasised about the ideal setting for creativity, and it always looked much like the room I now stood in. This place seemed impregnated with Oskar's talent and productivity. It would be perfect. I could imagine short stories, plays, perhaps even the start of a novel here. Clamped to the left-hand edge of the desk was one of those turn-handle pencil sharpeners that I associated with school. Directly underneath this sharpener was a steel bin. I peered into the bin, and was rewarded with the sight of – shocking lapse! – some pencil shavings and a discarded tram timetable. Rubbish. Debris, even, just casually left there for anyone to see. Oskar was plainly slipping. For a borderline obsessive-compulsive like him ... it was like catching Brian Sewell at a Britney Spears concert.

As if on cue, prompted by the timetable, a tram rumbled past in the street below. Hadn't Oskar written a piece called *Variations on Tram Timetables*? Pleased with my memory, I wandered over to the piano, flipping open the lid. This action caused a slip of paper to waft out and describe a swooping arabesque descent to the floor. I scooped it up and read it. Oskar had written on it in a prickly, pointy, fussy hand:

Please do NOT play with the piano.

That would be easy to arrange as I could not play the piano. I ran my fingertips gently, respectfully, over the surface of the keys. They were a nicotiny white and a simplistic black that defied adjectives. Brown-blue-*black*-black. But that's not quite it. I tinkled the same two high notes that musical philistines always tinkle when they are driven to fiddle with piano keys.

Box files, all labelled in Oskar's spiky black hand – *Solo #2, Comp '00–'02, Halle Aug '01, Misc '04,* Each one was stuffed ... no, stuffed is the wrong word. Each one had string-bound bundles of papers, newspaper clippings, folders, sheet music, financial documents, travel details and hotel bills meticulously *arranged* in it, as one would arrange a formal vase of flowers, stiffly and conscientiously. Oskar the organised. Oskar the organised musician.

Photos, Oskar with people I didn't recognise, bow ties, penguin suits.

I remembered that my bags were still by the front door and that I had unpacking to do. The door I hadn't tried yet had to be the bedroom. Opening it was a complex action involving holding my holdall with my left hand, hanging my flight bag from the ring and little finger of my right, and turning the knob with the remaining two fingers and thumb.

There is something primal in the sound of claws against the ground moving towards you, and an animal jumping. It fires something back in the lizard root of the brain, springs the safety catches off, triggering a reaction designed for survival and still operational despite being broadly unneeded; a working Betamax video recorder in the animal mind. Still it wired out its useless message like an aggressive lout shouting a drinks order at a defenceless gland – *A pint of adrenalin, and make it snappy, bitch.* I tensed involuntarily as two furry streaks cannoned through my legs towards the living room, two irresistible vectors of feline purpose. Late and unbidden, my Cro-Magnon fear manifested itself as a foolish and embarrassed sprinkling of sweat.

Ah, I thought, *the cats.* Oskar had mentioned cats, and here they were, or rather there they were, wherever they had gone. Afraid of cats! But not afraid, simply surprised and caught off balance, a simple shock. *And besides,* I thought, appealing to an altogether more recent section of the brain, *it's not as if anyone saw me being surprised by them.*

So that's all right then.

I could ingratiate myself with them later. For now, I walked into the bedroom and dropped my bags by the white linen of the large double bed. There was less to see here; the dominant features were the bed, an armchair and a large standing cupboard. The armchair was plain wicker with an off-white cushion, an item that seemed to exist solely for the purpose of injecting an air of homely domesticity into a room that was otherwise as coldly modern as the principal living area. It was one of those chairs that had a sad aura of futility, a regret that it had been designed to be sat in and never was, and had often suffered the indignity of simply being a prop to drape clothes over.

Furniture is like that. Used and enjoyed as intended, it absorbs that experience and exudes it back into the atmosphere, but if simply bought for effect and left to languish in a corner, it vibrates with melancholy. Furnishings in museums ('DO NOT SIT IN THIS SEAT') are as unspeakably tragic as the unvisited inmates of old folk's homes. The untuned violins and hardback books used to bring 'character' to postwar suburban pubs crouch uncomfortably in their imposed roles like caged pumas at the zoo. The stately kitchen that is never or rarely used to bring forth lavish feasts for appreciative audiences turns inward and cold. Like the kitchen here, I thought.

And there was a further indicator of this strange psychology of material goods in the bedroom; flanking the bed were two small tables, and whereas the one nearer the windows bore a light, three stacked books, a small notepad and a small stone statuette, the other was empty but for an identical light. So it was clear which side Oskar slept on and which had been taken, until recently, by his wife.

These musings were not a sign of growing gloom; far from it. My smile was broad and growing broader. I had taken up Oskar's invitation and come here to his city in order to write and to be inspired, and I was thrilled –

frankly, a sensation close to exhilaration – that in such a short space of time in unfamiliar surroundings I was already feeling more creative and the insights into detail were coming with the frequency they did. This euphoric state was given more lift by my next discovery. The bedroom's proportions demanded three picture windows, but there were only two and the place of the central set was taken by French windows that opened onto a narrow concrete balcony overlooking the street. As soon as I noticed this, I crossed the room to investigate. The window opened easily, letting in a blast of unruly city air and noise, and I stepped out.

Below, two storeys down, the flagstones and cobbles of the street throbbed with the constant effort of traffic. Another tram passed, shuddering and clanging as it nosed through a melee of battered and tubercular cars from a medley of unfamiliar marques: Ladas and Dacias and Oltcits. The few users of the broad imperial pavements moved with huddled and private purpose to alien, unknowable goals. Opposite was another apartment block, baroque, so grey it seemed moulded from a compression of ashes. Indeed, the four streets pushing away from the crossroads were mainly composed of heavy grey prewar buildings, apart from a few obviously more recent municipal-modern blocks perhaps intended to fill half-century-old bomb wounds or part of an ill-advised 1960s attempt at redevelopment. Washing hung drying from lines between balconies, potted plants spilled colour on sills and through railings, wallpaper in four dozen different styles could be spied through windows.

This exotic chequerboard of domesticity was enthralling after the cold touch of Oskar's Good Taste and Clean Lines.

Once again, I travelled in my mind's eye back to those walls that defined my space in Clapham. Walls dented by chair backs and grimed by the touch of human hand and hair. Carpets cratered by careless smokers at drunken parties and spotted with spilled red wine. A topology of blemishes and taints from myriad unknown miscreants. A slow-motion and inevitable despoliation by scores of hands. And did I notice it? No. These grazes sank into the patina of the background, the grain of my life. I had signed an armistice with entropy, come to terms. I let it happen. It was a rented flat – landlords expect wear and tear, and I supplied it.

But how did Oskar see it? He owned this place, had done for years, and the manner in which he kept it ...

In fact, I knew how Oskar would feel about it. He had not surrendered. He would not let these details sink into the background. He had fought entropy to a standstill and forced it to accept *his* terms.

I felt a sudden and foolish urge to declare my presence from the balcony, state that I had arrived, and that I would be staying.

Of course, Oskar had left a careful list of instructions on the dining table. Oskar did not do chaos. He did not do disorganisation. He did not do disorder. At university, we had a bad joke about him:

Q: Where does Oskar go on holiday?
A: The Coaster del Sol.

Ha, ha. This was a direct reference to Oskar's habit – treated with bafflement, ridicule and mild annoyance by the other undergraduates – of swooping down with a coaster whenever it looked as though a drink served by him in his rooms might come in contact with a surface. The crowning insanity of this was that the surfaces came with the room, were supplied by the college, and were already heavily pitted and scarred by decades of use by less conscientious members of the intellectual cream of the nation's youth. He even did it with beer mats in *pubs*.

The flat was quiet, and the cats – both a mixture of black and white – were grooming themselves on the sofa. I needed noise and stimulation before sitting down to read Oskar's instructions, so I returned to the study, propped the door open and tried to pick a CD.

There was no danger of being denied choice: the CDs must have numbered in four figures. As might be expected, the vast majority were yellow- and red-spined classical. Not being very familiar with classical music – its codes and sigils, the K341s and scherzos were a strange and threatening language to me – I hunted for the familiar, the recent. After a few moments I found, in a discreet and embarrassed corner of a shelf, Oskar's half-dozen popular discs: David Bowie, Simon and Garfunkel, Queen, the Kinks, and a 'Best of' the Velvet Underground, which I plucked and slotted into the hi-fi. 'Sunday Morning' in Lou Reed's wistful tones filled the strange flat in the distant city. I calmed.

Four A4 pages, closely filled with Oskar's script, anchored by a bottle of red wine. I read:

My old friend,

Again, thank you for your help in what is sadly such a difficult time for me. The flat is not large and what I need from you not great, it is mainly a business of knowing that there is a trusted soul in situ and that I need fear no break-ins or fire. As I sincerely hope you are aware, I would gladly repay this favour for you at any time.

First, let me address the issue of my friends the cats. They are called Shossy and Stravvy. They are fond of their activities and often very fast and busy, but they are good souls and happy to be picked up and very happy to be stroked. Please do this, it is good for everyone I think! But they must be fed and their hygiene must be attended. I have left tins of their favourite food, and their bowls, and the bag with their litter, and their tray, in the little room by the kitchen, with the clothes washing machine. They need half a tin each in the morning and the same in the evening, with a sprinkling of their biscuits, which are also in the cupboard with the food. Please remove their doings every day; there is a scoop for this not very nice job! Every week, change the litter.

When you go to bed, please shut them out of the front door, and in the mornings, you will find them back and hungry, ready for their breakfast! They are allowed on the bed for their sleep BUT NOT THE SOFA or the chairs in the living room.

Shit. I looked across at the sofa. The cats were still happily sprawled there, enjoying their illicit activity. Not a good start. Well, they were meant to be 'fond of their activities'. I broke off reading to banish them from the forbidden zone, watched them saunter sulkily back into the bedroom, then returned to the note.

> Please make sure that the windows and the front door are securely locked if you leave the flat and when you go to bed. I have written down some numbers of plumbers and other emergency people: ...

I started to skim. Emergency numbers, location of spare keys, the nearest pharmacies, supermarkets and so on. A few details about the city.

> While you're here, do make an effort to see something at the Philharmonic. They are very good, and I do not say that simply because of my connection with them! Their summer season has now begun and I would love to think that although I cannot be there to enjoy it myself, it might give you some pleasure.
>
> Oh, and finally what is perhaps the most important thing since the cats are able to take care of themselves and will tell you if they are in need of something: PLEASE, YOU MUST TAKE CARE OF THE WOODEN FLOORS. They are French oak and cost me a great deal when I replaced the old floor, and they must be treated like the finest piece of furniture in the flat, apart from the piano of course.

DO NOT put any drinks on them without a coaster.

ALWAYS wipe your feet before entering the flat, and take off your shoes when inside.

If anything should spill, you MUST wipe it up AT ONCE!!! so that it does not stain the wood. Be VERY CAREFUL. But if there is an accident (!), then there is a book on the architecture shelf that might help you. CALL ME if something happens.

The cleaner calls twice a week (you do not have to pay, it is a service of the building, so do not worry).

I do not know how long I will be in Los Angeles, no one will tell me, and perhaps they do not know. But I think I will be safe to return after about three weeks, and with any luck for me, less than that. I will telephone you at times and let you know how things are going.

And again my thanks. The wine is for you. I hope to see you soon.

Your old friend,

OSKAR

I stared at the note for a brief time after reading through it, to see if any deeper meaning became obvious. Was a note of this length, in this sort of detail, normal? Normal for Oskar, I supposed. How he must hate to leave his flat like this. 'A trusted soul' he had written. Really? Not so trusted that I could escape being micromanaged by notes, it seemed. So clean, so ordered. I thought of the pencil shavings in the wastepaper basket. Oskar's neat-freakery only made minuscule 'lapses' like that more noticeable. He had the assistance of a cleaner, of course. But how thorough was the cleaner? London was full of Eastern European women working as domestic cleaners, but I had no idea if they did a good job. Besides, did we get their 'A-team' or their 'B-team'? Did the best and the brightest cleaners head west? Or only the ones who could not cut the duster in their own countries?

The bookshelves that covered one wall of the room drew my eye. Bookshelves are a devil to keep clean – dust gathers on top of the books with surprising rapidity, and it is difficult and tiresome to thoroughly clean those areas. I strolled over to get a closer look. I also wanted to find a guidebook that would help me navigate this city, something better than the inadequate volume I had brought with me. I doubted I would find one, because I had nothing similar about London back at my flat. But perhaps.

Like the rest of the flat, Oskar's books were beautiful and carefully arranged. They were organised first by category, and then by size. At least four languages were present, with German and French accompanying English and Oskar's mother tongue. There was a large number of paving-slab-sized glossy, expensive books of art and photography and 'design classics'. The art emphasised the 'modern' and the difficult -ists, constructivists, vorticists, futurists; Diane Arbus and Nan Goldin; and a blast of warmth and light from volumes on Warhol and Lichtenstein, the sort of art that did not make me so uncomfortable. There was architecture, of course, again characteristically modern: Le Corbusier and Mies, Richard Neutra and Herzog & de Meuron. The Neutra, like the Lichtenstein, suggested a Californian hand here. Did

Oskar's wife have any input when it came to the content of the bookshelves? I doubted it. The mixing of the bookshelves in a relationship is a gesture of vast, almost foolhardy, mutual trust, and Oskar wasn't able to live on the same continent as his wife, let alone jumble up the contents of his library with hers. Just thinking of the idea made me picture him wincing. But there did not seem to be even a shelf for her – none of the books I imagined she'd read, auction catalogues and law journals, blockbusters for those interminable flights across the world, West-Coast self-help, yard after yard of management 'bibles' by 'gurus' – business secrets, the main habits of monied sociopaths, the utterings of successful salesmen and speculators. But not an inch of them was to be seen. Her mind had not established the tiniest beach-head in Oskar's mental world. Who cheesed her move? The rest of the bookshelf was filled with the typical and the expected. Shelf after shelf of the books I associated with Oskar. There were a variety of novels and histories, broadly twentieth-century classics: Koestler, Camus, Salinger, Solzhenitsyn. History, cultural history, books about World War II and the Nazis and the Soviet Union, *Schindler's Ark*, modern politics with an emphasis on America, Russia and Germany, stacks of books about music, biographies of composers and musicians. Not a hint of dust, anywhere, so another 'win' for Oskar there. But already it was settling all around me.

One book caught my attention – a big book about Oskar's orchestra, the Philharmonic, in German. It seemed to be a history written in celebration of a very recent anniversary – 150 years of something. I thumbed it open, planning on looking up Oskar's name in the index, and found that a leaflet was slipped into it – a programme for the present concert season. Oskar's photograph smiled out from the page. I grinned at the vanity of it – bookmarking the page with his own photo on it. He was standing beside another man, taller than Oskar, with receding ultra-pale hair revealing a bullet-shaped head. They were wearing the highly formal evening wear that infests classical music, and Oskar's companion was carrying a violin. It was a good photo – a warm smile from Oskar, a pleasure enhanced by its relative rarity. Oskar applied the same rules to interior design and facial expressions: less is more. A smile was a superfluous decorative extravagance; a grin was rococo excess.

There was something written on the concert programme, in Oskar's hand:

Maybe Useful?

'Maybe useful'? Why would he write that on a programme for his own orchestra? No one would know the schedule of performances better than he. Or was the note, and the programme, meant for me? If the programme *was* intended for me, then tucking it into a book like this was an unusual move – especially this book, this page. Unless he knew I would look in this book – but that was unlikely. Or maybe he thought that looking in this book meant that I was interested in the orchestra and therefore might attend a concert? The photograph of Oskar smiled at me. That smile now seemed teasing. Perhaps the leaflet had been meant for someone else (the wife?), or Oskar was in the habit of leaving notes to himself.

Taking out the programme, I closed the book and put it back on the shelf. Odd, odd. Inside, three performances were marked, their dates underlined, with an asterisk next to them in the margin. The season had started three weeks ago, I saw, but the highlighted concerts were all in the next two weeks, as if they were intended for me, suggestions of performances I might enjoy while I was in town, or ones that Oskar particularly wanted me to hear, for some musical reason that was beyond me. The soonest marked concert was two days away.

In a sudden thrill, the entire oddness of the situation, my situation, struck home; Oskar's home. Here, his flat, was the aggregation of his *entire life*; his collected works. And the collected works of Oskar that surrounded me not only displayed the mainstream of his personality, his ordered, taxonomic brain; they also displayed the interstices in that plane of self, the gaps, the discarded bus tickets, the quirks and wrinkles.

Flush with this weird sense of omniscience, I felt a growing need for domesticity, for a small obeisance to the household gods. I wanted to make myself a cup of coffee in order to test the kitchen. Also, I didn't know what time the cats had last been fed. Oskar probably fed them before he left this morning – he had certainly let them back into the flat – but that may have been quite early. They might by now be hungry, and I thought that feeding them would give me a bit of good PR. Aha, they would think, this is a man who knows how to use the tin opener.

But coffee first. The person in this relationship needed sustenance before the animals. Besides, a quick poke through the cupboards would also establish if there was anything tasty-looking for supper, and there was the horrible possibility that Oskar only stocked coffee beans that needed to be ground and percolated and all that tedious rubbish. It was the sort of thing he was capable of, and there was a coffee-maker-percolator thing on the work surface, its gleaming chrome winking impossibility at me. Those twisty detachable wrench-handle-cup parts pointed accusingly.

Thinking along the lines of the ergonomics of the kitchen, I tried the cupboard immediately above the treacherous mercury-shine gadget. The payload – a waft of dried beans and leaves, pressure-packed, freeze-dried, connoisseur-approved, corporation-imported caffeine for a dozen delivery methods – was hit instantly, but also released with that relieving aroma was a slip of paper that, sucked out of the cupboard by the air-pressure difference created when I opened the door, flipped, looped and swayed down to the worktop.

It read, again in Oskar's cramped black hand:

> Please help yourself to all tea and coffee, but if it should run out please replace.

I stared at the note, just the tiniest strip cut from a pad, for a little while. It was thoughtful. It also felt unnecessary, perhaps; it was pedantic. Did he fear I would strip the flat of the materials for making hot drinks, leaving him thirsty

and bereft on his return? Why did he feel another note was needed? The concert programme was still on that table, next to Oskar's instructions, which had seemed to me to be very comprehensive. But then, this was his flat, he above all had very specific ways of going about the business of existing. The sense of Oskar's very recent departure from the flat was a static charge in the air. Here was a man with very clear views on what should happen in his home. He had always been particular.

Perhaps it was appropriate that a composer should make notes. At university, Oskar had littered the staircase we shared with slips of paper, instructions, proscriptions, statements of intent, reminders, invitations and rebukes. In the first week of the first term, a little note appeared on the back of the door of the shared toilet: Please use the air freshener. O. On top of the cistern was a brand-new bottle of air freshener: pine. None of the other toilets had air freshener, but this was the one that Oskar used. He had bought it himself. As it was pinned to the back of the door, I was able to inspect this note at my leisure on scores of occasions. The O was hypnotic – a perfect circle, with no obvious beginning or end.

That was just the start of the notes. The emphasis was generally on the NOT. Please do NOT make so much noise after 1 a.m. Please do NOT leave dirty plates in the sink. On our staircase, eight people shared a kitchen. It was the scene and subject of endless disputes. Oskar was far from the only resident with a retinue of grievances and bugbears, and he was inevitably the most courteous in

settling them. But his clipped, frosty demeanour, the formality of the notes and the pathological neatness of his room put people on the defensive. The others engaged in volcanic screaming matches that were forgotten within hours. They screamed shithead and bitch at each other and went to the pub together that evening. Oskar never lost his temper, never blew up. He was regularly angry, but his anger was as controlled and modulated and systematic as the music he would later write. Similarly, he never erupted into riotous geniality or helpless laughter. I only ever saw him drunk – properly drunk, that is, different-person drunk – on three occasions.

Q: What does Oskar drink?
A: Neat vodka.

Neat. Ha ha. He liked neat vodka at less than zero degrees centigrade – its high alcohol content means that it does not freeze. He bought a bottle, the best the off-licence had to offer, for himself and guests, and had no other place to store it than the freezer compartment of the communal fridge. This was a big purchase for a student, and the bottle monopolised the minuscule compartment, reduced to a letterbox by a thick sleeve of permafrost. The girlfriend of one of our neighbours failed to appreciate that vodka has to be stored at below-zero temperatures, and transferred the bottle to the main fridge when trying to find a berth for half a tub of chocolate ice cream.

Moved from its small and little-used nook and placed in the view of half a dozen thirsty, thirsty students, the bottle fared as you might expect. Most of it disappeared within three nights. Oskar discovered this on the fourth, when he had company. He took this badly, and having established the owner of the ice cream ('Not even someone on this staircase!') restored the vodka to its rightful place – with a note attached, saying Please do NOT put this out of the freezer.

This dispute somehow sparked off an impishness in the others. It became their mission to remove the bottle, drink some of its contents, and leave the depleted vessel in an unusual place. At this point, Oskar and I became friends: he recruited me to help look for the bottle. I was a nonentity to the others – not unpopular, just uninteresting, only there to make up the numbers at parties. My peripheral status made me an asset to Oskar: he knew I was not among the conspirators, and enlisted me to help search for the vodka.

So we searched together. The first time it turned up in the toilet cistern. The second time it was eventually discovered tied to a light fitting in the hallway. The third time we couldn't find it for weeks. We had given it up for lost when Oskar found it. Somehow it had been duct-taped to the underside of his desk. The tiresome repetition of the theft did not enrage Oskar – if anything, he seemed to become calmer every time it happened. A few days after the bottle was returned to the fridge for the fourth time, Oskar knocked on my door and calmly informed me that it had disappeared again. Usually on these occasions he looked grim and disappointed – I often felt that he thought he could actually change the attitude of our peers with his little notes and chilly equanimity, an idea that was patently ridiculous, as I regularly told him – but this day he bore a small smile. I asked him if he wanted help recovering it.

'No,' he said. 'It is mostly urine.'

He raised a supermarket bag; inside was a bottle of Absolut and a bag of supermarket ice. That night was the first time I saw him properly drunk.

Only Oskar could have been certain of producing absolutely clear urine.

Neat urine.

There was, among the various coffee specialties and special teas, a jar of Maxwell House. The kettle throbbed and phlegmed. Milk was in the fridge door. Brown sugar in a bowl on the table. Mugs were on the shelf above the beverage-makings. A spirit of efficiency ruled in the kitchen. It was easy to remember the efficiency and economy of Oskar's music, and easy to imagine the exasperation and frustration of his wife, with her Californian outlook and kitchen that was primarily used as a platform from which endless boxes of take-out cuisine could be eaten. Look into these steel surfaces for as long as you want, you could never make out the blood-orange, blood-transfusion blaze of the Los Angeles dawn. Europe's skies are older than America's; Europe's clouds start over there and by the time they reach here they are tired and ragged from their journey.

Boiling water over granules, a tilt of milk, and I stared into the result. Pale clouds lived and died by an unknowable rhythm under the surface, storms pulsating, growing and shrinking in the atmosphere of a gas giant, updraughts and sudden sinks pulling in a convective pattern. A spoon obliterates the system.

Billows of steam and condensation rose from the mug as it cooled on the side and I began to look for the cat food. Again, this was a short search; the cat food was in the larder-style utility room, along with a martial display of tinned foods and sacks of dried goods.

On the floor next to two water bowls and two spotlessly polished dishes was a pallet large enough for sixteen cans of diced mystery animal remains in a rich sauce of whatever, with the shrink wrap broken at one corner and fourteen cans remaining. Each can bore, next to the incomprehensible Slav-ese (probably containing the words 'juicy', 'stronger teeth' and 'at least some % meat'), a picture of a feline with eyes that twinkled like taxidermists' glass and a tongue that, captured in illustration, would now forever explore that same corner of its smiling mouth. Cat rendered as brain-dead consumer, trapped in lockstep with thirteen clones, licking tongues raised to the right in a bank of Heils, eyes fixed without focus on an endless future of more of this delicious food every day. Next to this band of brothers was a sack of the miniature biscuits that gave this gloop some texture. And a slip of paper, neatly folded on one of the surgically clean dishes, that I had not noticed at first; bleached paper on bleached china.

INSTRUCTIONS FOR FEEDING CATS, *I read.*

Half a can of food in each dish in the morning and the same in the early evening. Each time with a handful of their crunchy mix each, and be sure to refill the water bowls with fresh each time. Move the tray with the dishes into the kitchen for S. and S. to dine, and then when they have finished clean the dishes and return the tray to the cupboard.

O.

That was fine. The general list of instructions had contained nothing specific as concerned the feeding of the cats, and this job was clearly more important than the making of tea or coffee, hence the fact that it had been honoured with a full sheet of notepaper. Oskar was the most attentive absent host I could imagine, even across half the world. The conductor, the composer of precise, clipped piano pieces, the lord of a minimalist and restrained realm, would not have left things to chance. My liaison with his flat, his world, had to be organised with far more care than he had arranged his liaison with a Marlboro-blonde art jockey from the history-less West Coast.

I freed one of the cans of food from the shrunken plastic and carried it with the tray through to the kitchen, where I set it down on the floor.

This must have been the auditory clue, the Pavlovian bell – the soft sound of tray with dishes meeting the dull glow of the kitchen's wooden floor. At once, before I had even straightened up, there were two dull thuds from the bedroom and the unmistakable skitter, slip and scratch of claws against shining plank. Turning towards the source of the sound, I saw something I never expected – heading full pelt through the glass-partitioned corridor separating the bedroom from the kitchen, the cats had accelerated so much in such a short time that as they rounded the corner they left the floor, pacing the white wall like a wire-assisted Jackie Chan in a medium-budget kick-'em-up, flipped and held by the invisible hands of momentum and centrifugal force. As the wall ran out, so they ran down, not seeming to lose a joule of energy, only to stop dead in the middle of the kitchen, at least four feet short of the tray. But they didn't stop – they slid with practised elegance along the trajectory they had set and wound up, kinetic energy burned off against wood, a neat few inches from their proposed supper, circling and making plaintive noises.

My jaw hung flaccidly, its tendons sliced by this display of athletics. As Shossy and Stravvy mewled and arched their warm backs against my legs, I fought the urge to try and recreate what I had just witnessed, to move them back to the bedroom and the tray back to the cupboard, to recreate the phenomenon, but it was clear that it would not work. The butterfly's wings could not be unflapped, the cloud would never again assume the same shape. Perhaps they would do the same thing tomorrow, but it would never have the same effect as it just had. It had been done. The moment had broken and could not be reassembled.

Still adrenalised, I hefted the sack of dry food from the larder, fetched a fork (the obvious drawer, obviously), raked the lumpy brown treats into the bowls, and sprinkled the biscuit bits over the portions. The cats were already tucking in as this finishing garnish was applied.

With the recent feline acrobatics still on my mind, I wandered over to the scene of the feat. The floor glowed in golden perfection – it was clearly necessary for the stunt. On a whim, I walked to the front door and kicked off my shoes. Toeing the floor, its silken finish betrayed only the tiniest natural imperfections of grain and warp; it felt almost frictionless.

The decision was made by some over-ambitious subcommittee in the lower portions of my brain and failed to pass through the proper scrutiny procedures before the action it outlined was already under way. I braced, devoted the slightest of moments to a complex calculation of forces in motion, and launched myself down the corridor. After four and a half paces at the maximum acceleration I could muster, I braked, laid my stockinged feet flat on the wood and locked into a slide to the far wall.

Some twenty or thirty minutes later, the pain in my left knee and big toe had – aided I believe by a broad-ranging swear-word monologue – subsided from crippling agony to merely irksome.

By the time I had recovered from my pratfall and unpacked my bags it was early evening. The light had yet to die in the sky but the sun was low. I made a sandwich with some cheese and salami from the fridge and opened the bottle of wine that Oskar had left for me. I ate on the sofa with the TV on BBC News 24. The rhythm and jangle of rolling global news is an odd comfort, but the flat was filled with British accents and familiar branding. The repetition of bulletins and headlines was soothingly metronomic, a lullaby more than an alert. Rolling snooze.

I don't know how long I slept on the sofa, or the exact time I woke, but it was night in the city outside and the room was washed with the Lucozade orange of sodium street lighting. Travel and unfamiliar places can be exhausting, and I was more tired than I had realised. One of the cats was standing on the sofa next to me, regarding me with a quizzical air.

'Meow?' it said, tilting its head to one side.

'Yeah,' I said, rising slowly to my feet and stretching. 'You want to go out. Time for bed.' Several joints complained as I twisted to free my watch hand from its awkward position. I was neither sitting nor lying; just sort of slumped. I must have dozed off. Struggling to my feet, I scooped the puss off the sofa and walked it over to the front door where its partner was waiting like a partygoer holding a taxi for a friend. They needed no encouragement to disappear into the night.

DAY TWO

There is a moment between sleeping and waking where one is free. Consciousness has returned, but awareness has yet to rip away the thin screen between the waker and his surroundings, his reality. You float free of context, in no place – not sleeping, not fully awake, not at the mercy of the unknowns of the subconscious, and not yet exposed to the dull knowns of care and routine. It is at this point, between two worlds, that I think I am happiest.

For a second, I was disoriented, uncertain of my location. I was surrounded by white, a bubble in an ocean of milk. Then, the details began to resolve. I remembered that I was in Oskar's flat, under his white ceiling, under the peaks and troughs of his white duvet, on his white sheets and pillows.

The regime in Iran tortures with white. Its jailers dress a prisoner in white clothes and place him in a featureless white isolation cell, filled with white light. Food – white food – is served on white paper plates, brought in by guards all in white, wearing white masks. This becomes unbearable for the prisoner, an almost-total deprivation of the senses. Snow blindness. A disconnection from the limbs, from scale and perspective – freedom from context as hell, not bliss.

It was a perverse torment for an Islamic country. I had heard that, under Islam, perfection is the preserve of the Divine. Striving for perfection is sinful pride. Imperfections are deliberately introduced in artworks as a gesture of humility. In each of those fabulous abstract Islamic decorative patterns, there is a piously deliberate mistake, a flawed iteration.

How those prisoners must crave that imperfection. A mark on the wall, a shadowed crevice, a stained ceiling tile. Apparently it is enough to unhinge the mind – enough to make one do anything to escape that featureless room.

'Why do they dislike me?'

'Oh, Oskar, they ...'

I wanted to say: *Oskar, they don't really dislike you, they just don't really like you, you're not like them, and you're not an easy person to like.* I didn't say that.

'... What sort of question is that?' I said at last. 'They're not out to get you.'

'I just do not understand the stealing of the vodka,' Oskar said, gesturing at the bottle he had brought with him, which was now heavily depleted. We had been drinking for hours, and my guest was showing worrying signs of being a maudlin drunk.

'You should know better than keeping it in a shared fridge,' I said.

'It is the only way to keep it chilled,' Oskar said. He looked almost comically morose, like Droopy the Dog, summoning up hitherto unsuspected jowls.

'I don't know, mix it with Coke or something.'

Oskar wrinkled his nose. His lip kinked in disdain. 'I prefer it neat.'

I sighed. 'It's a shared kitchen. You have to compromise. Live and let live.'

'But they do not "live and let live", they leave a mess, they leave the dirty plates ...'

'They're students,' I said wearily. 'So are you, so am I. Relax.'

Oskar frowned. 'And this is relaxing?'

Fogged by vodka, it took me a moment to register that he had asked a question. 'What?'

'This,' he said with a languid gesture around my room. 'This is relaxing?' I tried to see what he was indicating and failed. 'Well, it's relaxing to have a drink with a friend ...' I said. Oskar was unnerving me. I remembered that this was the first time I had seen him drunk. He was an unknown quantity.

'No, no, no,' Oskar said. His voice rose and he became energetic, rising from his chair, pacing the floor. 'This! Your room! The way you live! This chaos!'

This took me by surprise. In another frame of mind I might have been offended, but instead I simply found myself surveying the room again, trying to see through Oskar's eyes. The open bottle of vodka stood on my desk, or rather stood on the small canton of desktop not lurking beneath a thick carapace of books, papers and assorted detritus. Bookmarks bristled like tattered standards from forgotten wars, or the books themselves lay prostrate, open, held in the middle of a thought that could never be retrieved. Paper was scattered everywhere, but little of it had been fully used. Instead, each sheet bore just a couple of discarded sentences, or an arcane note, its meaning lost. Tired biros lay like pick-a-sticks. A plate, scattered with crumbs and waxy traces of peanut butter, lay atop one heap. A Frisbee lay at the bottom of another, and I had a vague recollection that it had served as an ashtray before being covered in notes. Another impromptu ashtray, formerly the lid of a jar of gherkins, now spilled cigarette butts behind the desk, into the lair of a medusa of extension cords. Above it all, my angle-poise shone cyclopically like the fire brigade floodlights at a midnight motorway catastrophe. The rest of the room displayed variations of the disarray of the desk in clothes, books, posters, bedding and the worthless paraphernalia that early adulthood attracts – dancing Coke bottles, inflatable guitars, purloined pint glasses, incense holders, broken CD cases, novelty bottle openers, a crippled cafetière.

I shrugged. 'I know it's untidy ...'

'It is not just the room,' Oskar said. 'A room is not just a room. A room is a manifestation of a state of mind, the product of an intelligence. Either conscious' – and he dropped dramatically back into his armchair, sending up a plume of dust and cigarette ash – 'or unconscious. We make our rooms, and then our rooms make us.'

I wanted to say: *There you go. That's why they don't like you.* I did not. I quit smoking. Much of the contents of the room would go into black bin-liners at the end of the term. After that room, there were other rooms, then shared houses, then a string of one-bed flats. I have regarded them all with the same dissatisfaction. This was Oskar's gift to me.

Gazing up at the ceiling of Oskar's bedroom, splashed by a fantail of sunlight from the windows, I felt most satisfied. I listened to the city edge its way in. A tram grumbled and clanked its way past, tinny leper's bell sounding, a protesting squeal at the points in the crossroads. The sound of duty also penetrated my sleepy mind, a scratching and mewing at the balcony windows. Shossy and Stravvy were hungry.

I flung open the French windows to the chattering, brilliant city air. The cats snaked around my legs in that odd feline way – why do they pass so close when there is plenty of room? – and headed straight to the kitchen with the expectant purposefulness of factory workers at the lunch whistle. I followed, stretching.

Shreds of the previous evening lay by the sofa – the papers, the wine glass. I attended to the cats and then filled and switched on the kettle. As it boiled, I tidied away my mess, the depleted bottle – with its note from Oskar – the newspapers and magazines, the glass—

I stopped. A drop of wine or two must have made their way to the base of the glass on one of my many refills. There was no coaster beneath it. (In my mind's eye, Oskar winced.) A 45-degree arc of red wine marked his precious floor, a livid surgical scar on pale flesh.

This stain held my attention for a moment or two, ice running through my veins. Red wine stains, I thought. I thought of Oskar's injunction. From nowhere came the memory that speed of response was the crucial factor in dealing with that sort of thing. Action was imperative, my brain insisted, disregarding the fact that I had been asleep for several hours.

Without panic, I turned to the kitchen and ran a dish-cloth under the tap, then returned to the scene of the crime. Kneeling as though in supplication, I started to rub and scrub. Satisfying; the mark seemed to shift quite quickly. After five minutes or so of work, I could not detect a trace of the wine. I waited a while for the floorboard to dry, and then inspected it, aided by the late-morning sun.

There *was* still a mark. The slightest, faintest curved blush, hardly noticeable in the natural grain of the wood. A birthmark awaiting its final laser treatment. But now my eye was unstoppably drawn to it – as if it was as large, as black, as inescapable as the sofa.

Clearing my mind, I attempted to appraise the area objectively, as if I was in the room for the first time. This was obviously not going to work. My work – my illustrious writing career – mostly involved composing and editing brochures for local authorities. Residents of Ealing may remember my acclaimed *Know Your Library Service*, but I consider my masterpiece to be *Bin and Gone: How, What and When to Recycle*, now in its fifth reprint in Southwark and translated into nine languages. (Want to know the Somali for 'compost'? I can tell you.)

Whenever one of these towering works hit the presses, there would almost inevitably be an error. Colossal, humiliating, *Private Eye*-worthy errors ('Council Launches Literasy Initiative') are very rare. But nearly every piece of printed matter contains an error somewhere. Most are invisible to the inexpert eye – a double space here, a full stop incorrectly italicised there. Only the editor will see these. But once he or she has seen such an error in the final printed product, that is all they will ever see. The beautiful clarity with which they explain the law on fly-tipping will be invisible to them – they will notice that a simple hyphen has been used where an en-dash was needed.

And so it was with Oskar's floor.

I was fixated on the damaged sliver of wood even when standing at an absurd distance from it. It was nothing, barely visible – if it was noticed, it could be taken for a natural variation in the colour of the wood. But to me, it stood out like the European wine lake.

The kettle had long since boiled and I made myself a coffee. The cats ate noisily. Again, I found myself trying to work out which was Shossy and which was Stravvy. It was impossible, of course. Even if I could somehow judge the personality of the cat, whether that better fitted a 'Shossy' or a 'Stravvy' was beyond me.

I decided to compress all of my sightseeing for the trip into one day, saving myself the mental and physical effort of trying to find something different to do every morning, when I could be writing. Such was the indistinction of this country that I had been unable to find a guidebook for it in the bookshop at Heathrow, but did manage to find a *Lonely Planet* that included this scrap of pointless autonomy as an afterthought and dealt with everything of interest in the capital and beyond in just forty pages.

Walking from the flat towards the Old Market – 'the city's ceremonial centrepiece' – I began to feel that forty pages was rather generous. The city may well have been of Roman foundation with an illustrious Medieval heyday, but the vast majority of this heritage had been ripped down in the middle and late nineteenth century to make way for endless mock-gothic and baroque buildings of such lumpen construction and poor repair that they all resembled Miss Havisham's wedding cake with an added layer of antique soot. The Second World War and the Eastern Bloc had also made their luckless debits and credits. I passed by the National Museum's Acropolis-with-gigantism façade, saving it for later, and pushed on into the Old Market.

In London, I was never alarmed by crowds, instead feeling that they were my milieu, the pressing discourse of humanity, the language of the Tube, the very soul of the city. Here, they were different; perhaps my nervousness was a product of not knowing the language (the phrase book in my pocket felt like a lead weight) or possibly of being such an obvious tourist. 'The bustle of the market is a charming counterpoint to the grandeur of its surroundings,' *Lonely Planet* informed me. However, it seemed that the enthusiasm of the commerce conducted at the market was a charming counterpoint to the utter worthlessness of the goods on offer. Meagre clumps of limp, filthy root vegetables were spread out next to mounds of Tupperware that seemed to have already seen one or more decades of heavy use; obsolete, tatty paperbacks jostled with worthless candelabra covered in peeling gold paint.

Unbothered by this absence of any clearly desirable merchandise, the market square was filled by what seemed to be the city's whole population. Never before have I truly understood the full significance of the word 'heaving' in relation to masses of humanity, but the market was heaving; one's direction of travel was utterly limited by crowd consensus, so that whole quarters were closed off by contrary flows of traffic, and often your course was entirely away from your intended direction, dictated only by a new shudder of peristalsis in the folds and crevices the stalls left for their wretched consumers. Godlike above all this, the first-floor windows of what I believe was once the state department store had been given over to titanic posters for a Western cosmetics firm, and the six-foot-high faces of beautiful screen actresses and models gazed down smugly on the teeming hordes. The new, free men and women of Europe were as far from this ideal as they had been from the ruddy-faced perfection in the propaganda of the old state. I swear I never once saw anyone under the age of sixty – a charitable estimate – and they were all hunched and aggressive of demeanour with eyes that gleamed, as I saw it, with some unspecified, unneeded, unmotivated malice towards me in ways that I couldn't even begin to quantify.

If only I had something to buy, I considered, some purpose to be moving around, then perhaps I wouldn't be so keenly aware of this sense of being, very literally, a foreign body. But what did I *need*? What could I possibly *want* from this place? Nothing occurred; and as I struggled towards the other side of the market the idea that I was simply there to take in the scene began to feel as absurd a notion to me as perhaps it did to the natives. It was not warm, but my skin thistled with sweat; I have rarely been less comfortable. Tube trains in stygian rush hours, supermarkets on the eve of national holidays; never have I felt so prickled and alarmed.

I pushed through the throng, shakily counting suspicious glances, leers and glares, to find my way to the National Monument, where the crowds eased. As if answering the moisture gathering in my armpits and at the small of my back, the sky began to perspire rain with the effort of pulling its dishrag clouds across the firmament. The jostle faded as I reached the steps to the monument and I was faced by a granite bollard, inflated to ten times its natural size and borne aloft by slab-like soldiers whose arms twisted in ways militated against by both aesthetics and anatomy. The monument was a stump awaiting prosthesis. It was a snapped bone piercing cobbled flesh. In the lee the monument caused amid the shuffling crowd, I turned to look again at the square.

Pristine secular gods and goddesses, sanctified by the airbrush, peered down at their flock. Their avatars stared like Egyptian tomb paintings – the crocodile, the half-man, half-horse (polo stick raised, ready to smite). They promised salvation, Because You're Worth It. Salvation, by Calvin Klein.

Behind the hoardings, stucco crumbled. The pallid stone guardians of the national monument stared out across the masses they had saved from an –ism on behalf of some other –ism.

Why did Oskar like it here? Did he like it here, beyond the accident of it being his birthplace? His immense talent, his success, meant he could work anywhere he wanted, yet he chose here, with its headscarves and ochre multi-zeroed banknotes.

Nearby, a vendor was selling bottles of water. I bought one and sat on the monument's steps. The growl of the crowds and the ubiquitous jingling rumble of the trams settled around me, and I felt more at ease.

Oskar had spoken of his home country that first time we got properly drunk together, after the great vodka hunts. We toasted his revenge, and toasted the quality of the unadulterated freezing-point vodka. Not that I understood its quality – it simply numbed and burned me. I had no mixers other than a room-temperature can of cola. This was mine alone, as Oskar considered it sacrilege, but he talked of how garlic was sometimes added to the precious spirit by his countrymen. I asked him about his background, curious about this figure who had become my friend almost by accident. I expected a soulful Mittel-European paean, sad and loving. Instead, Oskar approached the question with an odd air of disjointed gravity, thinking a long time before speaking.

'It matters to me,' he said. Then he sipped his shot. Another pause slid through the room. Oskar pre-empted my attempt to break the silence as I drew breath. 'After I finish my studying here,' he said, 'I may go for more study in America, or here, or look for a position here or there. Maybe I will go home. But ...'

Another pause, and sip.

'You are funny, the English. You are always in a worry for ... What? You say "going to the dogs". This fear, yet you have been happy sitting on this island and Armadas and Nazis cannot reach you. My country is a shifting shape on the map, and empires and armies walk across it, it disappears and moves, just a patch of colour, a story. Still I know, and my people know, that my country will always be there. But you English think the world has collapsed if they get rid of the old red telephone boxes.'

He drained his glass and refilled it, topping up mine, and proposed another toast.

'Our Motherlands,' he said with a sardonic smile. 'Let us get drunk enough to love them.'

And we did.

The National Museum was deserted, save for a brigade of scowling old women in headscarves. One sat on a wooden chair in the museum's atrium, selling tickets from a card table. Others sat guard in each of the echoing halls, knitting, reading newspapers or staring at me. Their gaze was stern rather than welcoming, but I was grateful for their presence – but for them, I would have been alone in the building. Not one other visitor could be seen.

From the exhibits, I learned which parts of the country were oolitic and which were pre-Cambrian. Stuffed fauna lurked in unexpected corners, all malevolent glass eyes and dusty fur. A wall chart explained the intricacies of lignite mining; another, the workings of a bauxite plant. Examples of local industrial production included most of the marvels of the modern world: washing machines the size of small cars, small cars the size of washing machines, telex machines, AM radios, aluminium frying pans, lead-based toothpaste, acetate pyjamas, asbestos quilts ... Few of the explanatory timelines mustered the strength to get past 1975. In a nod to the interactive, touch-screen age, many of the glass cases needed the dust wiped off them to reveal the treasures within.

One hall was devoted to depictions of traditional peasant life through the ages in different parts of the country. This led to an enfilade explaining the national story through serfdom, monarchy, industrial revolution, republic, fascist republic, people's republic and democratic republic. All these phases were packed into the twentieth century. The preceding epochs were simply a grim routine of invaders, pogroms and home-grown rulers with soubriquets such as 'the gouger'.

The particularly potent version of hell that the Nazis and Soviets inflicted on Eastern Europe was handled in a curiously modest fashion, with little bombast or horror. And the final three panels of the exhibition were visibly recent insertions, pale patches on the wall betraying the outlines of their predecessors. Presumably the originals had extolled the glorious strides made by the people's republic towards the socialist nirvana envisaged by its leader, the father of the nation. Instead, they extolled the collapse of the Soviet east. Walls fell. Assemblies were stormed. Street names changed. The advertisers arrived.

The history was the newest thing in the building.

* * *

As I was crossing the polished floor of the museum's atrium to the heavy wooden doors and the street beyond, the old woman who had sold me my ticket jumped up from her chair. I froze, suddenly nervous, as she rushed towards me, apparently eager to prevent my leaving. The brass of the front door's fingerplate was cold under my fingers – I desperately wanted to brace my shoulder and push out, escape, but held back. Perhaps one paid on the way out, I thought, except that I had bought a ticket on the way in; perhaps you had to pay to enter and leave, or perhaps she expected a tip of some sort. Or perhaps she suspected that I had hidden a stuffed owl under my coat. It seemed certain that she thought I had done something wrong.

She was ushering me towards the door in gestures that seemed half shooing and half encouraging, as though she wanted me to leave. All the while she was speaking to me, an incomprehensible torrent. Was this a simple send-off? Was she throwing me out?

We were through the door, and she still spoke, and gestured, now with a sense of eagerness or purpose. She took me by the sleeve of my coat and led me with a strange, quick, waddling gait around to the side of the building, where a narrow alleyway separated the museum from the neighbouring cube of stone. Decades of fumes from brown coal, retarded industrial adventures and pitiful automobiles had unevenly stained the museum's side wall, and it was etched with graffiti, mostly domestic and cryptic, some international (a swastika, and USA #1). Pockmarks like acne scars were sprinkled over this filthy surface, deep holes like missing divots.

The sentinel of the museum looked at me expectantly. This, this wall, was what I had been brought to see, but I did not know why. Her face, regarding me with a sort of anticipatory glee, carried no clues. In the 1990s I had been to a birthday party where the host's presents included a 'magic eye' print – a rectangle of coloured static that, if stared at for long enough, apparently resolved into an image of the New York skyline. A succession of other guests gazed deep into this picture and then whooped or gasped or similarly exclaimed satisfaction when the trick played out. It would not work for me, remaining a polychrome garble. Look more closely, the other guests, my friends, said, unfocus your eyes, cross your eyes, look past the picture, don't try too hard. I stared and stared, and they all looked at me with that same expression that the museum guide now wore, a sort of cultish eagerness.

I pointed at the wall. 'What am I looking at, then?' I said.

Before I could lower my arm or step back, the old woman grabbed my raised arm by the wrist and pulled it insistently towards the wall. I was stunned; a sick horror rose in me and I think I let loose a breath, a gasp of shock, but she still wore that determined grin. Her grip was like iron, and maybe I could have freed my arm, but not without a violent movement that was utterly beyond me. This woman was perhaps more than double my age yet I was completely unable to conceive of wresting free of this grip that terrified me. My muscles were heavy wads of wet toilet tissue. She pulled my hand forward so that the index finger, still extended, went into one of the holes in the stone. *How many years of filth are in there?* I wondered. And then my wrist was free – she left my hand with a finger pointing in this rough little hole. The hole was deep, maybe three inches or more – it almost swallowed my finger. It was too deep to have been made by some natural process of erosion, and there were many others like it.

'Pan!' the woman said, quite suddenly, a short, explosive syllable. 'Pan! Pan!' She was pantomiming firing a rifle. Maybe in other circumstances the sight would have been comical. But not now.

'Pan!'

I saw now, and whipped out my finger as if it had been burned. These pockmarks were bullet holes. The side of the museum had been riddled with bullets. From what war or revolution? Who had been fighting whom? Was it even fighting? They could have just lined people up in this alley and shot them. Revolutionary justice. Counter-revolutionary justice.

The museum guide was still grinning at me. She could see that I now knew what I was looking at, I was sure. Maybe she thought that this was what tourists wanted to see, the real history. She clearly had me pegged as a foreigner – maybe she thought, or knew from experience, that Westerners were likely to be unenchanted by the displays inside the museum and instead had a ghoulish fascination with the story drilled into its stone, its guts, the real thing. I still did not know if these scars were recent or not. But it seemed to me that most of the history here was recent. I doubted that their television schedules were cluttered with *I ♥ the 1980s*. Strikes and shortages, curfews and disappearances. The holes were a presence, not an absence. They awed and chilled me.

I ran my fingertips over a hole at chest level. Dug into solid stone at the bottom of that hole was a chunk of lead. What did it pass through before pitting the wall? The air, alive with shouts and commands and terrible noises; and skin, and muscle and sinew, and bone and blood? Had the blood been washed off, or was it now a component of the black filth that coated every inch of the wall? From blood to crud; vital motivating fluid one moment, dirt the next. Whose blood, though, if it was indeed there at all? Why spilled? What for? Fascist? Communist? Nationalist? Dissident? Loyalist? Monarchist? Collaborator? Resistance? Might this have been a freedom fighter's corpuscles, or were these terrorist cells? Whoever had won would now decide that. Faceless idealists flitted in my imagination. Or no one, nothing – a bullet hurled through air ringing with forgotten slogans only to embed itself in this dead rock, which remembers it still. And the slogans echo to silence, and a man from an indifferent country sees the mark but not the maker, his time, his cause. All gone, and damage and trash is left behind.

The woman from the museum, that strange creature who brought me here, wrinkled her nose as if to indicate *Ooh, isn't this fun?* and turned back towards the street, talking merrily to herself. I waited a couple of minutes until I was certain that there was no possibility of awkwardly re-encountering her around the corner, and then followed.

My stomach pinched and I realised with unwelcome timing that I was hungry. It was past lunchtime, the bulk of the afternoon was already gone, and my lower back ached from the walking. Doubly unwelcome was the realisation that I had a chore to run. I needed to buy groceries. Either I had to shop, or I had to eat out every night, and as I didn't know how long I would be here, eating out could become expensive. But the notion of shopping for groceries while technically on holiday was repulsive to me.

There was a small supermarket on the way back to Oskar's flat – I had seen it on my way out. But at some point in its history, a thunderingly incompetent acolyte of Baron Haussmann had had his way with this city. Its historic street pattern had been almost obliterated by an attempt to systematise it into a grid. This almost-grid had then been further complicated by a series of non-orthogonal avenues that stretched out from two focal points, the Market Square and the National Assembly. This carved the plan into dozens of flatirons, splinters and sawteeth. On the map, it looked a little like a sheet of reinforced glass that had two bullet holes punched in it, radiating fractures. On the ground, my path back to Oskar's via the supermarket zig-zagged in an uneven W.

The supermarket occupied the ground floor of one of the spearhead-shaped blocks, a wedge like the prow of a ship. A heavy antique iron clock was cantilevered out from the sharp point of the block, above the store's front entrance, layers of cellulite-lump black paint and hefty Roman numerals speaking of another age. And now it surmounted a buzzing mass of strip-lighting and ready meals. It was a purgatory of sticky linoleum and radium-blue insectocutors. I bought what I needed and left as swiftly as possible.

As I uncomfortably backed my way through the resisting front door of Oskar's building, I heard a disconcerting noise. At first I thought the door was creaking, but that was not the source. It was a sort of creak, though, but also more than that. It was the sound of the blade of a spade being dragged along a pavement, only changing in pitch, rising as it went. There was then a fraction of a beat of bright silence, a bit of rustling, and a savage metallic slam. It was the sound of a mechanical giant with a lame foot, limping towards some malign goal. The twin sounds repeated, rusted yowl and mantrap slam. They were coming from upstairs.

On the landing between the ground and first floors was a woman, hair tied back in the ubiquitous headscarf, her age an irrelevant point somewhere between forty-five and seventy. A life of poor diet and hard work had turned her into a huge callus, and her nose was pushed up in a way that inescapably reminded me of the squashed face of a bat. She was dumping rubbish-filled plastic bags into a metal-doored hatch in the wall of the landing, a rubbish chute with an age-degraded but still powerful spring on its opening. The effort needed to pull it down was clearly considerable, and it snapped shut with swift viciousness. Creak, slam. Hearing me climb the stairs, she turned and confronted me, demanding something I did not understand.

I took an instant dislike to this new person in my life, blocking my way. After the troubling interlude in the alley,

I did not care for further crone encounters. Also ... I look like nothing myself, and try not to judge on appearances. But this woman's physical ugliness seemed in my snapshot opinion to be matched by an ugliness of nature. Hair tied back under the ubiquitous headscarf, that nose of the order chiroptera, and the unforgiving gleam of the eyes behind it ... and she was fat, not the pillowy fat of overindulgence, fat like an armadillo. The bags of groceries I carried should have indicated that I was not some sort of burglar or rapist, but I felt like an intruder nevertheless. I put them down on the stone floor – the two bottles of red wine I had bought clinked and drew her disapproving attention – and pointed upstairs, pulling Oskar's keys from my pocket with my other hand.

'Oskar, upstairs,' I said, more than once, as I dangled the keys like a hypnotist. She stared at them with what seemed like scepticism, then slightly grudging acceptance. Then, pointing upstairs with an expectant look on her face, she said a word that I (obviously) did not understand. I adopted a quizzical look and pointed upstairs. She repeated the word, nodding the while. Then she said it a third time, this time adding a questions mark. Baffled, I smiled and repeated the word as best I could. She smiled and looked intensely satisfied. Smiling and nodding like a Japanese businessman, I fled upstairs.

At least modernity had taken firm hold in Oskar's apartment. The kitchen gleamed like a surgical instrument. The cats lay entangled and becalmed on the sofa – I shooed them off and sighed, then brushed at the hairs they had shed with my hand. It was obvious why they liked the sofa; direct sunlight warmed the black leather beautifully. They were hungry, and they orbited me, carefully making practised shows of being pitiable. I looked down at them, prowling around between the sofa and the coffee table, and my eye was drawn to the small blush on the floor my wine glass had left. The light was different now, and there was no escaping the mark – it was certainly there, undeniable, and I could not imagine that Oskar would not see it. I was an expert at deluding myself out of responsibilities, but this was beyond my powers. Oskar would see it, I was convinced. It was a blemish on my record, and made less than twenty-four hours into my custodianship of his home. Once, Oskar had astonished me at a dinner party by holding forth on my shortcomings with an exceptional eye for detail. My girlfriend at the time had been less than impressed, and I believed that the evening had contributed to the breakdown of that relationship. Oskar's girlfriend back then was the woman who later became his wife, a relationship that a dozen Californian lawyers were at this moment dismantling for what I imagined was a considerable profit.

That mark ... I went to the sink and wetted a sponge with a scrubbing patch on top, then dripped a drop of washing-up liquid onto it. Then, I attacked the mark with the ferocity of a wronged man. It was maddening, truly, to have a floor that could not stand the slightest flaw. A floor was made to be trodden on! It was where things inevitably fell. I scrubbed and scrubbed. That dinner party had been an odd evening. One of the reasons I liked Oskar was his truth-telling instinct, his directness about the failings of others, often without concern for social niceties such as their feelings. Really, it was only a surprise that he didn't apply his frightening insight and uncompromising honesty to me earlier. But then I thought of his open contempt for my housekeeping abilities at university. And he later apologised, made a point of apologising, to me in person; in fact, that dinner party had been the beginning of a chain of consequences that had led to Oskar asking me to look after his flat.

Once my elbow and shoulder began to ache, I stopped scrubbing at the floor. I rinsed the sponge, squeezed it thoroughly, and wiped away the suds. Was the blemish still there? The floor was wet – it was hard to tell. Besides, I was beginning to feel that this blemish was like a flash-shadow left after a photograph has been taken, a blob imprinted on the back of my eyes and nowhere else. I thought of Edgar Allan Poe's story 'The Tell-tale Heart', in which a murderer is driven mad by the imagined audible beating of the heart of his victim, concealed under the floorboards of his room. But I was no murderer, I thought, and it would take a lot more than a tiny mark on the floor to drive me insane.

DAY THREE

I was lying in Oskar's bed, not even slightly awake, when I realised that my surroundings had performed an unhappy transfiguration in the night. The bed now seemed to be of unlimited size. At first I feared that I had shrunk, but that theory did not stand up to close examination. The white duvet was as thick as it had been when I went to sleep, all the stitching and weave of the cotton was the correct scale, but the mattress and its coverings no longer had a visible end in any direction. Everywhere I looked, it stretched out to an invisible vanishing point, a white cotton horizon against a plaster-white sky. Sky, or ceiling? It was impossible to tell, and the answer did not seem to be important. Beneath me, I imagined a fathomless underworld of dusty springs. Above was the irrelevant nothing.

Slow panic. To crawl or walk out onto that trackless desert of duvet, or over the treacherous footings of boggy pillow-down, would mean losing my way, succumbing to snow blindness, and ultimately (in the boxer shorts and T-shirt I slept in) death from exposure. To worm my way under the duvet at first seemed a better plan; not so exposed to cold, at the very least. But a duvet that size must weigh thousands, millions, of tonnes, I feared, whatever its tog count. To crawl too far underneath it would be death – I would suffocate in the dark before the first mile was up.

It really was unfortunate. My immediate surroundings, in their proper place in the world and at sensible proportions, could not be more comfortable – I was simply in a bed. But as this bed had grown to encompass the whole world, it had become a deathtrap as alien and unforgiving as an Arctic waste or Asiatic desert. Any place, I realised, no matter how temporarily comfortable or inviting, is only rendered habitable by the promise of other places beyond it.

For want of anything else to do, I turned over. The horizon, a greyness that was really only a fresh, distant, horizontal quality of whiteness, swung into view. A tiny pang of seasickness came and went. Seasickness without the hint of an ocean; not so much as a drop of water. How long could one survive without water? Not that I could measure time – I did not believe that this ash-white dome above me varied its appearance according to night and day. I would have to conserve and 'recycle' my own fluids, I thought. The idea of drinking my own urine did not appeal. And I had no way of ... decanting it. Would I be reduced to using a cupped hand, or somehow ... *aiming*? The mechanics of the whole operation were not at all pleasing. Afterwards, I would have to move to a new place on the frontier, no doubt about it. I was not going to lie in the damp patch. Certain death in a prosaic wilderness was one thing, lounging around in my own waste was quite another. Fortunately, and this was the one bright spot that I could see: there was no shortage of identical spots to move to.

Incredible – I could not have been in this new situation for more than ten minutes, and already I was figuring out the practicalities of pissing all over myself. And right on cue, the question of fluids arose, and a mild complaint issued from the fleshy lower part of my abdomen. It was unmistakable, and it would only become more urgent. And there was something else wrong. A darkness was advancing in the distance beyond my feet. Maybe I had been wrong about the days and nights here, and this was dusk. But it was not dusk or gathering bad weather. It was spreading below the horizon, just a storm-like far darkness at first, but more resembling an incoming tide as it advanced. Storm-like, yes; it was the bruised blue colour of spilled red wine, a purple, thunderhead hue. It was Homer's wine-dark sea, seeping into the white cotton of the acres of duvet, darkening as it grew deeper. At first, it seemed to be a growing lake that was approaching my feet, but then, in a dreamy instant, I realised that it was to my left and right as well, cutting off escape. I did not want to look behind me. It was no growing lake, I was a shrinking island.

At this moment of intensifying crisis, my bladder also wanted attention. What had been naught but a twinge from the early-warning system a few second ago had now, unfairly, escalated into a full-scale case for immediate action. I was facing imminent peril of an unknown nature on all sides, thanks to the Wine Stain from Beyond, and the need to go to the toilet. I had two top priorities, both of them evacuation. But there was also something strangely reassuring about this sudden desire to urinate. It was the most familiar thing about these circumstances. It was a factor that appeared to come from beyond this contrived terrain of duvet and mattress and threatening darknesses. It was real; I was certain of it. I really did need to go to the loo – it was something that I could measure empirically and had experienced before. I began to suspect, very strongly, that everything else might be a dream. And as if detecting my lack of confidence in it, my new reality all at once felt far less substantial.

The stain had advanced to within two feet of my two feet. And with that, consciousness fell hard around me like a cookie-cutter stamping out the rectangular shape of a king-size bed in the cotton savannah, and then lifted to reveal the walls of Oskar's room beyond. Oskar's room! I was sitting up, unexpectedly, and my heart started to beat like a rubber ball dropped on a hard surface from a great height. It was morning; there was sunlight and street-sound. I was awake. I needed to go to the toilet. Outside, beyond the French windows, I could hear the cats whingeing. The demanding little beasts would have to wait.

I pivoted on my rear, swinging my legs out from under the duvet (which, although it had resumed its conventional proportions, I felt it would be prudent to treat with some suspicion) and put my feet on the floor. This manoeuvre provoked a hollow *bong* from the mattress. Something in its echoes brought to mind whales calling in the ocean depths. The floor was rugless and cool; hours of bed warmth seeped from my feet into the boards. I stood, stretched, and trotted off to the lavatory, crossing as I did so a rhombus of sunlight. Its heat surprised me.

An inexplicable misery had overtaken me at some point in the night, and the promise of a day of brilliant sunshine seemed only to sharpen the sensation. Maybe the desolation of my nightmare had followed me out of sleep.

It felt most likely, however, that my low mood came from the following apprehension: I had nothing to do. Of course, this wasn't strictly, technically true – there were various things to be 'getting on with'; I needed to shower, the cats needed to be fed, I needed to be fed as well. But beyond these quotidian tasks, no activities were planned. This empty time – I had mentally categorised it as 'relaxing' or 'pottering about', both of which names imply some activity other than just standing stock-still or going back to bed – had been deliberately introduced into my rudimentary schedule in vast quantities, and I had eagerly anticipated it when thinking about my trip before setting off. This, I thought, would be the point at which my better self, the improving-book-reading, poem-writing self, would emerge; the time when I had removed from my path all the obstacles that I considered to be the source of my lack of creativity and self-improvement back in London. I had no work to do, I was not going to be interrupted, my surroundings were congenial and my mind was (mostly) at ease. My sensitive soul was no longer held down by heavy chains of duty and distraction – it would now (I had theorised) take wing. But I was gripped by a kind of dull horror. Even in perfect conditions, I couldn't muster the perfect mood to be all that I wanted to be. I simply could not do it. If nothing was stopping me, then what was stopping me? Because I was certainly stopped. Something had me by the entrails.

Unfair friends of mine saw my ambitions as pretensions. They, I was sure, were wrong. Oskar had been worse than unfair – he had been savagely fair. I did not know what to think. 'I want to be a writer' *sounded* right to me, but with it came a kick in the guts from the you're-telling-a-lie goblin. That was my ambition presented as a proud thoroughbred when in fact it was a spavined, half-blind mule. Certainly, riding it had not got me far. I had never even left the stables. For pity's sake, I had roughly planned that I would be at least a proper journalist of some sort while attempting to write whatever it was I wanted to write, but I hadn't even managed that! What did I do? I wrote council documentation. I explained your bin collection schedule. The shower, at least, managed to refresh me and slough off some of these fears.

Household rituals. I put out the cats' food while the kettle was boiling for my coffee. What did they do during the night? Whatever it was, it gave them an appetite, and they chugged down their chunks of brown flesh with gusto. What did they do in the sleeping city ... fuck and prowl, no doubt, glory in streets without trams and human feet. They were active, most active, in the dark and cold corners of the night and then sought out the brightest parts of the room in which to sleep. It was as though they stored up the energy that fell on them during the day and released it at night.

Coffee for me, my energy source. I was hungry as well, lazy hungry. Breakfast would have been the obvious way out, but it was past eleven already, and too close to lunch. I switched on the television, and again had to chase the cats off the sofa in order to watch. Why did Oskar banish them from a spot they clearly loved? It seemed arbitrary and cruel. CNN prattled its anytime monologue. Television news, especially rolling news, especially *American* rolling news, is criticised for its incessant preoccupation with novelty, crisis, overthrow and calamity, lives violently stopped and systems at bay, but to me it seems to be a mantra of imperturbable continuity, the reassuring (to some) humming of the great wheel continuing to turn. All these horrors, it says, all these revolutions and tumult, they do not matter, my children, they have not altered the hourly bulletins, the opening and closing of markets, the drumbeat of the global system. It goes on with the supreme, hermetic self-confidence of the medieval monastic orders. It sings the hours heedless of day or night, matins and compline, business report and planetary weather. No wonder it seemed so suited to the international, interstitial spaces, the airport lounges and hotel rooms. These places are called bland, but they are not. They are the default, the canvas, the underlay, the transmission test card. Everything else is a localised aberration.

It seemed so unfair to stop the cats from sitting on the sofa, and in my low mood I felt that I would appreciate the proximity of their warm little minds. I lifted the nearest one – the one whose tail bore a white tip, the only distinguishing feature I could discern so far – onto the sofa beside me. It circled once, and then jumped back off again, apparently just to be bloody-minded. Fine. Be like that, see if I care.

Damn – I *did* care. I had been snubbed by a lesser mammal. Nothing snubs quite like a cat. What evolutionary purpose did it serve, this inherent disdain, this artful blanking? International weather revealed, to my chagrin, that London was also sunny. I wanted it to be raining there, and sunny here, so that I could properly enjoy the *Schadenfreude* of the holiday-maker. But they would be sweating on the Tube, and when lunchtime came not an inch of grass in the central parks would be spared the imposition of a secretary's pasty arse.

Time trundled on, trams rumbled by. No wonder they had served as muse to Oskar. They informed the air like the lowing of cattle, the same air of unthinking service of unknown needs. A tram is unaware of its timetable; even its driver, its guiding intelligence, is concerned only with his route. I decided that I would do at least one culturally improving thing today, if nothing else – I would find and listen to *Variations on Tram Timetables*, Oskar's great success.

Noon passed. The day was broken, cracked down the middle like a paperback's spine. I made a simple lunch, thick slices of Routemaster-red sausage, Land Rover-green cucumber, slices of cheese and bread, a sliced lunch conducted by a sharp, pointy little paring knife, a most surgical instrument from Oskar's surgical kitchen. Consciously avoiding thinking about my actions and their implications, I pulled the cork out of the half-full bottle of wine on the kitchen table and poured myself a glass. A glass at just past midday, only an hour from rising, not a healthy thing. But this was a holiday, of sorts, not a time to be concerned with the formalities of everyday life. I would have to be careful, though, not to spill anything.

The stain was still there, of course, that damn little mark. It was so small and pale, nothing at all. I was now worried that my fierce cleaning yesterday had, if anything, made it more noticeable. The scrubber surface of the sponge had left tiny scratches in the thin polish of the floor – an oval matt patch, with that cursed little blemish at its centre. The message was clear – no more scrubbing at it. There was nothing more I could or should do about it. I had to put it from my mind, ignore it. There was no way Oskar would notice it.

What was I thinking? Of course he would notice it. I knew that he would. I chewed on a slice of sausage ruefully, and remembered the effort I had made to clean my flat before Oskar had come round to dinner that time. It had made little difference.

What did he want, after all? Even he could do nothing about the inevitable degradation of all things, the scuffs and scratches, the smuts and drips, the fingerprints and dust. Fingerprints are universal, the calling-card of humanity. I loved those forensics shows, the television police procedurals in which criminalists painstakingly reassemble human incident from smudges and residues, the blood drop and lipstick trace, the soiled tissue and shed thread. In those, the most evil criminals were always the ones who left the fewest clues. When a killer left no trace, not a hair, not so much as a single helix, you knew that you were dealing with a real bastard, a psychopath, calculating, emotionless, outside the human. An intellect vast and cool and unsympathetic. As for dust, that was more human than anything. It is primarily dead skin cells. We are walking dust factories. However futile it was, Oskar's resistance to this inevitable grime was magnificent.

It was too early for wine. I sipped it with care. It clung to my lips, and to the sides of the glass. Winemakers call this the 'legs', and it's a measure of the alcohol content of the wine – the 'stickiness' is caused by the spirit overcoming the liquid's surface tension.

Surface tension – not a bad description of my fears for the floor, and Oskar's other perfect planes. His other plane of existence. What was he doing right now? Approaching 3 a.m. in California – he would be still asleep in a hotel room, in that city of hotel rooms and freeways. My mental image of Los Angeles was a sun-baked tangle of asphalt clichés. LA was the nest of his wife, his soon-to-be-ex wife, Laura. I had met her only that once, when she came to dinner, and I had taken an instant dislike to her. She worked for a large American firm of auctioneers, and made extravagant amounts of money overseeing the transfer of fine art masterpieces between members of the super-rich. A perfectly legitimate line of business, but my muddy leftism caused me to regard it as somehow discreditable. She drank spirits, Oskar said (neat vodka, perhaps), and I had the strong impression that she did not think very highly of me, that my dislike of her was reciprocated. But my impression of her was fair, of course, and hers of me was a monstrous error based on snobbery.

A discreditable profession, exhibit A: she had described herself as an 'oil trader' when we met. Commodities, I assumed, but it was her idea of a joke. Not an icebreaker – it was a ploy to put me off balance and seize the initiative. The art of conversation according to Sun Tzu.

It didn't help that this exchange took place just inside the front door of my flat, an area that reeked of chemicals from the bleach onslaught I had deployed in the bathroom. The bathroom was next to the front door, as is strangely common in small London flats carved out of Victorian terraces. Welcome to my home – it may smell like a gassed trench, but that's preferable to it smelling like a latrine. When I consider the placement of that loo, outhouses at the bottom of the garden start looking like a smart move.

Oskar's toilet did not smell of chemicals or latrines. His bathroom smelled slightly of soap, but mostly it smelled of water. Not the marshy, damp smell that sometimes builds up in bathrooms. Water, the smell of a pristine glacial stream splashing onto rocks, the smell of ice. What is one actually smelling when one smells that smell? Ozone or ions or something. Perhaps if I paid more attention to shampoo adverts I would know.

I ran water over the plate and the paring knife and left them in the sink. Then I drained my glass, hovered over the taps, and turned back to the kitchen table. Again without allowing my actions much thought (*another* glass? And not yet 1 p.m.?), I took the wine bottle and thumbed the cork out of its neck. With my glass recharged, and my spirits recharged by its contents, I decided to take another look at Oskar's study as a prelude to maybe doing something constructive, something worthwhile. It drew me because it was so perfect an environment for work.

It was as I had left it, of course; it was almost exactly as Oskar had left it. There was a subtle, near-imperceptible change in the air in here, the smell of paper, of newspaper clippings slowly turning brown (the printing press autumn), the smell of dust. I could hardly see any dust, but it had left its infinitesimal aroma, a ghostly trace in the air. Those motes in their lazy but restless diurnal migration of convection. A dust diaspora, banished from the surfaces. But Oskar had been away, now, for two days – it was settling. The finest sprinkling could be seen on the lid of the baby grand piano. The cleaner would be coming soon to move it along again. Cleaning products often have violent names – Oust, Raid, Purge. One could easily be called Pogrom.

I set my glass down on the blotter on the desk and drew my finger across the top of the piano. It trailed a path in the traces of dust. Next, I attempted to write my name amid the particles, but there were too few to make it out clearly, and I wiped it away. It's a strange instinct, to want to sign one's name in misty windows, wet concrete, snow. It is like animals marking their territory, particularly in the case of men inscribing snow. But I do not think it is a possessive, exclusive act: 'This is mine, keep out.' When we were a young species, the world must have seemed so unlimited and trackless, and to leave traces of oneself must have been to reach out, wanting to connect with others, strangers who would always remain strangers. To make one's mark then was an expression of how deeply we longed to see the signs of others.

Idly, I struck a piano key (I do not know which one – it was near the middle) and listened to the note ring in the air. On the far side of the door, the television was still on, near-inaudible, a soft rhythm of speech and jingle, and there was the street, cars (not so many), trams (regular) and feet.

The trams dislodged a thought in my mind. I looked over the shelves of CDs, with their serious, wordy classical spines, and found a small section of works produced by the local Philharmonic. Oskar must have had some role to play in many of these recordings and, sure enough, there were some copies of *Variations on Tram Timetables.* Lou Reed was still in the CD player; I evicted him and opened the case containing Oskar's *Meisterwerk.*

There was a slip of paper inside the case.

I hope you enjoy it! – O.
(There is better to come when Dewey is finished.)

How nice of him, I thought, or at least began to think as the sentiment stopped dead in my mind, like the needle being ripped off the surface of an old vinyl LP. This wasn't *nice,* or if it *was* nice it was nice in a sinister spectrum of nice that I did not have the ability to see. How many of these notes were there? Briefly, the thought of ripping the place apart occurred to me, before I shook it from my head. It was just creepy, not threatening, and no reason to go insane. And if you must go insane it's best to have a reason. If anything, Oskar was exposing a mental weakness of his own. I should feel superior.

The CD tray of the stereo was still sticking out, pornographically exposed. A tongue, a seedy player. I put in the disc of *Variations* and closed it, then scrumpled up the little note and dropped it in the bin. Was that a mistake? Perhaps I should have left the note in situ, so that Oskar would not know that I had been listening to his music. But the note had made clear that he welcomed my listening ('I hope you enjoy it'), so maybe it was good to show interest. Also, if I put the note back now, I would have to smooth it out first, and it would be obvious that I had opened the case, screwed up the note, and then returned it, an obviously lunatic course of events. In any case, maybe the notes were Oskar's way of keeping track of exactly where I had been in the flat. Faced with control-freakery of that order, what was the polite course – conceal traces, or helpfully leave them where possible?

But it was impossible to second-guess tactics of this kind. If they really were tactics; there was the strong possibility that Oskar's actions were entirely guileless and friendly, and my reaction was the aberration. 'Crazy,' I said to myself softly.

Play. Oskar's composition whizzed up in the player – his talent began its exhibition. The opening was very simple, a low metronomic note; then, with a higher double-note that sounded almost exactly like a tram bell, the piece suddenly became far more complex. What appeared to be three, or even four, different elements within the tune headed off in various directions, obscuring the composition with apparent chaos, then meeting and intersecting. They were simple, repetitive building blocks, like the beating of metal wheels over points, but at some moments it was difficult to tell how many pianos were involved.

Originally, of course, only the piano in this room had been involved. How did one do that – hear music that is nowhere but inside, and snare it, note by note? Was Oskar a genius? I had no way to tell. Being un-musical, a six-note advertising jingle is a work of alchemical, transcendent skill to me. But Oskar was clearly gifted, set apart from all but a tiny fraction of men and women. An agonising wash of inferiority swept over me – what had I ever done? Here was Oskar's skill, picked out in Dolby clarity. Thanks to my work, many London residents now knew the phone number of their borough pest control officer, and what to do with discarded white goods. I like to think that I had invested my work with a little élan, but it remained the case that if I had not existed, those leaflets would merely have been written by someone else.

I regarded the piano with a mixture of curiosity and awe. It was all bulk, mixed curved and straight lines, reticent surfaces and concealed capabilities, like a stealth bomber. Do not play with the piano, Oskar had said. That presumptuous 'with' – of course, you won't be able to play the piano, the most that can be expected is that you will play *with* it, like a child, and you shouldn't even do that.

With as much care as I could muster, I opened the top of the piano and propped it up. There were its workings, complicated but unmysterious, ranks of sleeping soldiers, a harp set on its side. I hit a key and one of the hammers leapt up like toast out of a toaster, a note that gatecrashed the still-playing CD. Such a clear sound from a congregation of clumsy elements – wood, string, felt. Another note, clear and anachronistic in the music.

A strident machine bleat tore the calm, sending a jug of iced water down my spine. I came very close to dropping my glass, and had it not been empty, I would have spilled some of its contents. To be careful, I put it back on the desk, and as I did so the electronic shriek repeated. The phone was ringing. What does one do in these circumstances? Answer another man's phone? It might be Oskar – what time was it in Los Angeles? My great fear was that, if I answered the phone, the person on the other end of the line might not speak English, and I would be taken for an intruder and the police would be summoned. How likely was this?

Third ring. Ring? It was like the death cry of a robot seagull. Eastern Bloc engineering, no doubt modified from the radiation leak alarm on a nuclear submarine.

Fourth ring. If it was Oskar, it was best to seem 'in', guarding the flat. If it was a non-Anglophone, I would just repeat Oskar's name like an idiot. I caught the phone in the first half-second of the fifth ring, an assonant hiccup cut short.

'Hello?'

A crackling, long-distance pause, the hiss of dust-covered copper cables. 'Hello, hello, it is Oskar.'

'Hello, Oskar. How are you?'

'I am fine, I think.' Electric emptiness loomed behind his words, and threatened to overwhelm them. I started to do mental arithmetic; Los Angeles is seven hours behind London, and I was two hours ahead; it was past 1 p.m. ... this was wrong.

'What time is it there?'

'It is late. Or early. I am jet-lagged. Are you listening to my music?'

Variations was still on. There was no room for 'no' in Oskar's question. 'Yes. It's very good.'

'Hrm. Is everything OK in the apartment?'

My eye strayed to the cats on the sofa and the stain on the floor. The stain was actually hidden from me by the coffee table, but I felt I could still see it; a flash burn on the retina, always in centre view until you tried to look at it, when it swam away.

'Yes, yes, fine. I meant to ask ...'

'Yes?'

'You mentioned a cleaner – when do they come?'

'Does something need to be cleaned?'

Yes, everything, always. 'No, but I just thought I should know in case I'm naked or something.'

A tram passed by, clunking into the distance, trailing with it my ability to take back what I had just said.

'Are you naked now?'

'No! But I don't know if I have to be here to let them in or something.'

'She has a key.'

'OK.' There was a cork on the kitchen table in front of me. My unoccupied hand picked it up and started to roll it back and forth between my fingers. Was this call really necessary? Was there some unasked question in the background, with the tinfoil shush of the line? Was Oskar waiting for some unknown reassurance from me?

'You are having a good time?' Oskar was in the habit of framing statements as questions – not in the infuriating Valley-speak manner of Californians, but in a more philosophical, European manner, as if preceding the quasi-query with the unspoken words *We can of course both take it as read that* ... This, however, was a straightforward question.

'Oh, yes. I went sightseeing yesterday – saw the National Museum ...'

'While you are there, you really should go to see the Philharmonic. You will go?'

'Yes, maybe, if I have the time ...'

'Time? What else are you doing? The Philharmonic is in its summer season, and I helped set the programme. It is very good. Will you go tomorrow?'

'Tomorrow?' I wanted to say that I had made plans for tomorrow, but that would have been an obvious lie. While thinking of a better lie (I almost had one), I let too long a pause bleed into the conversation.

'Tomorrow, then,' Oskar said, decisive and clearly cheerful at the thought of inflicting classical music on me. 'I will call them and make arrangements for a ticket in your name.'

'Oskar, you don't have to ...'

'Yes, I can always get free tickets, so I will call them. Seven-thirty. It is Schubert, "The Trout" and "Death and the Maiden". Very good. Very popular. You will like it.'

I squeezed the cork hard. Apathy and boredom fought within me. Going out seemed like such a chore, but at the very least, it was something to do. Another silence was emptying into the conversation. 'Isn't "Death and the Maiden" a film?'

This time, the silence unfolded on Oskar's end of the line. 'Ariel Dorfman wrote a play called *Death and the Maiden*,' Oskar said, with the air of someone explaining a point to a slow child. 'It is about this piece of music.'

'But there was a film as well,' I protested, somewhat wretchedly. A bubble of memory floated up. 'With Sigourney Weaver.'

'I remember it. I will make the arrangements. Goodbye for now.'

'Um, goodbye Oskar. Thanks for calling.'

The 'ling' of my last word was transmitted nowhere. The call had ended.

I put the phone down, and flicked the cork into the air, trying to catch it with my other hand. It evaded my grasp and skittered and bounced across the floor, startling one of the cats, which froze for a split second and then pounced, stopping the errant stopper. Ha! I don't know what it thought it was – a vole in a tiny barrel, perhaps. The discovery that it had captured a cylinder of soft bark didn't seem to disappoint the cat, though. Instead, it held its prize in outstretched front paws, hindquarters hunched and tensed; then it freed the cork, batted it to one side, and pounced again. Pow!

The bottle emptied, I set down my recharged glass and tapped the cork across the floor with my foot. The cat was on top of it like a furry slingshot. It was impossible not to laugh. I hooked the cork back with the side of my foot, the cat tensed like a sprinter, and I kicked again – a tailed comet streaked across the floor. (The other cat was on the sofa, ignoring all this. What fills a cat's mind in those idle hours of reverie? Where do they go?)

An idea occurred to me. For the third time, I retrieved the now slightly dog-eared (cat-eared?) cork – the moggie put up more of a fight this time – then punted it into the room's most remote corner. Then, I opened one of the kitchen drawers, an out-of-the-way one that looked as if it might contain string.

Inside the drawer was a note from Oskar.

> Corkscrew – in drawer by sink. Torch, batteries – in bottom drawer under sink. 1st aid box, aspirin – in bathroom. Cleaning things, candles – in pantry.
>
> This drawer: spices.

Indeed, the drawer contained spices, and that distinctive spice-rack melange of smells. And Oskar's note, another note. Did all the drawers contain notes like this? I had taken cutlery from a drawer, and there had been no note. Curious, I tried the next drawer along, and there was another little note, identical to the first one except for:

This drawer: Place mats. Coasters.

Two lines under coasters. It was very pleasing to see that even when he was surprising me, Oskar was, in a way, predictable. That made two notes – but they were not in all the drawers. Perhaps it was possible to discern Oskar's thinking here; maybe he thought that, if I was hunting through unexpected drawers, I might be looking for items on his little treasure-hunt list. I might need them in a hurry.

I wanted string. When might Oskar use string? It occurred to me that some of Oskar's papers in the study had been tied up with string, so I went through to look in his desk drawers and returned, triumphantly, a minute later with a piece between three and four feet long.

After a little work, the cork was tied to the end of the piece of string, and I embarked on my experiment. I flicked the tethered cork out towards my subject, the still-alert cat. It had not lost its killer passion, and went for the mark with vim, the deadly determination of a plain single girl going for a thrown bridal bouquet. But just as it reached the cylinder, I pulled on the string and yanked it away. The cat dashed in pursuit. It was a game; I wondered if the cat knew it. It cannot really have believed that it was chasing some sort of animal, a meal-in-waiting. Play – another thing that doesn't separate us from the animals. It was possible, however, that it separated me from Oskar. Did he play with the cats like this? That was difficult to believe, but I would not have considered him capable of keeping animals in the first place. Fish, maybe, because they kept to their real estate and had simple needs that corresponded well to his scheduled mind. Instead he had made room in his life, in his flat, for such an autonomous, deranging creature as the house cat. Two, indeed.

It was slightly galling that the cat tired of the game before I did. It was as if the illusion that it was snatching at a live quarry had suddenly dispelled, and it saw the situation for what it was – a man teasing a cat with a cork on the end of a piece of string. The fifteenth or sixteenth time I threw the cork, my playmate simply did not move. It studied the projectile with geological indifference and turned away, tail aloft like a raised middle finger.

This exercise had tired me, and the day had turned hot. I slumped into the sofa and fiddled with the knot that held the string to the cork. A headache was lingering above the top of my spine, a sickly, dry pang. Too much wine, too early in the day.

Emma had drunk too much, too early in the day, when Oskar and Laura came round for dinner. Someone in her office – she worked in PR – had left their job that Friday; the staff had gone out for lunch together and never returned to work, following the bistro with the pub. She had not returned by the time Oskar and the oil trader turned up, punctually, at seven-thirty. An anxious call to her mobile at six-thirty had yielded the information that she was 'on her way'. Shortly before seven-thirty, an almost panicky call to her mobile uncovered the fact that she was still 'on her way', despite the fact that she had evidently not left the pub – raucous laughter and the baying of a

West End tavern crammed with office types made her excuses almost inaudible.

Oskar asked where she was almost immediately.

'She's on her way,' I said. I was half sure that I wasn't lying. Emma had never met Oskar; he was my friend and she had been lukewarm about the dinner. Still, I had assured her that Oskar was 'really, really nice', so perhaps we were both only on nodding terms with the truth.

'I don't know how you Brits cope with such small apartments,' Laura said after we moved through to the living room. Maybe she was attempting to make innocent conversation, but now I was parsing her every word for barbs, and finding them.

'It's enough for me,' I said, and started opening a bottle of wine. 'London is very expensive.'

'Even Clapham?' Clap-Ham, not Clappam. I felt a surge of anti-Americanism, which snapped back as self-loathing – predictable bloody middle-class left-wing reaction. If I was even boring myself, it was hard to see how I was coming across as a charming host. I poured the predictable Merlot and put on a predictably banal bit of middle-class easy-listening dinner-party background music.

'It's considered very desirable,' I said, defending my chosen neighbourhood.

'*Really?*' Laura replied, clearly not convinced.

'Shall we discuss schools next?' Oskar interjected, all cool and continental. 'I think that is the prescribed second topic for these occasions.'

* * *

My minor headache was still minor, but other symptoms had developed – an acid swirl in the stomach, a general sense of metabolic unease. What this was, I realised, was a miniature hangover, a hangover in the middle of the afternoon, when I had been clean sober just a few hours before. There were therefore two rather depressing options – drink some water and ride through it, maybe taking a bit of a lie-down, or drink more, swamp it back into remission for later handling, aggressive vinotherapy. A catastrophe in Africa was being dispensed in bite-size nuggets from the television – generally disgusted, I switched it off.

At first, we decided to wait for Emma to arrive before starting eating. But the chicken breasts were drying out in the oven, the potatoes were softening in the pot, the conversation was not tripping along as nimbly as I wanted. By eight-fifteen, I surrendered, opened another bottle, and we started to eat.

Emma turned up shortly after nine. She was hardly able to stand. My anger with her served no helpful purpose, and I wasn't going to compound the situation by instigating a flaming row with her on the doorstep. Considering her state, it could have been disastrous, a road crash of screaming tears. Instead, I was icily accepting of the situation, and suggested that she might want to drink some water and have a bit of a lie-down. She agreed, and was out cold on top of the duvet before I had finished taking off her shoes.

By the time I returned to the table, embarrassment and untargeted anger were still stumbling about clumsily inside me. I had drunk a fair amount myself, we all had.

'I'm so sorry,' I said grimly. 'This evening has not gone as smoothly as I wanted. Christ.'

'No, I am very much enjoying myself,' Oskar said, smiling.

A bright tongue of fury flickered inside me. I glared at him. 'Of course. Of course you're enjoying yourself. You must be having a terrific time. It must give you considerable pleasure, seeing that I still can't organise a fucking thing. Well, I don't fucking care if you disappro— No, actually I *do* care if you disapprove, I care a fuck of a lot but I can't do a fucking thing about it. I don't like being looked down on, I really ...' Oskar wasn't smiling any more. I felt an urgent need to bring my remarks to a close. 'I really hate it.'

'As a matter of fact,' Oskar said, with the pedantic care of a non-native English speaker deploying an idiom, 'I was being sincere.'

I was already flushed, with wine and ire, but I felt the crimson deepen a shade. I had never actually killed a friendship before; mostly they just died of neglect or slipped into comas.

'I do not get very many chances to see you,' Oskar continued, 'and I enjoy your company. I do not care about Emma. It is "one of those things". And I do not look down at you.'

'Shit. I'm sorry,' I said. Laura was looking at me intensely, apparently fascinated.

'Honesty ...' Oskar began, and stopped, looking for words. I was struck by how old he looked – not geriatric, but mature, adult. Wise, not wizened. We are the same age, and I felt like an adolescent being talked to by a grown-up. 'Honesty is important. It is interesting to know these things about you, and how you feel.'

The air did not feel clear, however. It felt freighted with angst, my angst. 'I'm angry with Em, I suppose. I wanted this to be a much better evening.'

Oskar waved this away. 'Now let me be honest for a time. I do not compare myself with you. You are not a musician; I measure myself only as a musician against other musicians. Once, I cared what others thought, and now I do not greatly care. When we met I liked you because you were very "at ease", and I was not at ease, and I liked your tolerance of other people. But I do not think that you see that your tolerance has become ... a *poison*, a poison to you. You care too much about how others see you, and making room for them, and you tolerate, you tolerate everything; you live in this dim little flat, and you do not even like it, I do not think you like Emma very much but you tolerate her because you think you should have a girlfriend, and I am sure that you hate your job, but you tolerate it, and why? For money? There is no money! Because you work at home? Why do you want to work here? And the very bad thing is that you tolerate yourself. You are messy and chaotic and disorganised and to be frank rather lazy, and it makes you unhappy, but what do you do? You are tolerating the situation. Are you waiting to be forced into action by something outside? It will not happen.'

In the light of this, I was beginning to feel that my tirade had been justified. How could he not be comparing his life to mine? Every moment I had known him, he had been on the graceful and swift ascendant arc of his ambition. He was at all times a perfectly placed ornament on the plan of his life. I had no plan, just a series of problems and workarounds. 'Whatever you say, it sounds like you have a very low opinion of me.'

'No,' Oskar said firmly. 'You misunderstand. I do not have a low opinion of you – I have a low opinion of your circumstances. I really have no opinion of you other than the fact that I like you. My opinion is: you are my friend.'

He took a drink of wine. No one said anything for a short while. The CD had come to an end some time earlier; I didn't feel up to putting another on.

'What d'we do now?' Laura said, a sudden flare of brightness and energy. 'Play Pictionary?'

They didn't stay much longer. Neither did Emma, for that matter. We had a low-level passive-aggressive row about her lateness that hungover Saturday, a skirmish that did not have much significance among the conflicts that consumed the relationship as it collapsed over the next couple of months. Neither of us had firm reasons for breaking up beyond the fact that we did not have much reason to be together. She instigated the final severance; I did not mind, and did not mourn its passing. We are not in touch.

My headache nagged at me. I certainly was not going to have a bit of a lie-down. That was defeat, of a sort. The only option was to keep drinking.

DAY FOUR

I was woken by a shell-burst in the trench of sleep. Heart skipping, with eyes fighting light, my thoughts sprang up like a field of starlings startled by a farmer's gunshot, a thousand separate, autonomous specks that swirled into a single united black shape.

There had been a noise in the flat, loud enough to rouse me, but it had no characteristics in my mind, having occurred in the wastes at the edge of sleep. What had happened? And now there were more noises – shuffling footsteps in the hall outside, a thump with a rattle of bottles. The door to the bedroom now seemed atom-thin, and there was someone beyond it – more footsteps, a rough sigh like antique waxed raincoats being pushed aside in a long-closed closet.

I sprang out of bed, striking up a cloud of body odour and sweated alcohol, and prompting a wet slam of sick pain in the back of my head like the echo of the sudden noise that had woken me. A slam – the front door had slammed and someone had come into the flat. I was wearing boxer shorts, T-shirt and a sticky veneer of sweat; my trousers were lying near the foot of the bed, polio twisted. How much had I drunk yesterday? No memory of going to bed. Who was in the flat? What time was it?

The sun was already high in the sky, but there were no cats on the balcony; I must have gone to bed without letting them leave for their night out. It was alarming that I had been drunk enough to completely absent myself from the controls. As I pulled on my trousers, I found myself thinking that it was lucky that I had taken them off in the first place. A pendulum of nausea swung and rotated in my neck, just below my Adam's apple. And my bladder was full – a blessing, really, as it meant that I had not emptied it at some inappropriate moment in the night. At a New Year's Eve house party once, a friend of mine, mentally violated beyond reason by happy Russian quantities of vodka and finding himself in unfamiliar surroundings, had relieved himself in a wardrobe. Remarkably, very little was actually splashed around the wardrobe's interior, showing that some aiming had taken place. The urine was more liberally spilled the next morning, when the owner of the house had suggested a bracing walk around the local woods, and had gone to put on his wellies. At least they were warm.

Barefoot, conscious that my hair indicated that I had just risen from bed and had not been up since 6 a.m. studying Bible verses, I left the bedroom. In the kitchen, the bat-faced old woman I had run into on the stairs yesterday – the day before yesterday, my recovering brain corrected me, apparently determined that it would keep its owner up to date on the present status of the planet's rotation if nothing else, and invoicing me a jolt of queasy pain for its trouble – was tidying up the kitchen with the thoroughness of a secret policeman roughing up a dissident.

She saw me, and displeasure flashed across a face supremely adapted for displaying that emotion. Without saying a word, she turned abruptly towards the utility room, so that my 'good morning' was directed at the malignant knot of hair that was stitched to the back of her head. (A 'bun', although it had none of the pleasant bakery-fresh connotations of that word.) She dipped from sight for a moment and then reappeared bearing, to my revulsion, the cats' litter tray, which she thrust under my nose with an angry exclamation. Four or five little feline turds rocked back and forth on the litter, and vomit rose in my throat.

'Ugh,' I said, and turned away.

'——!' she said, repeating her opening remark with some intensity. '——! ——? ——!'

Her meaning wasn't hard to discern – I should have emptied the tray, freshened up the grit and raked it into a little Zen garden for Shossy and Stravvy to contemplate during their meditations. I liked the cats, but was now reminded why I didn't have any of my own. This woman, Batface, I did *not* like, and I wanted very much for her to go away. It was, however, now clear that she was the cleaner as well as the concierge of this building, and that she would not be leaving until she had finished whatever she was here to do. How long would that take? An hour? Two? Could I hide in the bedroom or the study until she had vacated the premises? She would presumably want to clean the bathroom at some stage, which meant going through the bedroom – I thought of the sloshing wellies. I had to get to the bathroom before her, to check nothing was amiss.

'——!' Batface continued. Waving the litter tray expansively around the kitchen. In my mind's eye I saw the tray spilling, scattering its contents onto the floor, the cats pouncing after the falling, cork-like turds ... another spasm of nausea. But not a speck was spilled. The cats were on the sofa (did she know about the sofa injunction?), sensibly pretending to be asleep, a strategy I wished I had adopted. The kitchen didn't look so bad to me – a couple of empty or half-empty wine bottles, hardly any washing up, but clearly well short of Oskar's scrupulous standards. There was an empty tin of tuna on the counter, with a fork next to it and some light smears of oil around it – I remembered that it had been my supper and the cats had clearly had a go at it in the night. Deep in my digestive tract, I feared that the tuna had turned salmon and was about to attempt to swim upstream.

The cleaner picked up a third-empty bottle of wine, showed it to me meaningfully, stuck a cork in its neck and thrust it into the wine rack on the kitchen counter.

'I'm sorry things are a little untidy,' I said. 'I've been meaning to ...' I had no way of finishing that sentence, and in any case the language barrier meant that there was no point. I smiled stupidly. My bladder, which had been politely waiting its turn, called for attention. I walked back through to the bedroom.

Things weren't that bad, surely. The disorder of the living room was minimal, and Batface's reaction seemed extreme. Perhaps it was not the state of the flat that she objected to, but the tendency it represented – it was on a vector of neglect, pointed at inevitable chaos, a Hobbesian anarchy of filth, disrepair and coaster negligence. I relieved myself, and – mind still fuddled with alcohol – the porcelain rim of the toilet bowl wobbled in my imagination, transmuting into green, vulcanised rubber ... The odd thing about that incident at the New Year's Eve house party was that I had some elemental sympathy with what it felt like to pee into a wellington boot. My friend had done it – he had taken the blame for it. He had, however, no memory of doing it, and somehow on some subatomic level, I did have a memory of doing it. It was not that I remembered doing it, but I felt certain that if I was to urinate into a welly now, I would experience a powerful sense of déjà vu. I didn't do it, of course. I didn't remember doing it. I was fairly certain that I didn't do it. There was no way that someone could do something like that and not remember it – but then my friend had done it, and he claimed to have no memory of doing it.

I wanted to have a shower. Not while she was in the flat, though. Did that matter so much, if there were two closed doors between us, one of them locked? Clearly it did, because I was uncomfortable: I would wait until she left.

Once I had washed my hands, I stared into the mirror. Stubble, and dark rings under the eyes. The strip-light above the sink was pitiless – my face was a tapestry of flaws. An extractor fan whirred. This was, of course, madness, to be trapped here simply by the presence of the cleaner. I felt deracinated. If I left the flat, there was nowhere to go. Maybe a local café or park, not that I knew of any. It was another warm day, even hot, so simply wandering was possible, unless I got lost. But walking aimlessly did not appeal. Another facet of paranoia sparkled in my mind – without a shower, I might stink. Last night had been heavy going. No doubt the smell of alcohol was still on me, seeping from my pores.

I brushed my teeth, taking far more time than the job required, and combed my hair. I splashed cold water on my face, and my headache seemed to recede into a dry shell around my brain. The nausea seemed to be in retreat as well, but the battle against it was not yet won. These little acts of grooming steadied me. It was clear, however, that I had to get out.

The bedroom seemed incrementally smaller, as if a thick layer of paint had been added to its white walls. It was as if the walls were reflecting my own feeling of griminess back at me, as if they too were covered in a veneer of drying sweat, my minor depravity externalised and inflicted on them. The subjective made objective. I snatched up my light jacket – it was probably too warm for it, but to leave the flat with nothing seemed uncomfortable, a display of my lack of purpose – and walked briskly into the hall, announced 'I'm going out for a minute', and almost threw myself through the front door.

It was another hot day, but an insecure and troubled one, spooked by occasional gasps of cooler wind. These stirred an atmosphere that was otherwise as thick and sticky as Turkish delight. The sky was an intense dark blue.

Wanting to explore new territory, I followed the tramlines away from the city centre. There were not many people on the streets, and this gave the city an evacuated, expectant feel. Three trams passed me, all headed into the centre. This directionality, and the closeness of the air, gave me a sense of pressure building to my rear. It was a relief, however, that not many people were around, as I was still self-conscious of being unshowered. It was even a relief when I began to sweat in the torrid heat; this fresh perspiration, it seemed, would dissolve and displace the stale. It had been my plan to stick to the tramlines as a precaution against getting lost – I could always follow them back. But after three blocks, I unexpectedly found myself at a small bridge. The street perpendicular to the tram tracks was divided by a deep canal, a narrow vein of filthy, oil-rainbowed water, unmoving and pocked here and there with reefs of rubbish. The water was a clear eight feet beneath street level, and girded by blackened stone walls. A flight of steps from some Piranesi dungeon fantasy led down from the bridge to a slender footpath. It was not exactly inviting, but I descended anyway.

A fetid, marshy smell rose from the water. The thought of rats sent a scurry of mild, irrational fear through my mind, which swiftly shifted focus – what if this was no canal but a storm drain, and a sudden downpour (which seemed possible in this tropical weather) flooded it, drowning me and sweeping my body out of the city with the other rubbish, flushed away to some remote hinterland? But, I reasoned once reason had jolted awake, this was not the climate for storm channels, and besides, they did not have towpaths. Los Angeles, that was the city that needed storm drains – a parched metropolis with intermittent flash floods. A city locked into a binge-purge cycle, bulimic urban hydrology, stunt rivers.

It was appreciably cooler by the canal. For some reason its near-dereliction, the mature weeds sprouting at intervals where path and wall met, the undredged water, the corruption in the air, appealed to me, matched my darkened state of mind and calmed me. There was romance to it, just as Piranesi had found romance in prisons. Neglect had a kind of gentleness to it that plucked at the sentimental. Time had passed here, undisturbed; I passed time there, undisturbed.

She had gone by the time I returned to the flat. The slight smell of bleach lingered behind her, and the cats were fed. All the clothing I had taken out of my bags had been folded with ostentatious care and stacked neatly on the chair in the bedroom, clean and unclean items mixed. This intrusion irritated me intensely – it might be forgivable for the anonymous cleaning staff of a hotel, but here it felt like a deliberate violation. The bathroom also smelled slightly of bleach. I took my shower, at last. Tonight, I was going to a concert, I thought as the previous night washed down the drain. A concert. Schubert.

'It is Schubert,' I said to myself, mimicking Oskar's voice. 'It is Schubert. Very good. You will like it.'

The water swirled and circled around my feet, which looked pale. They didn't look like the sort of feet that would typically walk into concert halls. They didn't look like the sort of feet whose owner would say, in a clear voice, 'I would like tickets to tonight's concert, please' and mean it. No, not the sort of feet that would stay still for two hours under an uncomfortable seat in a darkened room while their owner did nothing, nothing but listen to classical music.

'Schubert,' I said to myself. 'Shooby shooby Schubert.' Shossy, Stravvy, Shooby. Was there any way of getting out of this concert? I could just not show up. But Oskar would certainly discover this – if he wasn't offended by the no-show, he really should be, it was an act of calculated rudeness. No, I would have to take my punishment like a man. Besides, there was an entire day to waste before then.

The shower blasted most of my hangover away, but did not wipe it entirely. A sticky residue seemed to have formed on the inside of my skull, around the bottom of the back of the brain, and subversive elements were still abroad in my elbows, knees and gut. The day itself was tacky to the touch, with the humidity rising. As the afternoon wore on, I became aware that the quality of the light had changed, as if the real thing had been replaced with a synthetic 'economy' brand in the hope that daylight savings could be made without anyone noticing. But I noticed, and I looked up from what I had been doing – stroking the fur of a snoozing cat on the sofa – to see that the buildings on the opposite side of the street looked peculiarly bright, as if their stone or stucco was suddenly luminescent under its layer of filth, a lightbox piercing an X-ray smoked with tumours. Indeed, they were bouncing back the now-slanting rays of the descending sun, but the peculiarity of their illumination was a matter of contrast owing to the abrupt, unheralded darkness of the sky behind them, which had turned an intense slate grey, pregnant with blue and purple tones; an embolism of a sky, a dam behind which unimaginable pressure had built. But still the sun shone on the buildings across the street, transforming their façades into shining lies, Potemkin structures keeping up a pretence of fair weather when the storm was coming, without doubt, with no compromise in its inevitability.

And the storm came, with thunder like a starting gun, triggering marathon rain. I had to run to the bedroom, certain that the French windows there were open (they were not), such was the pervasive noise, the crazed applause of a million falling raindrops. Lightning on the white cotton duvet lit up the bed like a giant UV bug killer blazing with the death of a small creature, and in the study (where the windows were also closed), the water running down the panes appeared, by reflection, to be cascading down the open, obsidian lid of the piano.

It was exhilarating, this sudden burst of rain, it was action after stasis, a motive kick to an inert body. To my inert body: my heart was beating faster after the dash from room to room, and the activity had infused me with a sudden elation. To my surprise, I found that I was actually looking forward to going out, in the storm, to hear the concert, that I felt energised about it, that the *sturm und drang* pounding at the windows made me feel positively Wagnerian. *Götterdämmerung*! 'Death and the Maiden', it sounded good, bombastic, stormy ... 'The Trout', of course, did not. It was not even a very dynamic fish, not predatory like a shark or a pike, but then what did I know about fish or, for that matter, classical music? For all I knew, the trout might be one of nature's trick questions and, like the whale, not a fish at all but a kind of rat or swan or something.

The cat I had been stroking on the sofa had been stirred up as well, possibly by the downpour, more probably by me jumping out of my seat to check the windows. It was now standing, turning a slow, tired circle on the black leather, white-tipped tail periscoping left and right. Our eyes locked, feline on the Swiss sofa, me by the study door, and I had a sense that something passed between us, some iota of information or moment of understanding. In this premonitory nanosecond I knew that the cat was about to do something.

With provocative, lingering lack of haste, the cat arched up its hindquarters, stretched out its front legs, and exposed its claws, which it then raked back across the leather with a terrible ripping, popping noise.

I think I made some wordless sound of horror, some throaty, gasping protest, because the cat stopped, paused halfway through its steady act of vandalism, forelegs still extended, claws still exposed but for their points, which were dug into the hide of the sofa seat. It looked at me; I looked at it. It seemed, as it often does, so unfair and limiting that life does not have a little switch or dial that can turn back time a short way. A mere thirty seconds would be enough for most situations like this, not much to ask, but it seemed we were stuck with the tedious, unrelenting tyranny of linear time.

'Fuck! No, fuck, shoo!' I exclaimed, lunging towards the sofa. The cat took the message and bolted. I was left inspecting the damage – two ranked sets of tiny tears in the leather, strung together by scratch trails. It clearly could not be repaired, saving some arcane process known to a shrinking number of wizened old men that I knew nothing of. Why can't leather simply heal up, I wondered? It is just skin, after all. I ran my fingertips across the scars, caressed them, but I did not feel them scab and seal under my touch. The surface was not completely broken, just deeply scratched. Maybe there were secret, invisible menders out there ... but I didn't like my chances of finding such a person in London, let alone in this foreign place. Looking down at the sofa, my eye of course strayed to the wine stain, beautifully framed by its pale, scrubbed penumbra. If the cleaner had seen it, she had either done nothing to it, or whatever she had done had made no difference.

My grandparents had a small pond in their suburban back garden, a pond that used to fascinate me, full as it was with slimy life. Frogs mated there, leaving great slicks of spawn. This was my childhood Serengeti. The pond was circled by concrete slabs. My mother used to tell me, the five- or six-year-old me, not to lean out too far while kneeling on the slab, a warning that I thought made no sense. I knew my own centre of gravity, precocious child that I was. There was no chance I would just fall in. But the slabs were not held in place with mortar or cement – they were just resting at the pond's edge to anchor the black plastic waterproof lining. Years of moss and the encroaching lawn made them look like permanent geological features, but they were loose, and one day I leaned over too far, the slab see-sawed on the edge of the pond, and I was dumped into the water.

I remember being told once that, on average, a man will spend twenty-four hours of his life having an orgasm. This is no doubt apocryphal, but if you did tot up all those explosive seconds, you would probably arrive at a surprising length of time. And I imagine that we spend a similar lengthy period, over a lifetime, in the middle of an accident – in the act of tripping over, or dropping something breakable, or otherwise engaged in routine slapstick. While on my way into the pond, an appreciable amount of time between the moment when balance was definitively lost and the moment when contact was made with the surface of the water, a perfectly articulated thought occurred to me: *This was why Mum warned me not to lean over too far.* It made perfect sense now. Such a pity, though, that this insight should only strike at this moment, when the tipping point had been passed, when the situation became irretrievable. It was as if the thought had been waiting, fully formed, underneath the paving slab, waiting to be released and flit into the cortex at the moment of crisis.

This was why Oskar did not allow the cats on the sofa. This, this was the reason, not the hair, and it was only now the damage had been done that the reasoning became clear. It had oozed like a bead of blood from the gashed leather. Regretful, after-the-event wisdom; the Germans must have a word for it. Oskar would know. If they didn't have such a word, they should. We rely on them for things like that.

The cats were off the furniture; the stable door was firmly closed as part of standard equine post-bolting procedures. The damage done could not be undone, and I felt a numbing calm. The storm had broken, the tipping point had been passed, and that was that. Things were as they were; lessons had been learned. We were all a little older and a little wiser. It was a scratch and a minor stain. It was not a matter of life and death. Outside, in the rain, trams still throbbed their dreary, reassuring bassline, an overhead spark and visceral rumble to match the spark and rumble of the storm.

The sky lightened for a short time after the worst of the storm had passed and the steady rain thinned out the clouds, but the heavens never cleared and the rain never ceased, although it did diminish from a torrent to an insistent and steady stream. When seven came near, the recovering daylight began to retreat again as the sun sank somewhere behind the thick duvet of cloud that smothered the continent.

It was a short walk to the concert hall, as I had known for a while. I could not imagine Oskar elbowing his way onto a tram every morning with an *International Herald Tribune* and a briefcase full of fresh batons, perhaps individually wrapped in hygienic paper like the chopsticks and toothpicks in Chinese restaurants. The pavements were slick with water, their surface animated by the raindrops beating upon them. I carried an umbrella from the stand under the coat-hooks by the front door, a cheap collapsible obviously intended as a spare – next to it was a bayonet-straight, mahogany-handled patrician number that was clearly Oskar's first choice. I considered umbrellas essentially disposable items, an opinion forced on me by the fact that I have unintentionally disposed of so many through the years, and so I always buy cheap ones and strive not to become too emotionally attached to them, as soon they will be making their way in the world without me. Oskar's umbrella looked simultaneously brand-new expensive and antique expensive. There was no way it was leaving the flat in my company. There would be no more screw-ups, not tonight. Tonight, I was not even in the flat to screw anything up.

Brooks ran in the gutters, seeking lower elevations. The canal would be refreshed tonight, I thought. Most of the route to the concert hall was along one avenue, a tree-lined axis of uncompromising straightness drawn to connect two cardinal points – a triumphal arch that led nowhere and which commemorated an entirely imaginary triumph, and a plain roundabout of no apparent significance. Either the palace or monument that had formed the other anchor had been removed – a distinct possibility in a country that could only function if it periodically forgot the colossal contradictions inherent in its history – or it had never existed in the first place.

The age that had had the confidence and power to smash these lines through its own capital had apparently balked at tweaking God into compliance. Like the Islamic carpets that contain a deliberate flaw, the avenue was disrupted by the Divine. An Eastern church erupted from a square bisected by the boulevard, a heavy castellated cube covered in antiseptically white plaster that seemed pulled in tight to every angle and leading edge, a starched bed sheet tucked impossibly tight by some psychotic matron, surmounted by a fungal mass of time-green copper domes. Generous, almost Catholic, gilt glinted through the rain miasma, and even in the grim light the whitewash shone in a way that suggested it was producing its own energy, throwing off a kind of Cherenkov radiation into the cooling tank of the city. It was possibly ancient, but so perfectly maintained that it might as well have been built yesterday, a fresh cube of tofu swimming in the city's murky tetsu broth.

On the other side of the avenue, the square had been greatly extended to accommodate the twentieth century's contribution to the scene. This was a looming stack of stained concrete boxes, badly streaked by the falling rain, simultaneously giving off an impression of awful, imposing weight and of moth-eaten fragility. It was as if the innocent grey halls on the South Bank of the Thames had swollen in the rain, bloated with multiplying cement and asbestos tumours, and suddenly started to broadcast ineffable malevolence and alien-ness. It was the poster child of a public safety campaign against modernism. Something about it screamed 'A gift from the Soviet people'.

For a single ghastly moment, frozen in the rain, I thought that this was the home of the Philharmonic, Oskar's Philharmonic. It was, after all, clearly a cultural facility of some sort. But the address did not tally, and instead I was directed behind the bulk of the church (which blocked, thank goodness, my view of the concrete monstrosity) to a modest Beaux-Arts façade in the adjoining street. Despite Oskar's domestic fondness for modern minimalism, this well-mannered assemblage of columns and caryatids was exactly what I had imagined his workplace would look like. It was a building that, with its time-polished wood and shiny brass around the doors, ever so slightly resembled a musical instrument itself. Inside, the steep and tightly curved flights of steps that led up and out of the foyer, with their gleaming banisters and carpet rods, gave an impression that one was standing inside a tuba, and the bowed windows behind which the ticket-sellers sat resembled the pipes in an organ, complete with half-moon aperture in place of the notch in the windway.

I was in good time, and joined the short queue to collect tickets. Other concert-goers stood around, mostly in ones or twos; there was a buzz of anticipatory conversation, but muted to an almost subliminal hum. It was an aged crowd and a conservative tendency in apparel was evident, with almost all present wearing suits and ties, and more than a few bow ties and waistcoats. In a similar crowd in London, I might have felt uncomfortably underdressed, but here I could safely wield the International Naïve Tourist Waiver. Plus I had absolutely no doubt that had Oskar considered a necktie obligatory, he would have mentioned it.

It was perhaps my imagination, but for all the efforts to keep up appearances there was a certain shabbiness to the crowd. Many of the gentlemen's jackets were patched at the elbows, polytechnic lecturer-style, and there was a note of exhaustion about their cuffs and other edges. Many of the ladies' dresses were shinier around the exposed bluffs and headlands than they were elsewhere. In terms of style – I am no judge of fashion, mind – I had the curious sense of gazing into the past, as if I had come to the end of a recorded programme on an ancient video tape and a curtain of static snow had fallen to reveal a far older programme underneath, halfway through, a Narnia beyond memory where the Berlin Wall still stood and all was reassuringly wrong with the world.

The shuffling shoes ahead of me in the queue were certainly cheap, fashioned out of recycled bakelite and perished tennis balls around the time the *General Belgrano* was taking on water. And there was a charity-shop smell in the air, a strong top note of dust with the slightest hint of incontinent mortality. But might the crowd simply be picking up these characteristics from their surroundings, the way that over-enthusiastic fluorescent lighting could bring out every infinitesimal sign of wear and distress in a face, simultaneously draining away colour? Certainly, I doubted that a dustbuster had ever attended to the richly folded rococo décor. The heavy red fabrics that were draped here and there looked a little as if the shadows in their folds might not disappear if the fabric was pulled taut; some of the gilt had eczema. Could the foyer be exercising some form of negative Dorian Gray influence over its patrons, whereby the saccharin cherubim and seraphim painted on the ceiling remained young by sapping all that was new, youthful and stylish out of the music-lovers below?

My ticket came with a strip of paper, blue-lined and possibly torn from an exercise book, wrapped around it. I unfolded this slip with a feeling of weary familiarity, but the handwriting that greeted me was not Oskar's: it looped and slipped its leash like an over-friendly dog.

Meet me in bar afterwards!
Michael. (friend of Oskar!)

OK then.

How was the concert? I have been asked this before by people, on the rare occasions that I have attended concerts, and I have never known what to say. Normally, I would just reply: 'Oh, very good.' By this I mean: 'There were no obvious mistakes. No notes were missed in such a clunkingly apparent fashion that I was able to detect the error. No one forgot how to play their instrument halfway through. No one ran amok in the audience. Nothing caught fire. Music played and I was so bored that my *hair* was bored.'

How was the concert? Not intolerable. I surprised myself by recognising the music. All classical music is recognisable in an oh-isn't-this-the-tune-from-the-Kenco-advert way, but I knew that I had heard 'Death and the Maiden' before – possibly from the Sigourney Weaver film – and 'The Trout' turned out to be the theme tune to a BBC sitcom from the 1990s that I had only the faintest traces of a memory of. Thus culturally anchored – and reassured that I wasn't about to be exposed to some two-hour experimental piece consisting of a crying baby and the sound of a shovel being dragged along a pavement – I was free to enjoy myself. Still, it was hard not to consider the nature of the psychological characteristic that others present possessed and I did not, the characteristic that meant their enjoyment was immersive and rapt, and mine was partial at best. When listening to classical music, I want to be able to read the paper at the same time, or potter about. If forced to devote my attention wholly to the music, I wonder what I am missing out on, what secret channel of sublimity I am not receiving, what tiny disposition of cartilage in the inner ear means that classical music is little more than nice background noise to me, high-quality aural wallpaper. Obliged to gaze upon this wallpaper for a couple of hours, my mind will always turn to other things.

With soaring heights of aesthetic joy apparently denied to me, my thoughts strayed to the corporeal. I started to think about my legs, and whether they were comfortable or not; I wondered if cavemen had sat like this at all, or whether it was a more recent thing. My legs were like sullen guests whom I had dragged along to this concert and was eager to please; my concern for them only intensified their grumbles. The focus on them grew sharper, soon pinpointing problems at microscopic level; a rogue fear that half a dozen blood cells had died and fused together, a newborn clot roaming the legs' circulation, searching blindly for some vital system to lodge in. All of a sudden, I was aware that I was a pulsing sack of blood, relying completely on the cooperation of millions upon millions of individual cells; these teeming workers had had little opportunity to make any grievances known to the controlling mind as their feedback and petitions were reduced to nonsense twinges and discomforts that I ascribed to either hypochondria or a hangover or dismissed entirely. But even now an enraged delegation of blood cells might be marching up a major artery, bearing at their processional fore an encrusted mass of their deceased brethren, intending to cram this clotted protest deep in the cerebrum and bring about a permanent industrial stoppage. Strike, meet stroke.

But the music did not stop suddenly, as I feared it might, an abrupt silence brought on by the cessation of my life. ('Rebellious legs,' the coroner would remark, gravely. 'It was the sitting down. They wouldn't stand for it.') The performance came to its natural end after little more than an hour. The musicians stood for applause, and I scanned them for potential Michaels. They looked very pleased with themselves. I remembered how Oskar looked after performances I had seen him give – a tightening in the cheeks at either extremity of a perfectly horizontal mouth, a feline narrowing of the eyes; a mask, a self-imposed rictus of satisfaction that looked as if it might snap into an expression of anger, or loss, or humour, the instant it relaxed in private. But it never relaxed, in private or otherwise, it just switched seamlessly back to his normal face, the pine doors of a cabinet closing on a dead TV set.

* * *

The bar was not decorated in the same thrombosis red as the rest of the building, but hung with dark green embossed wallpaper. A green room. Green rooms in theatres were green because that colour was most restful on the actors' eyes after an evening spent gazing into the limelight – burning lime was once used as stage lighting, with blinding effect. This was a generous, high-ceilinged room made strangely claustrophobic by the fact that the wallpaper continued above the top of the walls and covered the ceiling, in the process apparently smothering what I imagined were plaster cornices and mouldings, which now appeared as vaguely malignant lumps and ridges. A communist-era chandelier dangled from a particularly prominent tumulus of wallpaper in the centre of the ceiling, distributing a kind of restless surgical light. It was an obvious triumph of proletarian aesthetics and wiring over bourgeois conventions of beauty and safety; a cuboid entanglement of metal struts and sheets of yellowing fabric, it strongly resembled a box kite hitting an electricity pylon, and would have been far more comfortable in the brutalist megastructure across the street. With the wallpaper, it was like an abstract ice cube floating in a glass of congealed crème de menthe.

The bar was original, though, an ornate teak longboat in dry dock, staffed by the best-dressed people in the room and backed by huge mirrors in gilt frames. But a long portion of it was topped by an ageing sneezeguard, the plastic of which was beginning to fog and craze in places. I ordered a gin and tonic, in English, a language that the barman clearly understood. A mobile phone trilled behind me; the till that my money disappeared into was new. The West, home, at once felt closer than it had done at any time during my stay here, and very far away. I felt as if Oskar's flat was a bathysphere submerged in alien depths, and I had just briefly surfaced, an isolated bubble of humanity bursting into the atmosphere of others. An awful sloshing wave of homesickness caught me, trailing misery. How much longer would I be expected to stay? Oskar had said at least a week, almost certainly two, possibly more. At this moment, even the end of the first week seemed an impossible age away. The beginning of the week also felt distant; time telescoped away in both directions. I found a place to sit and sipped my G&T. Was I still hungover, perhaps? The gin, I thought, would revive me. Maybe it was the hair of the dog that I needed. Yes, the hair, the hairiest hair of the hairiest dog. Let the hangover be deferred, thin out that clotting blood with a dash of spirit, get things moving.

The crowd was also unclotting. A few concert patrons had bought drinks and settled at tables, small groups, husbands and wives, and a line of men had taken up positions along the bar, in pairs and threes, adopting the slight deviation from the vertical that indicates that they were there to stay, not simply to purchase refreshments. The mood was intelligent and self-satisfied, two things that I did not feel. I felt self-conscious, a lone drinker. Not a rare sight in this country, perhaps, a state of alone-ness. It was a state of alone-ness. It was the kind of place that started shooting political prisoners because it suspected that they would enjoy solitary confinement and internal exile too much. The zinc surface of the table at which I sat was covered in little dents, as if it had been used for target practice by a Lilliputian firing squad. These little dents in the pinkish metal pulled my reflected face this way and that, obscuring my eyes, pulling my jaw into a John Merrick parody, making it look as if a whole second head was swelling up behind mine ...

My name was spoken. Clearly, very close behind me. I didn't even hear it as a word – I simply started at the sudden knowledge that I had been identified.

I turned. There was a tall man standing behind my chair, the owner of the second head I had seen swelling from my reflection. It was a long head, and prematurely balding, with wisps of incredibly pale blond hair arranged over an inescapable pink dome. An intelligent forehead presided over an assortment of young, pink features, animated with a liberal smile. Underneath this affable face was a black dinner jacket and a white dress shirt, open at the collar. Sweat gleamed on an equine neck.

'Ha ha!' said the dome. 'I made you jump!'

'Uh, yes, miles away,' I said, twisting out of my seat and standing with the easy grace of a newborn giraffe.

'I am Michael,' said dome in German-accented English. His smile did the impossible and broadened, revealing a parade of white teeth of American splendour. He extended his hand, and I shook it.

'Would you like a drink?' I asked, gesturing towards my glass in case he was unfamiliar with the concept.

'Yes, yes!' Michael enthused, before his features darkened: 'But not here.' He scowled in the direction of the bar.

'OK,' I said, feeling a little dazed. I had been moving in the direction of sitting back down, and I straightened instead.

Michael stared intently at me for a moment, as if fascinated. Then he pointed at my glass on the zinc. 'Finish, finish.'

I picked up the drink and drained it. The ice hurt my teeth.

'How much money do you have with you?' Michael asked.

'About a hundred euros,' I said.

'OK. We can get more.'

'OK,' I said, pulling on my coat. 'Uh, what?'

Out, out through the ventricles of the lobby, out into the rain-soaked street.

'He owes me money,' Michael was saying, 'and he is being fuck about it. How is it said? He is being a fuck about it. Or he is being a fucking thing, a something, about it? A fucking something. Noun and verb and adjective – very useful, the English fucking; fucking useful.'

This monologue had been kept up since we left the bar, but as Michael had charged ahead of me, I had not been able to follow much of it.

'Who?' I asked.

'Who? Victor!' Michael said. We were passing the cathedral, crossing the great square. 'He owes me money, and is being a fuck about it. So I will not drink there. I do not want to look at him. No more money for him!'

'The barman,' I said, filling in the blank for myself.

Michael stopped at the avenue's edge, to my relief – I had been worried that he was going to march straight into the hurtling chasm of traffic, such was the momentum of his trajectory from the concert hall.

'Yes, the barman,' he said, looking at me as if I were a cretin. 'The bar, man. *CHANGE!*'

This exclamation startled me, but it was not directed at me. Instead, Michael was apparently addressing the torrent of cars. It was past nine, and rush hour was long over, so that the city's motorists were now able to pick up speed along its triumphal axes. This increased velocity added to my sensation that the pace of the evening was, if anything, picking up. I wanted to relax, not pick up the pace. It was an anxious experience, meeting a stranger in a foreign city – by now we should be making awkward chit-chat over a modest supper, but instead I was being startled by this frankly startling individual, Michael.

'*CHANGE!*' Michael bellowed. The city did not listen. The traffic continued to race past, tyres hissing on the drenched asphalt, beating up mist. Across the avenue, water was gouting from several points on the concrete monster where its gutters and drains had failed. I wondered that it hadn't dissolved entirely, like a grey sugar cube. The lights of the pedestrian crossing changed and the traffic grudgingly halted. I now realised what Michael had been yelling at.

'Interesting building,' I said as we drew nearer the brutalist lump.

'Horrible,' Michael said, jerking out his left arm in the direction of the structure as if he sought to waft it away. 'A gift from the Soviet allies. They built it on the graveyard of the church. On the bodies of the dead! But the bodies, they had their revenge. It is too heavy. It is sinking.' He stopped abruptly, and I almost ran into him. 'Big cracks in the floors,' he said with a grisly grin. 'You can smell death.'

Unaccountably, I felt drawn towards Michael. I was starting to like him. He had flicked off the safety catches of the evening.

'Where are we going?' I asked, joining his smile.

'Near,' he replied.

The bar was a brick vault below ground level, unexpectedly dry and not too stifling. It was filled with cacophonous jazz from a CD player with a stutter, noisy chatter, and cigarette smoke. The lighting was jaundiced and inadequate; with the smoke, it killed depth. Back in the bathysphere, sinking. We sat at a table in a vaulted booth, and a waiter brought us a bottle of red wine on the basis of a raised index finger from my host. No money changed hands, no price was indicated. The thought that Michael might consider a hundred euros inadequate funding for this evening nagged at me. Did he want me to pay for him, as well? Was this my treat? I detested my meanness.

'Now, Oskar's friend,' Michael said, pouring the wine. It irritated me that he didn't use my name. 'Tell me about you.'

'Well, I'm a writer,' I said.

'Aha! You write books?' Michael said, eagerly.

'Um, no,' I said. I hated conversations that progressed in this pattern. 'I write leaflets, press releases, that sort of thing.'

Michael's brow knotted up. He had an expressive forehead. It would be an impressive feature even if he still had all his hair. 'What are "leaflets"?'

'It's ... like little books,' I said.

'Short stories?'

'No! no ... like ... information sheets, eight, twelve pages ... for local councils.'

A blaze of light issued from that articulate face. 'A-ha-ha! Pamphlets! Political, yes? Jonathan Swift, Tom Paine ...'

'No, no,' I said, exasperated, 'leaflets ... about recycling, and environmental health, and noise nuisance, and how to pay your council tax in instalments by direct debit, how to vote ... all the things a council does.'

'This is writing?'

'It's called copywriting,' I said, emphasising the *-writing.*

'You are copying it?'

'No, the writing is called copy. But it's very samey stuff. It might as well have been copied. You notice that the leaflets from one council read much the same as leaflets from another council. It's all the same bollocks. Online is worse. But online it's not called "copywriting". It's called "content provision".'

'"Content provision",' Michael echoed. A smile spread across his face. 'This is writing. "Content provision." You provide "content", yes? This is fantastic. Then I am not a musician. I am no longer a musician. I am a "noise organiser", yes?'

I laughed, and raised my glass. 'To noise organisation!'

Michael returned the toast, and we drank, and he topped up our glasses. 'The concert was good,' I said.

'Uff,' Michael said, wrinkling his nose. 'Some of it ... I drink to forget.' He drained his glass with amazing speed, refilled it again, and poured more wine into my already-full glass, bringing it to the brim.

'Well, I liked it.'

'When we play, we are imitating the dead,' Michael said. He had darkened with astonishing speed. The rapidity of these emotional oscillations reminded me strongly of Oskar. 'Noise organisation after the fashion of the dead.'

I decided to disregard this. The English model of conversation – in which death either did not exist, or was a very limited phenomenon happening only to absent third parties – seemed far preferable to me. 'What's it like working with Oskar?' I asked, with what I hoped was a devilish expression. I gulped at my wine, eager to keep pace and nervous of being seen as a lily-livered Westerner.

'What is it like working with Oskar!' Michael replied, with what seemed to be delight. 'Ha ha! What is it like being *friends* with Oskar? I like Oskar, Oskar is a very good man, he ... in music ... he is a genius. He is fantastic, superb. It is good that he goes to Los Angeles. It is the correct horizon for him. He will be famous there.'

'He's only there for a couple of weeks,' I said. 'For the divorce.'

'Yes, divorce ...' Michael said. 'Did you meet her?'

'Laura? Yes.'

Michael wrinkled his nose, again. 'And what did you think of her?'

His expression made it clear that I was safe to tell the truth. 'I didn't like her.'

'Yes! Yes ...' Michael beamed. 'My God ... She is a *bitch*, yes?'

Such was the savage, savouring joy that Michael put into this word, he forced a laugh out of me. 'Ah, ha, yes, well, I didn't like her.'

'She came here and she was rude about everything, the food, the wine' – he tapped the bottle – 'We have Italian wine here, we have French wine! This isn't Communism now! We have Australian wine and the' – the vitriol reached a corrosive crest – 'Californian fruit juice. Chateau Minute Maid, Cuvée 7-Up! She was rude about everything. I think she thought the city was very dirty, and she did not like the people here.'

I was beginning to feel guilty about my own private musings on Oskar's home, but at least I had kept them to myself. And Laura had clearly considered Britain to be an unwashed, anarchic backwater, sliding backwards into dereliction and despair, so what she made of this place, well, the mind boggled.

'I did not like her,' Michael continued. 'But Oskar, I like Oskar. But I work with Oskar. You are friends with Oskar? Because I think perhaps we all work with Oskar. We are all his co-workers. He lives his life like a job. He does this job very well, he is very efficient and successful. You are his colleague, too. He does not go home from this job. He is working when he is sleeping. You see?'

'I think.' I noticed, with a degree of horror, that my glass was already halfway empty again; it wasn't this fact that horrified me so much as the fact that Michael had also seen the approaching dearth, and was reaching for the already heavily depleted bottle. But then all the horror dissipated suddenly and totally, so totally that I was left wondering if I had felt it at all; instead I felt ... good. I felt warm and relaxed. The atmosphere in the bar appealed to me, it included and enveloped me. The smoke and hubbub cushioned me. Some music was playing, appropriately Weimar-decadent, all accordions and clarinets and a sense of civilisation sliding towards catastrophe and the fact not being too important. I felt as if I could be a poet or an intellectual here, sharing a drink with a musician friend.

'What is it like to be Oskar's friend, then?' Michael asked.

'I haven't seen him very much recently,' I said, 'since he's been living here. Only when he has come to London. I've known him since university, though. We were quite close at university.'

'Why do you like him?' Michael asked. At first the question sounded perfectly straightforward. I opened my mouth and suddenly the answer skipped out of view. I was left with an inarticulate knot of intangibles and contradictory emotions. Then I realised that I had to say something, anything, just to break what was becoming an embarrassing pause. I had to start talking.

'Uh, I, well ...' I attempted. Then: 'Why do we like anyone? I like him because he's different to me ... he's very intelligent and, I don't know, I like his loyalty. Not his loyalty, that makes him sound like a dog. Maybe what I mean is that I like that he seems to like me despite the fact that there's no reason he should like me; at least, no reason that I can see. You know, he makes me believe I have likeable qualities. And maybe that's what I do for him. I think that mutual reassurance is probably a big component of all friendships, really. I mean, I don't choose to like him, I don't think you really choose who you like, who you're friends with. There may be reasons for your friendship, but they are never wholly clear to you. You can like someone without knowing why.' *Like you, for instance,* I thought – *I like you, Michael, but I cannot think why that might be.*

I stopped talking, concerned that I was rambling. Michael seemed to be mulling over what I had said. Either that or he hadn't been listening and was trying to figure out what he could without making his inattention obvious. I sipped my wine, which was a little harsh, but growing on me fast.

'Why do you think he likes you?' Michael asked.

'Maybe he doesn't,' I said, figuring that self-deprecation rather than honesty was the quickest way to end this little analysis session. *I'm sorry, our time is nearly up ...*

'Clearly he does like you,' Michael said, intently. 'You are here, after all, are you not? He has given his flat to you.'

This was true. I shrugged. 'Only while he's not here,' I countered. 'He has not sought my company.'

'But here you are, after all,' Michael persisted. I was beginning to feel uncomfortable again, but not threatened or under pressure, simply outside my comfort zone of thought. It was a sensation that was neither pleasant nor unpleasant. 'You must have some quality, Oskar has trusted you with his home.'

And look where that has got him, I thought. In a way, I realised, I was pre-emptively ending my friendship with Oskar. I knew that there would be trouble over the floor, over the sofa, over the cats, and I was fairly certain it would have a malign effect on our relationship, and would change it always. Technically, our friendship was still perfectly intact, and Oskar felt the same way about me he always did. But my feelings towards him were changing as I stayed in his place, and there would inevitably come a time when he saw the results of my stay and his feelings would change. Our friendship was a dead thing that was still breathing. It was like Schrödinger's cat, stuck in its box, neither dead nor alive. But when Oskar opened the box, opened the front door of his flat, the wave would collapse, and our friendship would be at an end. I was certain of this, and the certainty was liberating, refreshing.

'We lived in close quarters in university,' I said. 'He knows my habits.'

'Close quarters?' Michael's brow turned corduroy.

'Um, close together. In crowded circumstances. You know, student digs. Lodgings. Dormitories.'

Michael obviously wasn't listening. He was signalling to a waiter, and indicating our depleted bottle. Concern rose in me – a bottle each? More? My companion had easily exceeded my alcohol intake, even counting my gin at the concert hall. But he seemed, if anything, to be becoming more incisive and articulate as the drink went down. By contrast, I felt befuddled and ready to ramble, a weakening dam holding back a reservoir of malapropisms and faux pas. The hangover was gone, at least, and I was loosening up.

'What is Oskar like to work with?' I asked. I didn't want the conversation to revolve around our only mutual friend all evening, but this was a unique chance to find out more about my absent host's carefully hypothecated existence. I was also keen to shift the focus from me.

'He is very demanding, of course. He wants everything to be perfect. When things go wrong, he can be very angry. Very, very angry. When things are good ... Perfect. You have heard *Variations on Tram Timetables*?'

I nodded, silently grateful that my curiosity had overcome my apathy and I had played the CD yesterday.

'Amazing work,' Michael continued. 'It must be played with great precision, or the effect is ruined. It is Oskar's way of making other people play like him. You have to do it his way, see? Like a tram, it has to run along fixed lines, to a fixed timetable. If a tram misses a stop, it makes everyone late, and they miss the next tram. If a tram leaves its tracks ... it is a disaster, there is destruction and death. So in the piece, you must do everything right or it is a disaster, there is no room to improvise or be ... what is the word? Slopper.'

'Sloppy,' I said.

'Sloppy, yes,' Michael said. 'Hm. Sloppy.'

'He told me he is working on something new – "Dewey"?'

'Yes. Ha. Oskar, he is always ... He wants more. A symphony, on the Dewey decimal system.'

I smiled. 'A symphony based on the Dewey decimal system?'

'Yes.'

'The library index system?'

'Yes. Why do you smile? It's not a joke.'

'It just seems like such an odd thing to write a symphony about.'

Michael shook his head, grinning indulgently at what he clearly saw as naivety on my part. 'You are completely wrong. It is a system for the organisation of all knowledge. It is educational, dialectical. Every piece of knowledge that man knows, every fact, given a number, given a place: 200 is religion; 220 is the Bible; 222 is Genesis and 228 is Revelation and Apocalypse; 500 is science; 520 is astronomy; 550 is Earth science, and 551 is geology; 570 is biology, and 576 is genetics and evolution. Alpha and omega, in all different systems, without contradiction and in powers of ten. The Dewey system arranges everything. It is the perfect muse for Oskar. He will arrange the world. A symphony of everything. A Grand Unified Symphony.'

Michael's smile was positively messianic by this point. He did not strike me as a person who shared Oskar's organising impulse, but he was clearly smitten with the ambition that the Dewey symphony represented. The dream was Oskar's, but Michael had obviously become its servant. The world, ranked and classified in nesting subdivisions of ten. It was an encompassing vision, and at first it seemed generous and inclusive. But there was also a darkness to it. It excluded the possibility of thought outside the system. It imposed conformity. Bad ideas had taken root in beer cellars in central Europe, very bad ideas. The soil all around us was crowded and cold.

'You see?' Michael prompted. I had not spoken for a while. I raised my eyes, which had been fixed on the dark red liquid in my glass, to meet his.

'Yes, it's very clever,' I said, manufacturing a smile that I hoped did not look manufactured. And I feared that my compliment sounded weak, or forced. It *was* a clever idea, after all. I wondered when it had occurred to Oskar. In a library, no doubt. But inspiration seemed too spontaneous an act for Oskar, a little chaotic and unplanned for him. Maybe he had always had the idea, he had always had all of his thoughts, numbered and planned, and he had just been waiting for the correct moment to deploy this one. He had arrived on Earth with a lifetime of thoughts already installed, like index cards in a file, and then took them out one by one when the circumstances suited. At times every act, every possession, every achievement, every friend of Oskar's took on the appearance of an ornament carefully placed on the ascending curve of his life trajectory. Education, career, marriage ... but ...

''F course, he's not doing his job so well,' I said casually.

'Who?' Michael asked. 'Oskar?'

'Yeah, Oskar. I mean ... You said he lives his life like a job. And I agree. It's like he has it all planned. He likes timetables. But, like, the plan's gone wrong. The job's not working out. He made a bad hire. And now he's firing her.'

Michael, who had frowned through all of this, now fired off an affirmative laugh. 'Yes, yes! Yes,' he spluttered, turning suddenly matador red. 'Yes, but I think perhaps she is firing him.'

'Huh, yes,' I said. I wasn't clear on the details of the divorce, but I had the strong impression that Oskar was on the defensive. In fact, if proceedings had been filed in California, then it was clearly her doing – surely Oskar would file, or sue, or whatever it was one did, in Europe, and save the Los Angeles lawyer-hassle? Perhaps you had to file in the country in which you tied the knot. 'Yes, I think she is firing him. But I think he was the employer in the relationship, maybe?'

'What is it called in England when you sue your employer, when you quit, and they have been bad to you and you want money ...?'

'Um, tribunal,' I said. 'She's taking him to an industrial tribunal.'

Michael was disintegrating into purple-faced laughter – near-silent total laughter, the laughter that manifests as muscle spasms, paralysis in the lungs. He could hardly articulate the thought that had provoked this attack. 'To a ... a tribunal ... for sexual harassment!'

I also laughed, and it turned into laughter for its own sake, the laughter of simple pleasure.

Michael recovered himself. 'Do you know really why they are divorcing?'

'Not really,' I said. I only knew what Oskar had told me the last time we met, on Whitecross Street, that awful drunken afternoon. 'It was very hard on them, him here and her in California. They spent all their time on planes, and when they met all they did was fight. She didn't like it here and, I don't know, I think he didn't much like California. You probably know better than me.'

'That's what I know,' Michael said. 'He was quite often away, and he did not like his work to be interrupted. He was most content without her around. When he was going there, or she was coming here, he was very anxious and agitated for a week before and after. At other times, she maybe did not exist for him, you could forget he was married. It got worse and worse. And it seemed to go on for so long, you could forget the time when they were happy together.'

'Yes,' I said. 'I forget that. I saw them once in London, and they seemed quite happy then.'

'Maybe London would have been all right for them,' Michael said. 'Oskar did not like it much, though. But I think she would have liked it.'

'She didn't like it,' I said. 'Not much, at least. But maybe they would have been equally unhappy there – a good compromise. An equal sacrifice.'

'I do not think Oskar was happy to make a sacrifice,' Michael said. 'I think he already saw everything, all his life, as a sacrifice to music.'

'She didn't strike me as the self-denial type either,' I said.

'But you are right,' Michael said. 'The plan has gone wrong. It must be very difficult for him.'

'Yes, yes,' I said. Michael was absolutely right, more right perhaps than he really knew. It was obvious that it would be extremely stressful to see one's marriage collapse. But I felt, somehow, that Oskar must have felt it particularly keenly. The disruption and lack of control that went along with it would strike directly at the kind of security he appeared to value in life. And to get married in the first place must have required a great deal of emotional investment from him. He must have been obliged to open himself up to another human being to a hitherto unprecedented degree; and now that investment had gone bust. It might suit my prejudices about Oskar to consider him a bloodless, ratiocinatory creature and to think his marriage an unemotional, businesslike affair based on cool analysis of the costs and benefits, but he was human after all, in pain. I was disgusted with myself for not appreciating this earlier. Sympathy and self-loathing welled up inside me and I felt, even, the heat of tears readying themselves behind the bridge of my nose. But then I recalled the amount I had drunk – a bottle of wine by now, perhaps, not counting the gin – and I recognised that the drunk's emotional pendulum had swung to misery. I had to clear my head. I stood, and went to the toilet.

The toilets stank terribly, the reek of shit and piss competing with the astringent odour – a flavour, almost, coating the back of the throat – of some low-grade cleaning product that scoured the sinuses and pickled the eyes. A couple were in the only stall, very much engaged. I breathed ammonia and chlorine. Gas, lads, gas. An ecstasy of fumbling. There was an ecstasy of fumbling going on in that stall, all right. Graffiti was, apparently, tolerated, and the walls were larded with it, interleaved with yellowing pictures clipped from newspapers or magazines and pasted straight onto the brick. The pictures were mostly of girls – swimming teams, starlets. There was an unsettling fetishistic air to some – girls in wetsuits, raincoats, gas masks. Over and under this collage, graffiti. Most of it was impossible to translate. The only parts that were understandable were arrowed hearts, the initials of English football clubs, and angry extremism: swastikas, hammers and sickles, JEW PIGS, FUCK ISLAM. These latter slurs were often blotted out or appended by criticism from later writers: FUCK THIS SHIT, and so forth. In some places, the accreted epidermis of posters and clippings was peeling away, revealing it to be many layers deep. Perhaps there was no brick beneath, and this crust had been plastered over the bare earth. The concave ceiling was exposed brick, though, and the graffiti continued there, scorchmarks from cigarette lighters.

Holding my hands under a stream of cold water from the tap of the filthy sink, I began to feel a little more clear-headed. But as I wove my way back through the bar towards my seat I still felt distinctly unsteady, and oddly disconnected, as if I was actually elsewhere, steering my body with an unresponsive remote control. I had a morbid fear of barging into another drinker and receiving a beating. That did not seem very likely, though, as overall the atmosphere, oppressively thick as it was with noise and smoke and humid, human heat, was blearily friendly.

When I approached the table, I saw that Michael had ordered another bottle of wine, our third.

'Michael, this has to be the last one,' I said weakly.

'Yes, yes,' Michael said. 'The last one here. After here, we'll go another place.'

'I don't know ...' I tried urgently to think of a compromise. For a moment, I considered asking Michael if he wanted to come back to Oskar's flat, so we could have a drink there – then I could safely go to sleep. But I did not want to invite back company, least of all when we were this drunk. The risk of another accident was too great. Nothing further could happen to the flat if I stayed out.

'We will go dancing,' Michael said. 'Do you like dancing?' He mimed a boogie in his seat, wiggling his hips.

'Sure,' I said. At least if we went to a club, the quantity of drink would drop. I could slip away in the melee. I detested clubs, and had not been in one for the better part of a decade. But still, this was meant to be a holiday of sorts, and if I got into the spirit of it, it might be fun.

Michael leaned in towards me. He looked serious, even stern. I blinked at him, and suddenly feared that the wine and heat were making my face red.

'You know,' the musician said, 'Oskar first asked *me* to look after his cats.'

'Really?' I said. What was this? Did Michael feel he had some sort of grievance with me? Even if he felt sore at being passed over for cat-watching duty, surely he couldn't hold me responsible?

'Yes. I would have taken them to my rooms. It is quite suitable. There is a little garden, a courtyard. Oskar thought this a good scheme. It has worked in the past.'

He was obviously as drunk as I, and I feared it was percolating into bitterness and enmity.

'Oskar didn't mention this to me. He just asked me to come over, and I was able to, and so ...' I had nowhere to go with that sentence. 'I didn't mean to offend you, or anyone.'

Michael seemed surprised by this. Incomprehension flashed over his face, and then a natural smile.

'Oh no, I am not offended,' he said. 'It is, you know, a *chore,* I am happy to be saved from it. But it is strange, don't you think? The cats are the only things that need help every day, and I am here and was ready to look after the little furry bastards. I love them. Without them, the flat is quite safe – the building has a caretaker, I think, who cleans ... But in fact he says to you to come, he brings you all these miles from London, so that you can live in the flat. Why?'

I blinked. 'I, I don't know.' My lips felt dry, very dry, and I sipped my wine. 'There is a caretaker,' I confirmed. 'A woman. A cleaner.'

'Maybe he does not trust her,' Michael said. 'Sometimes they steal. But I could have come in every few days ... And there are others, he has other friends in the orchestra. It is a mystery, no?'

'Yes, it's strange,' I said, thinking on it.

'So, as I said, he must certainly trust you,' Michael said. 'His precious flat!'

Wine had splashed onto the wooden surface of the table in front of me. I dipped my index finger into a puddle, and drew it out into a line, connecting it to another drop. Join the dots.

'I spilled some wine,' I said, quickly, candour ambushing discretion. 'On the floor, Oskar's floor. Not very much, less than this, but I didn't clean it up in time and it left a little stain.'

Michael's eyes were wide. He looked gleeful, which irked me. 'Aha!' he said. 'Oskar will not like that.'

'Maybe he won't notice it,' I said.

'Maybe,' Michael said. He did not look at all convinced by this.

'The cleaner saw it,' I said, adding: 'I think.'

'She will tell him,' Michael said, definitely. 'She will want to make sure that he is not angry with her. They are like that. In communism, these caretakers were big informers. They knew things. They would go to the police if they did not like your face, and then *pfft!* That was the end of you. They get a flat with their job, but they are paid almost nothing and they could get money from bribes and rewards ...'

He trailed off, his eyes fixed on a point beyond the brick vault, deep in the ground. 'Sometimes I think they miss the old times.' Then, with a barely perceptible frisson, he roused himself, and refilled our glasses.

Later – after the third bottle had been finished, I think – we were back on the street. It was not raining, but it had clearly been pouring while we had been in the bar, and the streetlights swam in filled gutters. Most windows were dark. Grand buildings slept. I did not know what time it was, but certainly past midnight. We moved at speed, on foot – it felt as if we were heading deeper into the city, and further from Oskar's flat – and Michael was singing, but not loudly. The traffic had practically disappeared, but for the occasional hurtling car slashing, then shushing, through the wet, red tail-lights converging. There were no trams that I saw, but small soaked groups in raincoats huddled in pools of white light at each stop, untalking sentinels at strategic spots. As soon as we came out of the bar, I stepped on a loose paving stone where water had pooled underneath. It splashed explosively, a liquid landmine, and filled my right shoe with cold muddy water. Normally this kind of mishap would have crippled my mood, but instead I felt indomitably happy. I had broken through, I had second wind. Oskar was a good guy, he wouldn't care about the floor, everything was going to be fine. There had been, however, something sickening in the tilt of the slab, the momentary loss of balance, the sudden wetness ...

Michael broke off singing and turned to me, squelching along in his wake.

'Oskar does not come dancing any more,' he said. 'Not since he got married. Only once or twice since he got married.'

'Well, it doesn't seem his sort of thing.' Walking and talking at the same time was an act almost beyond my remaining powers of coordination. Wine swirled acidly behind my words.

'He was not as keen as some of the others, maybe.'

'I think it's mostly for young people,' I said. *Younger than us, for instance,* I thought.

'Really? No, there are all ages of guys.'

We stopped at a black doorway with a neon sign above it and a heavy-set man in a black leather jacket outside it, arms crossed and feet firmly apart. *STAR'S* said the neon, and a loud, repetitive bassline thudded behind it. Michael nodded to the bouncer and pushed through the door. Inside, a dimly lit flight of bare concrete steps led downwards. The air smelled as damp inside as out.

'Underground again,' I muttered.

'What?' said Michael.

'Never mind.'

Footsteps ringing, we reached a narrow corridor space, curiously empty, red-lit, vascular. A woman far into middle age, but bare-shouldered and peroxide blonde, staffed a little ticket and cloakroom counter in a doorway halfway along the space. For our cash, we handed over our jackets and received four tickets each – admission, cloakroom, free drink and free dance. I looked at the last one, vaguely aware of a missed connection somewhere at the back of my mind.

'I don't think I'll dance,' I said. 'My foot is wet ...' The blood in my ears and pooled under my eyes throbbed with the music.

'You don't have to do anything,' Michael said. The red light gave his grin a terrible aspect. His eyes were lost in shadow. 'You just sit there and watch.'

My brain felt thick with scabs, old and new. It was full of wine, it rotated, looked close to spilling. Michael pushed through the bead curtain at the end of the hall and disappeared around a corner. I followed.

We emerged into a surprisingly large square space. Semi-circular booths lined three of the walls, and small tables filled the floor, each with one or two spindly chairs. At first it was hard to tell if the club was brightly lit or swamped in scarlet gloom. In fact, it was both, mostly murky, with a dazzling spotlit island at its centre. Under the spotlight was a stage, on the stage was a pole, and on the pole was a girl. On the girl was very little. She had the bored, focused expression of a forklift truck driver. Her body writhed and entangled itself with the pole in a way that was simultaneously animal and mechanical.

Oh, dancing, I thought.

Michael looked intensely pleased with himself. 'Come,' he said. 'We have a booth.'

There were other girls around the club, carrying trays or in the booths, some gyrating, some kissing men, some just sitting with men. There were not many men, most of the tables and more than half of the booths were empty. Dancers outnumbered clients. Almost all these clients were on their own, but there were a couple of groups, one noisy and suited, the other noisier and in jeans and T-shirts. This might be a British stag-do, I speculated. I hadn't seen any compatriots since the airport. The air smelled of 40% air freshener, 40% cigarette smoke, 10% stale beer, 5% sweat and 5% genuine evil.

We slid into the curved crimson leatherette-covered banquette of our booth, behind a circular table that had a black and red yin-yang symbol laminated onto it.

'I don't know about this, Michael,' I said. In my imagination, cancer cells encircled dying flesh. A clot formed. Wine drying, leaving a dark tidal mark. Sitting down made me dizzy. My muscles all felt incorrectly briefed, as if I had lifted a box that I expected to be very heavy and found it, with a lurch, to be empty. I felt powerless over events.

'What, what?' Michael said, emollient. 'Relax, relax, we'll have a good time.'

'I don't know,' I said again. The kissing bothered me. A lot of things bothered me, but the kissing was at that moment top of the list. 'Isn't there normally some kind of no-touching rule?'

'No, no,' Michael said, putting his hand on my shoulder. 'If you want to touch, you just pay for it. We'll have some champagne.'

Another platoon of concerns and objections marched into view. Rip-offs, clip joints, £200 glasses of orange juice, knuckle dusters. But a girl, wearing nothing save a red satin bustier and hotpants, teetering on a pair of clear plastic high-heels, had arrived at our table, and Michael was placing an order. In fact, he appeared to be doing more than that. He was chatting.

'Do they know you here?' I asked when the girl wiggled off.

'Yeah, sure,' Michael said. 'We often come here. Some of us, from the orchestra.'

'Oskar, too?' I said. It was nearly impossible to mentally place him here.

'Sure,' Michael said, 'but not so much since he was married. As I said.'

'OK,' I said. My head spun.

Another girl appeared, wearing even less, just a pink two-piece swimming costume and the ubiquitous heels, and carrying a bottle of champagne and four glasses. Her breasts swung forward as she bent over to put these things on the table, exhibited themselves, full and heavy. I found myself looking, and averted my eyes. Then I looked again. I felt composed of 5% sweat, 5% genuine evil. I thought of water balloons. Then I thought they were filled with blood. I wondered if I still had any blood in me, and realised that part of me was filling with it.

'It's OK to look, yes,' Michael said in a voice thick with encouragement. I had been staring, and he had caught me. He nudged me, a salacious caricature.

'This really isn't my thing,' I said. The words came slowly. My brain, I felt, was losing some sort of struggle, fatally undermined by drink, betrayed by my own instincts, devoid of reliable allies. I didn't know what the results might be if I just let it lose. I didn't want to become some sort of leering beast, but I also feared being a PC-hobbled wet.

'I know, you look like shit!' Michael bawled with laughter. 'Like a little mouse! It's OK, it's OK.' He squeezed my shoulder. I wanted a no-touching rule.

The swimsuit-clad 'waitress' opened the bottle with a squeak and a giggle as the cork blew and the foam ran over her knuckles. It would be chilled, at least, I thought, and the bubbles would be refreshing. I took my glass. It was not very cold. I think I must have flinched or grimaced, because I found the waitress frowning at me in a pouty, comic way. She said something I didn't understand. Her breasts were magnificent.

'She is worried that you are not having a good time,' Michael said.

'She is very perceptive,' I said. 'Do you think I could have a glass of water?'

'We have champagne!' Michael exclaimed, as if there was a chance I hadn't noticed. He said something to the waitress, who departed. Almost immediately, two other girls appeared, one blonde and ample, in a red bikini top and hotpants, and the other with short dark hair, elfin looks, wearing a gold boob tube and short shorts. The blonde squeezed in next to Michael without waiting for an invitation. The elf hovered on my side of the banquette, clearly attempting to seem both appealing and sexily aloof at the same time, a titanic contradiction that she embodied like a plucked guitar string turned into a transparent blur by its rapid oscillation between two limits. The part I was expected to play was obvious. I ushered her in, trying to look friendly and genuine without looking like a sex case. I do not think I managed this balance, and I comforted myself with the awful thought that she had met far worse men than me.

The blonde had curled an arm around Michael's shoulders and was stroking his hair. 'If you don't like this girl, we can get another,' he said.

'Would you like a blonde?' Michael's girl asked. 'We can be matching? A black girl? A Japanese?'

'What's her name?' I asked Michael. 'Does she speak English?'

Michael – whose girl was now kissing his ear, wetly, in a way that I could not imagine was pleasant for either of them – said something to the elf, who said something that sounded like 'Connie' to me, tapping her chest between her small, apple-like breasts.

'Connie?' I replied. 'Your name is Connie?'

'Yes,' she said. *Yis*. 'English?'

'Yes,' I said.

'I speak English,' she said, with extreme care. I felt reassured that we could at least talk, before I realised that there was nothing I could imagine talking about.

'Perhaps Connie would like a drink,' Michael prompted. 'We buy champagne for the girls and watch the dancing, have some fun. Have some beers too, or Scotch. The champagne is very weak, so the girls don't get drunk.'

I poured a glass of the sparkling liquid for Connie, conscious that it could be horribly expensive. She put her hand on my knee, and gave me a smile. We clinked our glasses together awkwardly, and drank. The bubbles scoured my throat. I felt like chewed gum. Connie caressed my chest, which I was certain had all the tone and masculinity of a clammy rubber bathmat. Then, Michael said something to her.

'Ticket,' she said to me. Sluggishly, I took out the four chits I had been given, which were now folded up with various other bits of ephemera – banknotes, the stub of the concert ticket, a tram timetable. Connie separated out two of these scraps, entitling me to a free drink and a free dance, and disappeared with them.

'Relax, relax!' Michael urged. 'You'll get your dance. Just have a good time. We'll have a drink.'

'I don't know,' I said. I felt anything but relaxed. I was trying to add up how much money had been spent and how much was left, a process like trying to fold a soggy newspaper in a high wind. My heart was running like a wind-up tin toy. I was sweating, and I was certain that I did not smell too fresh. I couldn't stand the thought of attractive female strangers being under financial obligation to throw themselves at me if I wasn't entirely clean. Prickly heat and fever cold pushed and shoved inside me, and wine swirled, alternated orangey blood red and Guinness black, oily rainbows on its stagnant surface. I wondered if I was going to be sick, the question one of distant relevance, an essay title in an academic journal.

'How do we pay?' I asked. I didn't want to ask about the economics of the whole business. To ask was to remember that economics was all there was to this. It was nothing to do with love, or chemistry, or actual attraction, and little to do with actual sex. This was all a profit margin. We were titillating ourselves on the intersection of two earnings curves on a graph.

Connie returned with yet another girl, an amber blonde with a ferocious straight fringe over her eyes, which made her hair look like a helmet. Her eye make-up was heavy, giving her a sluttish scowl. She was wearing a pale blue top and a micro miniskirt, both in PVC or latex. Connie sat down again next to me, setting a bottle of beer in front of me, and Amber started up a sedate routine of sexual display. She was not a natural blonde.

A spike of nausea and testosterone-laced blood ran straight through me. I marvelled at the male body's ability to feel disgust and desire in equal measure and its pulsing tempo of shame and shamelessness. A sexual guidance computer was competing with me for sovereignty over my inner controls. I thought of slabs of meat in cold basements. I thought of trafficking and sexual slavery, a mental coup de grâce that crashed the guidance computer, forced it to reboot, and detumesced its peripheral. Girls were shipped out of countries like this for lives of unimaginable servitude and horror in the West. I had redrafted local authority policy statements about it. So where did that leave these girls? Were these women lucky, or unlucky? Where did we all stand on the scale, in the cosmology of human suffering? What was their level of consent?

The tide of alcohol was coming back in, dissolving these arguments, mushing them into short-circuiting feedback loops, eating away at ethics, at second thoughts, at broader contexts, at tomorrows and consequences. Amber bumped and ground, and the drink revealed a simple formula on the smeared palimpsest of my mind: seek pleasure. Connie slipped a hand between my legs and I suddenly felt self-conscious, embarrassed even, of my recent reverse down there, as if I had failed to leave a tip. And with that, its presence returned. I swigged my beer.

'Not bad!' Michael said loudly as Amber's devotions drew to an end. It could have been either a statement or a question.

'Great,' I said, not very enthusiastically, tipping five euros. Connie leaned into me, and was now rubbing between my legs. She licked her lips. She smelled of a recent shower. She clutched the hair at the back of my neck with her free hand. I was caught in a dilemma, not wanting to appear either interested or uninterested. With some difficulty, considering my entanglement, I took another deep draught of the not very cold beer. As soon as the neck of the bottle was out of my mouth, however, Connie moved in. Her lips clamped around mine, her hot tongue pushed in. I tasted beer, champagne, wine, smoke, metal, blood. My hand went to her waist, thin and fragile, and up to her breast. I was repatriated to a tyranny of desire. Stale fireworks blew in my head, and yeast stirred in my belly.

I disengaged. Connie was beautiful, and her lips sparkled with moisture in the complicated red light. She was so beautiful, and if this whole process was disgusting her, she was doing an excellent job of concealing it. I wanted to feel free. I wanted to feel an open spectrum of possibility. But instead, I felt bound by many threads, each tied to an action in the past and a result in the future. The beer was not helping me as I thought it had been – it had been lying to me. I thought of fermentation, of yeast, of gases, of microbial processes. The wine churned, and came close to spilling. Many of the threads pulled at once.

'Oh, God,' I said softly. 'Michael, I think I have to go ...'

Tiredness and the urge to vomit crashed through me. My bowels liquesced. 'Oh, God,' I said again. I stood up, and pushed out of the booth, past Connie. 'I'm so sorry. I have to go. I've had a really good time. I'm very drunk. Tired, and I'm very tired.' I didn't want to talk. Talking, bringing forth things from within, felt risky. I fumbled through the scraps of paper I had dropped on the table and left some money there, more than enough. Then I turned and left at speed.

The entrance corridor smelled of bleach and water. It smelled of Oskar's bathroom. I wanted to be in that bathroom right away. I collected my jacket in a frenzy of impatience, and turned to see where the teasing sound of running water was coming from.

A stream was cascading down the concrete steps and into the club, where it flowed into a grate. The steps were a running gutter. The corridor was a sort of storm drain. And it was a storm up above – a biblical downpour, one that threatened to float away flagstones and snuff out streetlights. I was instantly drenched to the skin, and I did not care. I needed to get back to Oskar's flat, urgently, a priority that cancelled all other considerations. The threads tugged and pulled; many of them appeared to be anchored to my stomach.

I jogged and stumbled through the streets, guided by instinct, soaked thoroughly, skidding and tripping over the sliding paving slabs. Then, my legs felt washed away from under me, and I staggered against a rough wall. A terrible battle was lost inside, and I belched awfully, then doubled over and retched. A red liquid stream splashed out and spread into the puddles. Then it happened again, hot and acid. And again. I was propping myself against an abrasive surface, surrounded by water, feet almost submerged to the ankles. I felt the sandy roughness of the wall with the same hand that had, a short time previously, been warm and dry on Connie's waist and breast. Water was in my shoes and ears. Was it a short time previously, or hours? Another retch, I hoped the last. I was lashed to a rack of exhaustion, but the struggle was over, the threads now pulling me to bed, not pulling open my innards.

I looked up. Geometric forms in black and sodium orange meshed above me. It was the brutalist palace of culture, a revelation that forced a yelp of happy recognition from me. I had been vomiting against its concrete wall, but the rain was rapidly destroying all traces of my disgusting lapse, dissolving the results into the enormous puddle I was standing in. This puddle, more a pond, surrounded the palace like a moat, and I remembered what Michael had said about its subsidence into the burial ground beneath.

Across the avenue, in a pool of light at a tram stop, a silent, static group of half a dozen human forms of shining raincoats stood, looking across towards me.

I remembered Connie's face looking up at me, filled with bafflement and mild concern, when I had risen to leave. The long-dead planners, I felt, had cut their avenue, rebuilt their city, for me, for my convenience in that moment. The road stretched out ahead.

DAY FIVE

White noise. Indistinct sound, beneath hearing, the growl and whoosh of blood forcing through tight passages. A two-part beat, the slave-driver's padded drumsticks rising and falling as an exhausted muscle trireme heaves across a treacle ocean. A heart, pumping hot, thick goo in place of blood. Cells striving and dying. The electricity of the brain whining like an insectocutor. A cascade of neural sparks, an ascending, crackling chain reaction, synapses firing. Sensation – the sensation of no sensation. Then, awareness.

A cosmos of pain, discomfort, sickness and weakness. I was awake. At first, everything seemed to be pain, but this was an illusion brought on by apparent damage to the sensory apparatus. The brain. The brain hurt. It was a sinkhole of pain, dragging all other senses in. Each beat of the drum, each stroke of the oars, simply scooped more sensation towards that pulsing black point of hurt. My heart was going to give up and get *sucked* into my head, it would explode, and I would die in bed.

In bed. So I was in bed. I realised that this was a good sign. In bed meant that I had got home all right. At the very least, I had made it to a bed before losing consciousness, even if I was not home. This meant a degree of safety. It reduced the number of bad things that might have happened to me from infinite to a manageable few tens of thousands.

My heart was still beating. Whatever its troubles, I didn't think it was likely to stop unexpectedly. It was bound by several hundred dirty rubber bands, though. Moving was bad, it seemed. Any movement set off the pain in the head like an earthquake in a bulk discount china store. The pain in the head was worrying. At a rough guess, there were fourteen or fifteen tumours in there, and they were fighting in the lubricating pus like angry meatballs wrestling in custard. The thought of pus and custard set off a shudder of nausea. I realised how precarious everything was, how delicate, everything interlinked with tendons in complicated, secret patterns, so that the slightest wrong move might set off some sort of catastrophic unravelling.

Sensory information was now arriving in an unsteady stream. The news was not good. Systems were coming back online one by one after some sort of florid and spectacular trauma, not fatal, but crippling. Some symptoms were identifiable – a headache, and nausea. I began, in a detached way, to speculate about what might be wrong with me. A headache, nausea, and comprehensive general wrongness. But it was all on such an epic, Technicolor, Ben Hur scale. Committees of investigation formed.

It was possible that I was hungover. Yes, that seemed plausible. To be hungover, I would have had to have been drinking. Had I been drinking? A salvo of memories. No actual details or situations were entirely clear, but drinking was definitely involved. Yes, the committee agreed on that. There had been drinking, and other people.

Another shudder shook the plates in the china shop and they jangled, sending out waves of pain. I may have groaned. My body was made from wads of soggy material inexpertly lashed together with stringy sinews. The wads composed of the worst stuff possible – bad milk, wine turned to vinegar, chewed gum, earwax, the black crud that accrues on the bottom of computer mice. The connecting sinews all strained and ached. It was a bad scene.

My experience was expanding slowly outwards. Eventually it reached the gaping pores of my skin, oozing greasy sweat, and pushed into the world. The duvet of Oskar's bed had been twisted into a rope by some night-time exertions, and was coiled around my legs. My throat and lungs rasped with complaint, shredded by smoke. Chemists would have found it impossible to recreate the taste in my mouth without taking a sample jar on a trip to the zoo. A solution of lemon juice and envelope adhesive had been squirted into my eyes at some juncture in the night. I was neither dry nor wet, swaddled in evaporated perspiration.

The shell of perception around my body was continuing to expand, and I wanted very much for it to stop. The room was light, it was day, it was a day in a succession of days, it was the next day. I needed to know more about the previous day. More information was becoming available, sensory information, from the nose. It appeared to be bad, but I couldn't really understand it.

There had been drinking. I had been out drinking with Oskar's friend Michael. We had drunk a great deal. I had accompanied him to some sort of lap-dancing place. These were the preliminary findings of the committee that had been hastily assembled to determine the causes and nature of the recent calamity. The committee believed that further investigation was needed. The committee had reason to believe that I had been sick.

I inhaled sharply and my nostrils filled with the unmistakable smell of vomit. There was something very bad in the room. I jumped out of bed and a violent tremor hit the discount china store, setting the stacks of plates clashing and scraping. My brain pressed against my skull. I had to inhale again, and there it was, that awful smell.

There was no obvious pool of ejecta around the bed, where my clothes lay tangled. I explored my face with my fingers and found nothing on it but a thin residue of oil and sweat. The white sheets no longer looked quite so white after four nights of my presence, but they had not had an evening's red wine consumption emptied over them. I must have made it to the bathroom. But the bathroom was even cleaner, and I stood there gratefully, breathing in its glacial air, letting it sweep out the badness within. If there had been puking in here, I had been very careful about it. The smell trickling in from the bedroom made my stomach lurch, but I felt less at risk of throwing up now – which suggested that I had done so already, at some point in the night. The smell was inescapable. There was no other explanation for it. It was the smoking gun. But there was no body.

A shower would help, I thought. A strange calmness had me. My head cleared as the water poured over it, and more memories returned. My clothes would be damp, because I had been caught in the rain. I had been sick in the rain, and if I had been sick in the rain, then I had been sick outside the flat. A concrete vastness loomed in my mind, chandeliers swinging, carried on the chests of the dead, and receded like a passing Channel ferry. I remembered digested wine swirling into a puddle. I raised my face under the shower head and let the water splash into my eyes. I was born anew, sin washed away. My sick headache improved; an angry, tar-covered octopus of pain became an ugly and badly positioned trunk in the attic.

There was still the matter of the smell, though, and it tricked its way into my nose again as I dried and brushed my teeth. Back in the bedroom, it was as strong as before.

I checked last night's clothes for stains and, although the smell did seem to strengthen when I leaned to pick them up, I found nothing. They were still damp, though, and had left a patch of wetness on the floor. Could that damage it? I leaned over again to inspect the area, and again the stink swelled. The sheets, I thought. I would wash the sheets. Some nausea still stalked my system, and getting a nostril-full of the smell sent it scurrying. The laundry would have to wait until I recovered.

My shoes were sodden, brown leather darkened and fleshed with water. I picked them up and took them out to the balcony, leaving them in the bright, breezy day.

There were no cats on the balcony. A little landslip of memory fell, shifting the mental scenery and revealing ... nothing. I had no memory of letting them out the previous night. They were still in the flat when I left for the concert – I had expected to be back before ten, in plenty of time to expel them. Was I composed enough to show them the door when I got back from the club? It seemed extremely unlikely. My mental image warped, expanding and narrowing like a reflection in a fairground funhouse mirror, when I considered that I had been to a lap-dancing venue the previous night. Guilt prickled. I felt smaller and less evolved. And stupid – why hadn't I grasped the opportunity and enjoyed myself? Because, I thought, I would have been sick over that poor girl. I remembered the black-red fountain splashing into puddles in the impassive sodium light. And the state of the toilets in the bar, the eye-watering breath of old urine. My stomach flopped, and a black, bitumen-scented tentacle of pain pushed out of the heavy trunk in the attic. It was clear now – I was in for a day-long buzzing bolus of a headache, right behind the eyes, with an occasional icepick-blow to the back of the head. I groaned again.

The cats. Where were the cats? If not outside, then inside. I hurried into clean clothes, and went through to the living room.

In the later days of the recent spring, Oskar had been in London. He had been involved in a concert at the Barbican – a quartet, comprising members of the Philharmonic, had played one of his compositions. He called me and urged me to attend the concert, and I put up a firewall of increasingly wild lies to get out of it. At the time, I reasoned that even the best classical music – Bach, say – was barely interesting to me, and so to make for an entertaining evening a composition of Oskar's would have to be better than Bach, and even the most charitable guess at my friend's talents left me with the feeling that this was unlikely. Supper with an imaginary and terribly frail relative quickly filled the evening in question. We were both most chagrined. Before I could suggest it myself, Oskar was insisting that we meet the day before the concert. I eagerly agreed, and suggested a pub in the neighbourhood, a shabby little place on Whitecross Street that I was reasonably sure would be uncrowded and quiet.

Oskar was there before me, and I was there ten minutes early after putting a huge logistical effort into being punctual. Despite my earliness, I felt certain that his eyes would drop to his watch as soon as he saw me enter. I was wrong. He was staring at his pint, which he twisted to and fro with his thumb and middle finger, causing the remaining half of his lager to slop against the grey marine foam that adhered to the sides of the glass.

I had seen Oskar dejected before, but not since university. The memory of his forensic examination of my flaws over dinner was no longer fresh in my mind, but we had had little contact in the year since then, so it remained the most recent major development in our relationship. However, this was the insecure Oskar I remembered from the earliest days of our acquaintance; seeing him like this, I forgot more recent events and was taken back to those early intimacies. We had been friends for almost a decade and I realised that my affection for him had survived the ugliness at dinner.

'Is everything OK?' I asked. There was – as had been normal at university – something demonstrative in his depression, something that called out to be noticed and remarked upon. It was meant to be seen. In answer to my question, he shrugged, palms upward.

'The rehearsal goes OK,' he said. 'They know the piece. They are perfect. And now it sounds ... I don't know. Maybe they know it too much. But ...' He paused. It was not one of his typical laconic breaks, used for effect; this was a genuine inability to find the words for what he wanted to say in any of the languages he knew, a void betrayed by the panic that quickly gleamed in his eyes. He opened his mouth, and nothing happened. One of the hopeless cases at the bar coughed, and Oskar glanced over, jaws snapping shut. Then he said, firmly: 'I do not write *jazz*.'

I didn't know what he meant, and was myself momentarily at a loss. 'I'm sure it'll sort itself out,' I said.

He looked at me. There was something quite fragile in his expression, an atypical wateriness. Either he had been drinking or he had been crying. Perhaps both. 'How is your work?' he asked.

'Not bad,' I said, carefully measuring out a tiny portion of candour. 'Quite slow, actually. Not very busy.' In truth, my professional boredom was starting to manifest itself as a lack of dynamism in generating new work.

Oskar nodded. 'In your work ...' he said, carefully, '... how do you have holidays?'

'Well, I'm freelance,' I explained. 'So it's pretty easy to arrange time off, but I don't get paid holidays. Any time off is essentially unemployment.'

Again, Oskar nodded. 'Do you have a holiday planned for this summer?'

'No,' I said. I was anticipating a holiday on my own, and was not enthusiastic about the prospect, forcing my way through sensible books in a worthy northern European city, drinking expensive coffee and beer in expensive cafés or bars in order to get out of my expensive hotel room. Dutiful trips to cathedrals. Prix fixe. 'Not yet.'

Oskar spread his hands on the grimy table and looked into my eyes. Seriousness glittered in place of vulnerability, which had for the minute evaporated. 'I need someone to look after my flat for a couple of weeks, maybe three weeks, maybe a month. In the summer. Flights are cheap now. Are you interested?'

I was interested.

A miasma of evaporated alcohol hung in the living room's air, a haze of expended volatiles, the unquiet memory of long-dead sugar. The living room stank of stale wine. This wasn't the sweated trace of last night's drinking, it was something else – direct exposure to the atmosphere, with no human mediator. I moved swiftly, but as if caught in a dream, my sense of self shrinking back, reduced to a spectator as my body explored what had happened. There was no chaos or mystery – as I saw the disaster in the kitchen, it was immediately clear how it had come about. It was like seeing the scene after it had been dissected by the forensic experts, seeing the coloured string that linked the bullet holes with the position of the shooter, strands of narrative that connected everything I found with an instantly obvious explanation of its cause, its meaning.

There was a puddle of red wine, about one foot by two feet at its greatest extent, on the kitchen floor, with dark rivulets running down the bottoms of the cabinets and along the joins between the floorboards. It occurred to me, from afar, that the shape resembled a jellyfish – a bloated, formless body of hostile intersecting shapes, trailing long tendrils, seeking out weak points. Around this shape, this pool, this reservoir of disaster, radiating out in all directions, were purple paw prints. There were so many, it seemed impossible that they could have been made by only two cats.

The scene was static. The open neck of the bottle, on its side in the rack on the counter, was not dripping. The wine lake was already half dried, a reduced Aral of pink far behind the black-cherry coast that marked its one-time greatest extent. The strength of the alcohol odour was proof that a good part of the liquid was already in the atmosphere, leaving only pigment behind. It must have been like this for hours already.

I had a clear picture in my mind of how this had come about. After I had left the flat yesterday evening – in my imagination, as soon as I had closed the door – the cats had decided to resume the cork game that we had played on the previous day. One or both of them – in my imagination, again, both of them cooperated efficiently in this – had chewed or clawed the stopper from the bottle on its side in the rack. It can't have been pushed in that firmly; that was the cleaner's lapse. Then, a gout of wine, a splash, a glugging torrent as the bottle lost about half of its contents. I thought of the gush of wine, and a tight glass ring of nausea slid up and down my oesophagus. The rest of the scene plays out: the cats, startled, darting away, maybe being splashed; cleaning themselves, circling on the floor, reeling their nerves back in, and padding back to the newborn red lake when the effluxion of wine has diminished to an occasional drip, drip, drip.

Where was I at the crucial moment, when the grip of the cork against the walls of the bottle neck was diminished to the point that it was pushed out by the weight of the liquid stopped up behind it? In the concert hall? Afterwards, in the bar, pouring wine down my throat? After that, in the lap-dancing place, or when I was spilling out wine on the street? It was not impossible that everything had still been perfectly orderly when I had returned to the flat, and the flood had taken place when I was asleep. That seemed worse, somehow; that scenario suggested that there was something I could have done to prevent disaster. I doubted that there really was anything I could have done. I would only have picked up that bottle if I wanted another drink. That didn't seem likely, so nothing could have been done to stop this from happening.

I stared at the ruined floor. It was certainly ruined. The wine had had plenty of time to soak in, to dry, to work into the wood, the stain. Around the great lake were those paw prints. What had the cats been doing? Paddling in the stuff? An image suggested itself to me: the trampled dirt around a watering hole in a parched scrubland. Had the cats been *drinking* the wine? Did cats even drink wine, or any alcohol? It didn't strike me as something cat-like to do, but I could not think of any reason why a cat might not drink wine. I pictured two drunken cats, sliding around in the wine puddle, singing at each other as they haphazardly kicked about the mangled cork. Pissed louts skidding about on the wet, washed floor of a deserted London railway terminal in the early hours of the morning. The whole scenario started to take on the complexion of a student prank, an inconsiderate and calculated gesture of vandalism and theft topped off with an alcoholic debauch. They were probably sleeping it off somewhere. I fervently hoped that they were both suffering terrible kitty hangovers.

I walked from the kitchen to the sitting room, and sure enough there was a cat there, asleep on the chair. I woke it with a forceful stroke. It eyed me lazily. I half-expected there to be a telltale purple stain on its paws and around its mouth, but there was nothing. The fur around its paws was black, anyway. There was no evidence of a feline morning-after, no pained look, no tremors, no retching or pools of regurgitated cat food.

Regurgitated cat food. The thought of it, the idea and look and *smell* of it, brought another clench of nausea. The smell of it, though, I felt I knew exactly. I knew it.

There it was, in the bedroom. It seemed to have been gathering strength behind the closed door, waiting to assault me when I walked back in. A cat had been sick in here, I thought. But where? The results were not in plain sight.

Such was my burgeoning paranoia about the apparent malice of the cats that my first instinct was to check my shoes. But they were airing outside, and I would have noticed that they were full of cat vomit when I moved them. The wardrobe seemed, briefly, to be a possibility – the memory of the piss-filled welly may have guided me there – but even in the unlikely event that the cat had been able to open the door to get in, I doubted that it could have closed the door on its way out. Besides, the stink wouldn't be half as bad if the source was shut up in there.

No, I knew where the smell was coming from. I dropped to my knees to look under the bed. The blood rushing to my head as I brought it to floor level triggered a heavy throb of pain, a wet sandbag dropped onto my brain. It was dark under the bed, too dark to see clearly – I could make out a stack of papers, nothing more – but the force of the stench that hit me confirmed my suspicions. One of the cats had been sick down there.

I stood up again, and was rewarded with a bout of dizziness that ignited stars in my field of vision. Tension was spreading over my body, tightening up muscles and locking bands around my chest. I had spent the past few minutes – a tiny span of time that now seemed to stretch to encompass weeks and months, so distant was the era before this morning – in a state of total, unreal, peace. Nothing could be done to undo these events. But nevertheless, something had to be done. I had to respond somehow to what had happened. Reality was crowding in on me.

Kitchen first. Maybe the stain wasn't so bad, I thought. The bed situation could wait; it was, at least, out of sight.

The sight of the wine lake at once filled me with dismay. How could I have looked upon this calmly? It was more than a lake, it was an ocean. The pre-spill, antediluvian, age was so recent, and already it was an entirely vanished epoch, a golden age that I had dwelled in unconscious.

Acting with the extreme care that seems to come naturally to the hungover – for whom every movement must be made to count – I tilted the neck of the open bottle upwards, so that no more wine might spill out, and slid it out of the rack. Setting it on the counter, I pondered finding the cork and putting it back in. But instead petulance and regret hit me, and I poured the remaining wine down the sink.

I soaked a tea towel under the kitchen tap, wrung it out, and used it to mop up the still-wet central puddle. A lot of the dried wine yielded as well. However gratifying that fact was, there would be no miracle escapes, the stain was permanent. I rinsed the towel, squeezed it out over the sink, and went back to cleaning. The second bout made a pathetic amount of difference. I wiped down the long, spindly trails drawn along the boards by gravity over imperceptible gradients, traced along invisible valley floors defined by incredibly subtle changes in elevation, nudged, flicked and halted at points by the arcane whims of surface tension. Whatever wine that could be removed by a damp cloth had now been removed. What remained was the substratum, the stain. There it was, the stain, the physical manifestation of an event that by now felt almost metaphysical – the chalk outline around the corpse of my friendship with Oskar, the shadow cast on today by the confrontation that now loomed in the future.

And yet the stain itself – its proportions and intensity still obscured by the drying damp patch around it – did not seem, in itself, malevolent. Instead, I felt hostility radiating towards me from the floorboards themselves, seeping up from beneath like radon or fungal rot. They, not the stain, were against me. They lay there, welcoming the red deeper and deeper into their substance, like self-conscious, passive-aggressive martyrs. If they had been lino, or even sealed wood, this would never have happened. But Oskar had to have everything just so. He had to have everything perfect. He had to have this one kind of wood; any other kind would have been as ruinous as an incorrectly struck note. Everything had to be balanced, perfectly, always, on the edge of disaster, without the slightest margin for error. Wasn't this kind of calamity inevitable, given enough time? Didn't he realise that? His precious, delicate floorboards had their fate written into their absorbent grain.

It was, at least, not getting worse. The still-liquid pool had been mopped up, and no more could merge irrevocably with the wood. There was the matter of the bedroom, though, and whatever lurked under the bed. Kitty binge, kitty purge. But I still could not find the effort needed to confront that. A heaviness was holding my legs. I moved, a shamble, over to the sofa, and sat down.

The headache stirred inside me, and the nausea moved like custard under a skin. I felt tired; I wanted to sleep. But that would mean confronting whatever was under the bed.

I was exiled. My head drooped, and settled into my hands. There was a long list of things that had to be done, a list that seemed to be continually growing, actions that were needed to go a little way towards setting things straight. The energy was, however, wanting. And there was something else going on, a psychological barrier to action, like a bulkhead door sealed tight by the pressure that had built up behind it. I didn't want to do anything more. I wasn't the one who caused this destruction, and I did not want to be the one to clear it up. Even if I tried, even if I invested my best effort, there was no way that I could wholly succeed. The damage was done, the bridge was cinders. I was exiled, from the bed, from Oskar, from the flat's state of grace.

I could call him. There was still that. I could call Oskar and explain what had happened. *Oskar, there's been an accident ...*

'Thank you so much for this; you're a real friend for helping out.' Oskar's relief at my agreement to look after his flat had been palpable, an effervescence cutting through his dour mood. 'I don't feel comfortable leaving the flat for so long, not with the cats ...' he was momentarily transported elsewhere at the thought of the cats; I wondered how much trouble they could be.

I smiled modestly, enjoying the flattery I was receiving for what seemed to me to be a pretty good deal. 'I'm happy to help,' I said. 'Are you going to see Laura?'

At once, the light vanished from Oskar's manner like a bulb blowing. 'Yes,' he said, sharply.

His sudden reversion to gloom alarmed me. I had missed some subtle cue and fouled up, I thought. I had said something out of place. 'I'm sorry ...' I began, automatically, not yet certain what I was sorry about.

'No, no,' Oskar said, waving his hands and flashing me a pale smile. 'I am sorry. I will explain. I am going to Los Angeles to be divorced. We are getting divorced.'

For a moment, I didn't have anything to say. Then: 'Oskar, that's terrible, I'm so sorry.' In fact, my emotions were a logjam. It wasn't that I was happy to see Laura excised from Oskar's life. Instead, it was a combination of fellow-feeling for Oskar and the sort of wild, exhilarating interest that comes with something bad happening to a close friend – a mad glee at the opportunity to go on emotional safari in a passionate place for the span of a conversation, and then step back into a milder climate with no lasting implications. These feelings were overlaid with an acute fear that I might not be seen to be reacting in the correct way, and the usual British horror at the possibility that someone might start crying.

'I do not know if it is terrible,' Oskar said. 'It is very sad for me. Of course. But it was too complicated. Her in one country, me in another. And the distance makes life difficult when we are together. We argue. I do not like Los Angeles. It is unruly. And she hates my flat. This I do not understand – you will see, it is a very nice flat. And it is big! Too big for me alone, so I have the cats. And now I discover that it is too big for me but it is too small for two of us. One is lonely and two is crowded. Maybe it is like life.'

'I've never had a long-distance relationship,' I said, 'but I know that living together can be difficult.'

'Difficult!' Oskar appeared incensed by the word. 'Yes, I hear this. Why should it be difficult? People say, this is difficult, that is difficult. It is an excuse for failing, for doing something wrong. It is not difficult – it should not be difficult. As long as there are some rules, some agreements, people know how to do things, then everything should be easy.'

There was a bout of Dickensian coughing and throat-clearing from one of the hopeless cases at the bar. Oskar had finished his pint, and what remained of mine was warm. I offered to buy him another, and he agreed.

'Oskar, there's been an accident,' I said, out loud. The cat lying on the chair across from me looked up, as if to say: 'Oh? What's happened?'

'Oskar, there's been an accident,' I said. 'Some wine ... quite a lot of wine ... was spilled ...' No, that was no good. The passive voice would not do – he would automatically attribute blame to me. And this was unfair – it was not my fault.

'Oskar, there's been an accident,' I said. 'The cats spilled some wine on the floor.' But that was no good, either. It sounded absurd. I could see the eyebrow raising in response, the migration of tension in the upper lip, I could imagine the sound these things would make over the phone line from Los Angeles. I could hear the sceptical 'Oh?' – a syllable with so much acid that it would strip the insulating plastic off the communicating copper cords all the way to here. He would think I was lying. I would have to explain the details – the cleaner not pushing the cork in firmly enough, the fact that I was kept out late. I would have to blame everybody but myself, like an adolescent unable to take responsibility for their actions. But it *was* their fault! I was *not* responsible!

It was just all so *unfair*.

I straightened my back, and flexed my shoulders. Whoever was to blame, now it was my responsibility. I was the adult here. The cats weren't about to put on the Marigolds and muck in. Besides, if the mess under the bed was as bad as the mess in the kitchen, only so much could be done. At least it was out of sight there.

Standing up, I saw that the cat on the chair had followed my lead and was stretching; when it saw me stand up, it too stood up, and did a little pirouette. The anger in me ebbed back, and I ran my hand along its spine.

'You're still cute,' I said. The cat squinted and wiggled with pleasure. 'Where's your little buddy?' I asked it. The cat didn't respond, and squirmed happily under my hand.

I fetched together some sheets of newspaper, a pair of rubber gloves, the damp tea towel and a bowl of warm water with a squirt of washing-up liquid in it. The smell was waiting behind the bedroom door like a mugger. I crossed the room to the French windows and propped them open, something I realised that I should have done earlier. But earlier I was dying, not thinking. The city air rushed in, fresh and invigorating, its rain-washed exhaust fumes as sweet as Chanel No 5. I put on the gloves and took hold of the foot of the bed. It pulled away from the wall easily, not too heavy, moving smoothly along the floor without threatening to scratch it. Once it was clear of the bedside tables, I pushed it to the far wall.

Underneath, to my surprise, was a bright pool of happy, guileless colours – blues, yellows, reds, purples, and many pinks. A breath from the street, and papers rose up like jaunty wind-breaks on a festive, polychromatic beach. I was looking at a disordered heap of maybe four or five dozen pornographic magazines.

Inane smiles winked up at me from a mass of flesh tones, bad page layout and probing fingers. I stood there, gawping, full of a completely unexpected fear, unknown since my teenage years and now quickly back, as fresh as ever – the fear my parents might walk in. Then, another sensation, more familiar and commonplace, but every bit as unexpected: mirth. I laughed.

'You old dog,' I said, chuckling. Flirty smiles shared the joke, not understanding it.

There was the vomit, a fairly neat and discrete purple-grey pool affecting only four or five of the magazines. A very precise bit of journalistic criticism. With a little care, I was able to wrap up the mess in the skin-zines it had reached, before ushering it away to the bin in the kitchen. Walking with it, however, held in hands at the end of maximally outstretched arms, I found myself downwind of a fresh assault from the odour, curling out of its swaddling of sexual display. I stuffed it deep into the bin, coughing with nausea. Then, fearful of the reek polluting the kitchen, I pulled the black bin-liner out, twisted its neck tightly, and tied it off.

I looked at the knot of the bag, and the crushed black flower opening slowly above it. The taint lingered in the air. That knot did not look all that tight, already it was teeming with intestinal molecules tunnelling their way determinedly outwards to the air, the designer coffee-scented steel-edged air of Oskar's decreasingly pristine kitchen. And then I remembered the rubbish chute in the hallway.

It was cooler in the hall than in the flat, and opening the front door brought a conscious sense of decompression. I half expected the door to hiss like Tupperware. The inside-outside air, the drab ocean tones of the painted walls, and the hard, echoing sounds generated by tiled floors and stone steps put me in mind of school, in an age before high-tech composite fibreboards and brightly coloured laminates. There was something infantilising about the garbage chute, too – the way it seemed designed for taller, stronger beings, its grinding squeak like the complaint of an old man, and the vicious slam, which made me want to check my fingers. It was the sort of thing that parents warn their children not to play with. And as with all those forbidden things it performed magic, a disappearing act. Even the sound of the falling bag, if there was any, was lost in the groan and bang.

But there was one other sound, in that quiet hall, as I turned back to the open entrance of Oskar's flat. On the floor below, a handle turned with the minimum noise, and a door opened. I halted, waiting for footsteps, voice, a jingle of keys, neighbourly sounds. There were none. I became aware that I was not breathing. And then there was a faint note of a hinge, and, softly, the door closed. I shut Oskar's behind me firmly, with a slam, like a warning shot.

Back inside, the air was clearer. In the bedroom, the bed was still shunted to one side, and the low pile of pornography was naked in the middle of the room. Naughty boy, Oskar, I think. It felt good, very good indeed, to have come across this stash. Normally, a chance discovery of something like this in the possession of a friend would have embarrassed me, and made me eager to clear things away again and beat over my traces. But I felt no embarrassment, not for Oskar. I was delighted; he was human after all. His nightclub excursions with Michael could be read as the product of peer pressure, but this was undeniably private desire. So private, in fact, that it did not really feel as if I was dealing with Oskar. The whole situation was un-Oskar-like. It was strange that he should keep physical magazines at all, in the pixelated, diverse bounty of the Internet age. Even though there was no computer in the house, I had no doubt he had a laptop of some kind, something discreet and portable. That aside, the collection itself was just so untidy. The publications were a disordered sprawl on the floor, and individually they were dismally trashy – cheap, noisy, unappealing. Oskar's pornography had never figured in my imaginary inventory of his possessions, but I knew exactly what it should be – exquisite models decorously draped over carefully chosen pieces of designer furniture, photographed in black and white by skilled men (women, even) treating their subjects with the same professional detachment that they would accord the

Eiffel Tower or a flower arrangement. At the very most, taking a creative leap, I could see Oskar hunched over glossy photographs depicting smuttified stagings of the raunchier moments from great opera.

Not this eager, explicit junk. I squatted to get a better look at it, picking up a nearby title with the tender caution of a naturalist selecting a specimen of a new, exuberantly ugly and possibly venomous species for examination. The paper was thin and shiny, and stuck a little to my fingers. It was a slippery, loathsome thing, seemingly eager to escape my grip. I could see why it was said that this sort of publication treated women like pieces of meat. It wasn't a figure of speech, it was literally true. They were simply the fastest route between two points, an attempt to make flesh instantaneous, stripped of society and individual agency, reduced to its simplest form. Not just any flesh; only the cuts considered choice. These were unfailingly angled directly at the camera and made blatant, a simplified vocabulary of sexual display. Two expressions were almost universal: smiling and bored. When another cast of face appeared, sneaking past the picture editor's veto, it was a rare surprise – a flash of candour far more revealing than any nakedness. Quizzicality. Bashfulness. Doubt. Concern.

Where the eyes of the girls actually met yours, and had something in them to communicate, their gaze was uncomfortable to hold. Even with the expressionless ones, I did not like to stare. With the same pink poses repeated monotonously, they became invisible, lacunae on the page. The eye slid to the side, and background detail jumped to the fore. And the background features were far worse.

These brash beauties frolicked in the graveyard of good taste. The sets they reclined against were jammed with wickerwork, velour, padded headboards, animal prints, artificial fur, artificial plants and artificial leather. Around the images was a slaughterhouse of page layout. Working as I did in local government publications, I thought that I had seen all the evil that could be done when powerful desktop publishing tools were placed in inexperienced hands. I had, it seemed, been living in a fool's paradise. An insipid, spindly, badly spaced, machine-default sans-serif type predominated, in places tracked in so tightly that letters, words and sentences joined together into single streaks of text, and elsewhere justified so that a single short word stretched across a whole column. Headlines were set in a kitschy salmon-pink cursive that was merely ugly against white, and actually illegible against pictures. These typographic elements flowed into a jumble of wonky, garish boxes. The sheer artlessness of the arrangement commanded a kind of perverse respect; it was hard to comprehend the kind of inverted genius it took to get every element of the composition so perfectly wrong down to the last lost margin and grinding ligature. Maybe, for Oskar, this was the truly pornographic part; the loveliness of the unclothed lovelies tuned to a pitch by the overwhelming ugliness of their surroundings. Maybe this was Oskar's kink – the blush of sweat on an avocado-green vinyl sofa.

A troubling thought occurred. Would he miss the magazines that I had been compelled to throw away? How closely did he keep tabs on his little library? It would be typical for him to keep an exact mental record of the titles in his possession, but then it would also be typical for him to keep the magazines in chronological order in a series of slipcases, and instead they were heaped without an obvious system or care. Would he know that I had 'taken' four? If he did, his range of response was limited – he would not be able to acknowledge the loss without admitting to ownership in the first place. And besides, the disappearance of these magazines was nothing against the destruction of the floor.

In a way, then, I could do whatever I pleased with the porn. If it was over between us, if we were now simply counting the hours until Oskar despised me for what I had done – or rather, for what had happened on my watch – it would be satisfying to walk away knowing I had left signs that showed I had discovered his collection. I would be leaving evidence that I had found a flaw in him. I scooped an armful of magazines closer to me and began to arrange them into piles by cover date.

Something immediately stood out amid the smut – a sheet of paper. It had been tucked into the heap on Oskar's side of the bed. And, in his handwriting:

> You should respect my privacy. But I expected you to poke about a bit. See: we are all human. Clean up after yourself.
>
> Oskar

My grip on the note must have loosened, because it fell from my fingers and slid across the floor, disturbing a couple of lazy dustballs.

I wanted to swallow, but my mouth was again an acid waste. Dehydration, a consequence of the hangover and also the cause of the muffled banging in my head. What I needed was a glass of water. I stood up, and my legs almost failed me, causing me to lurch. My knees were drying glue.

With more effort than should have been necessary, I made it through to the kitchen. The cat on the chair, hearing me come in, jumped up and started meowing loudly, and head-butting my suddenly enfeebled legs. I realised that it was now the later part of the afternoon, and the cats had not yet been fed. Sod them, I thought, they can wait, a bit of a delay before their breakfast wouldn't kill them.

I twisted the tap over the kitchen sink forcefully and a quick blast of water hit my glass and fountained up, splashing onto my shirt and down onto the floor. After shutting off the flow, I stood there a moment, legs quivering at the knees, breathing heavily.

This wasn't just dehydration. I was angry, more than angry, furious, shaking with rage.

How dare he? How dare he assume that I would look? That tone – the affected air of weary tolerance, an adult addressing a child. As for the offensiveness of 'Clean up after yourself' – the only reason I had been down there in the first place was to clean up after *his* pets. They were the ones with the incontinent personal habits, he was the one with the porn, and yet *I* was the one who was expected to feel guilty.

The cat was still nutting my legs. I looked down at it, and it looked plaintively up at me. For a moment, I hated it, I despised its dependence on me. But for all the insolent entitlement in its attitude, it was still quite cute. I bent down to stroke it, and it stood up on its hind legs to meet my hand.

'Were you the one that spewed under the bed?' I asked the cat. It ignored my question. 'I'll get your food when I've tidied up in the bedroom,' I said.

Clean up after yourself. I would certainly do *that*. The truly detestable thing about Oskar's note was that he had no idea if I was snooping or not. He had been content to accuse me in writing of invading his privacy, comfortable in the knowledge that I wouldn't discover the contempt he had for me if I didn't discover his porn, and apparently not even considering that I might find the stash without meaning to intrude. Well, I had tripped into his little trap without meaning to pry, something he apparently didn't think possible. The stained magazines were gone now, so I had no way of proving my version of how I came to find his collection; so, I thought, I might as well eradicate any doubt he might have about whether I had discovered it or not. I wanted to make sure that he knew that I knew.

I returned to the bedroom, and started methodically organising the magazines by title and date, ending up with half a dozen neat stacks. My plan, at first, had been to simply leave these in a disciplined row under the bed, but I was concerned that Oskar might not appreciate the effort that I had put in on his behalf. What was needed was some sort of series of files and folders, and I was pretty sure that I would find some in the study.

The door to the room where Oskar composed his music was ajar, and pushing it open disturbed the still air beyond.

I was struck, again, by the peace of the study, its focused calm, its illusion of isolation from the rest of the flat. It had not been ploughed up by the jangling energy of my busy activities in the other rooms, and the street noise seemed muted. Even the light here was different – it seemed to slant most attractively, italicised for emphasis, soft and pale as vellum, enlivened by the pirouetting points that rose from the seams of dust cultivated by stockpiles of paper. It was restful, but wholly awake.

Nevertheless, stepping into the study unnerved me; a loose end uncoiled deep in my base memory. I had forgotten ... it eluded me. My pulse raised its tempo. Had I been in here last night? I sniffed the air, and there was something at its edge. My eyes went to a sharp focus and started to roam the detail of the room. And I stopped. I had been in here. I must have been very drunk because it seemed I had taken off my socks and left them hanging over the edge of the piano. I moved to retrieve them.

It was not my socks. It was feet. Feet and legs and tail. The top of the piano was a couple of inches open; holding it open was the body of one of the cats, leaving its furry hindquarters dangling on the outside. The rest of the cat was hidden from view, but the limp legs, the straight, heavy tail, and the uncanny angle of its spine where it met the piano lid clearly showed that it was dead.

I stepped slowly over, and stroked the back of my fingers down the side of one of the hanging legs. The fur was still soft, but cold, even in the bowing sunlight. And I was cold, I shivered, feeling the shadow of a great bulkhead of duty falling across me.

Nothing happened for a short time; I know, because I stood there, watching it not happen. The legs did not suddenly kick, the tail did not curl, warmth did not flood back into those sad flanks. The cat was still dead. Any chance for that outcome to be averted had slipped away, a chain of bubbles exploding in the wake of a departing ocean liner, the white end of the tail pointed straight down, the stopped weight of a stopped clock.

The piano lid had dropped onto the cat, breaking its spine. So the piano had been open – I had left it open. The cat must have jumped up and dislodged the strut that held up the lid; maybe it had stood on the edge, rubbing against the strut. The caricature drunk supporting himself on a lamp post. Slam. Had it been quick? There was no blood on the outside, no scratch-marks. The body would have to be moved, I thought. I made a mental edit: *I* would have to move the body. It could hardly be left like this. But where?

There was also the question of Oskar. He would hardly be happy that I ... that his cat was dead. He had, with pedantic predictability, been right: I should not have been fiddling with the piano. But, I recalled, the lid was left up because I had been interrupted by a phone call from Oskar. If he had not insisted on sending me to a concert, this might not have happened. If the cat had been drunk when it had its accident, then really the cleaner had to shoulder some of the blame for its death – she did not check the cork in the bottle before placing it on its side in the rack. And that was before we came to the cats themselves, that pair of whiskered saboteurs. If you are going to share your world with stupid animals, you have to make allowances for the fact that they are going to do stupid things.

But now the stupid thing was dead. Putting aside what Oskar might want to do to me, what would he want done with the body? Burial? Where? That was senseless, there was no garden and no way that I was venturing into a park with a dead cat and shovel. But did it have to be me? Maybe Oskar would rather conduct the solemnities himself. In which case, it would have to be the freezer for puss. There would be no lying in state on the kitchen counter. And imagine the homecoming, once I had left notes of my own – 'an accident ... unsure what to do ... flight to catch ...' – with, perhaps, a note on the bag containing the carcass, as if identifying a leftover casserole. Those labels never stayed stuck. And I didn't much like the thought of the body lying in there while I was staying in the house. Was it hygienic to keep a dead cat in a freezer? It could be wrapped up, of course, in a bin-liner, but was it even hygienic to keep a bin-liner in the freezer?

Of course it was. I shook myself to derail that decreasingly sane train of thought, and paced over to the window, looking away from the little feet and their little furry toes. Of course it was hygienic to put a bin-liner in the freezer, they did not come pre-slimed with garbage. It was perfectly sanitary itself, even if it was meant for an unsanitary purpose. That was the advantage, I thought, of living in a building like this: not having to deal with the bins.

I could drop the cat down the rubbish chute. That way, it would simply disappear. Oskar would not have to know how it died – maybe *I* did not have to know how it died. It just didn't come back one morning. Very sad. Maybe it had been hit by a car ... I didn't even have to put it in a bin-bag. It was better not to – if the body was discovered in the dumpster, it wouldn't look like foul play, it would look as if it had fallen from somewhere, or someone had found the body and slung it in there. How much forensic effort would be devoted to it, really? Besides, my conscience was clear. It wasn't as if I had killed the thing.

So, it was the chute for whiskers. Unless, of course, he had left something inside the piano. Crime-scene horrors of blood and vomit flashed in my mind – if anything like that had happened, then the jig was up.

I slipped my thumb under the lid of the piano, using the gap left by the wedged body of the cat. Then I lifted the lid.

The cat moved. I saw it raise its front paws and quickly begin to slide back out of the piano. Its head reared up. A spasm of panic flowed through me and I slammed the lid back down, hard, onto the cat's neck and front legs and the beefy base of my thumb. A flat, hellish chord sounded from the piano's jarred strings and hammers and pain shot up my arm like an electrical discharge. Blood sounded in my ears as the echo of the slam resounded in the small room, and my knees buckled. I think I must have cried out, and a spray of acid rose in my throat.

The weight of the lid had been holding the cat in place, stopping it from falling onto the floor. Now, again, it was being held in place by the lid, this time because I was pressing down on it, and my agonised thumb underneath. Lifting the lid, or even relieving the pressure on it, would cause the cat to drop on the floor, an act that seemed unthinkably profane. But I had to release my thumb. The only course of action was to hold on to the cat, something I had no desire to do. But the radiating waves of pain from my crushed digit left me no option.

I took hold of the cat around one of its rear legs with my free hand. The fur felt fake, the limb underneath cold and thin. For no reason, I feared that the body might just fall apart in my hands, unspooling into a heap of guts and strips of muscle. I freed my finger, and the body slipped out of the piano, a tug of weight on my arm.

Finding an unexplored avenue of pluck, I lifted the cat above my head to inspect its face. A bead of black blood had dried under its nose, and the short white fur near its mouth had traces of purple. Its first drink, and it gets itself killed.

I opened the front door a crack, keeping the ex-puss out of sight, and listened. The air in the stairwell was cool and still. If my neighbours were in, they were staying quiet. I could hear no TVs or music, no banging crockery or crying children. It occurred to me that I had not seen or heard anyone in the building since I arrived here. The block might as well be abandoned. Apart from the cleaner.

She was nowhere. No sound, no movement. I could see the rubbish chute, a worn metal hatch losing its paint at the edges, like a prison door or a washing machine from a Laundromat. I remembered the washing machines at university, in the basement, drab, faintly military, things, their chemical reek, their thunder in the bowels of the building, the steamy heat they pumped out, turning that small, poorly ventilated space into a sauna. Water would drip from the ceiling, which had a shiny yellow-white coat of paint at the start of each year and an ascendant rash of black mould at the end. There were no dryers – instead, clothes were dried on stands in one's room, infecting it with damp. For me, more often, the clothes stayed wetly tangled in their plastic laundry bag, where they sometimes cultivated mould of their own. I remember Oskar looking at the pink and white cube of that bag and his lip wrinkling, testing the air for mildew.

Why think of this now? Proustian procrastination. I was stalling. There was no one in the hall, now was the right time to move, to rid myself of the cat's body, the fur and flesh of its leg now warmed by my hand, the bone like something from the butcher.

Now was the right time to move. If I waited any longer, it would be the wrong time. Or would it? Now.

No.

I could see the rubbish chute on the landing between floors. I knew exactly what it would take to get there, get it done, how little it would take. I could break it into a small number of actions, each nothing in itself: a push through the door, a score of brisk steps, an arm to lower the hatch, an arm to hoist the cat, release one, release the other. Or I could stand here all day, a dead thing in my hand.

Now now now.

A lead weight swinging in the pit of my chest kept time as I strode out of Oskar's front door and onto the stairs, and the body of the cat swung too, brushing against my side. I did not want to look at the sorry thing, not in these last seconds we were together, especially not at its sad little face as I dumped it with the other rubbish. The metal hatch of the chute opened easier than I expected, with an affirmative squeal. As I lifted the cat up, ready to drop it in, I found I could not resist a final look. It seemed only courteous to pay something a little like my last respects. I part closed the hatch to relieve the pressure on my other arm, which was battling the powerful spring that strained to close the chute, and examined the skinny corpse. Its fur was disarranged in places, revealing swatches of pale grey-pink flesh, and its eyes had nearly closed. It was no longer cute.

The hatch was only open by a couple of inches; I didn't want it to slam shut with the usual big bang. Carefully, I slotted the cat's dangling front paws into the aperture, lowered in the lolling head, and let go with both hands.

Some feline hairs had adhered to my palm, and I was clapping my hands to dislodge them while turning to walk back up to Oskar's flat when I saw the cleaner at the bottom of the stairs, looking up at me. Her eyes and mouth were circles of shock.

Neither of us moved. How much had she seen? Her expression made it clear that she believed she had seen something bad. But was there time to see anything with any certainty? Could I simply deny everything? Scant seconds had elapsed – it had all been over very quickly, she had definitely not been there when I emerged from the flat, and her vantage point wasn't good enough to see much more than my back. There was no way that she could have caught more than a glimpse, a blur, and surely it would be simple to claim (to whom?) that all she had seen was a plastic bag, not ... what she was alleging ... to whom? To the *police*? It's ... it was only a *cat*, and it died in an accident ... she had seen nothing, this was an outrage, she was in no position to accuse, to judge ...

She was still looking at me, and her mouth opened and closed like a goldfish. Then, she took a step towards me, onto the stairs, and I instinctively flinched back. She raised her hand; she was pointing at me, eyes wide and mad, as she ascended the stairs. Her mouth opened and closed again, formed a word, and she was still pointing at me, or past me, transfixed in some sort of visceral, muscular motion of accusation and condemnation. I thought of Donald Sutherland in the final scene of the 1970s remake of *Invasion of the Body Snatchers*, arm raised like a rifle, face contorted with hatred, alien and loathsome. I thought of the ghost advancing on Don Juan at the end of the opera. She was approaching.

'What's the matter?' I stammered, attempting nonchalance. I was frozen to the core; no part of my body could make a movement that did not seem like an admission of some kind of guilt. And yet standing here in this spell seemed to be the guiltiest act of all. I did not know what an innocent action would look like, or what an innocent word might sound like. 'Is there a problem?' I asked.

The cleaner was nearing the top of the stairs now, almost on the landing with me, still pointing, still staring, still mouthing something. She was, I realised, surprisingly intimidating, wrapped in a protective binding of gristle and rind and ancient artificial fibres, an armoured hulk in a headscarf, especially with that stumpy, meaty arm stretched out towards me. Except that it wasn't really pointed at me at all. As she drew closer, it became obvious that she was pointing past me, to something behind me, towards the chute.

Reluctantly, I looked over my shoulder. It was obvious what had caught her attention. Protruding from the closed hatch, caught in its metal grip, was a four-inch length of white-tipped tail. The rest of the cat was, presumably, hanging on the other side of the door, suspended in limbo without completing its final descent. With the limp mass of the rest of the body out of sight, this little cigar of fur looked faintly comical, a prop for a violent cartoon or something that should be dangling from a car aerial. I thought for an instant of the terrible plastic fingers that made it appear as though someone was trapped in your car's boot, a novelty that was briefly popular in the 1980s.

Quickly, surprising myself with my own decisiveness, I tugged on the hatch handle, opening it a little, and the black and white sausage of tail disappeared like a startled rodent, accompanied by the receding slither of the dead cat falling down the chute.

The cleaner stopped only a couple of steps from the top of the stairs. She said something loud and accusatory, and then repeated it, this time labouring its syllables. I had no way of knowing what she meant, but her body language was unequivocally angry and she clearly had a low opinion of me. Her pose was stiff, tense, and her face had flushed an unhealthy red, with the nostrils of that ugly batlike nose flushed wide.

'It died,' I said, doing my best to seem calm and serious. It didn't really matter what I said, as far as I could see, but my tone and bearing did count for something. Whatever I said, she had obviously already formed a very comprehensive version of what had happened and who was to blame. 'It was an accident,' I continued. 'I was out, there was an accident, and it died. I didn't ...'

I didn't know what to do. I didn't kill it.

She had, at least, closed her mouth; indeed, it was clamped shut, as if she was fighting the urge to vomit. Her eyes bulged like ping-pong balls.

Then, abruptly, she made a dismissive gesture, waving both her hands at me and turning away to stamp angrily back down the stairs, muttering to herself.

I didn't move for a little while. It felt as if I hadn't taken a breath in several minutes, so I took one, suddenly cold and shaky. Clear, chilly fluid sloshed against my insides. I bolted for Oskar's door, and slammed it behind me.

A tram rumbled by in the street as I leaned against the door, gulping in breaths and listening for sounds from the other side. There was nothing. The word 'deniability' bumped around inside my head, then inflated emptily until it filled the space between my ears, pushing out everything else. Deniability. I needed deniability. The word buzzed and multiplied. What did it even mean? I had heard it in a political context, attached to some controversy or other. The precise definition escaped me but I grasped the basic inner meaning of it. It had to do with the command of truth – the understanding that objective reality is never wholly seen by anyone, and around it we weave our own subjective and false stories. What had actually happened was irrelevant and unknowable – what was important was the construction of a compelling story that could shoulder aside competing versions. After all, I had little doubt that the cleaner had by now concocted her own completely false version of events: that I had killed the cat and then disposed of its remains in a disrespectful, indeed outright inept, fashion. This was a flotilla of untruths, so what did it matter if I too tailored the historical record a little in order to sink it? I would be working in the service of a greater truth, even if it appeared to some that I was doing everything in my power to thwart genuine understanding of the events. I was certain that wrongdoing on my part was completely deniable, and deny it I certainly would.

I took another deep breath and looked back over my last train of thought. I was panicking. There was, at that moment, no need to deny anything or enter into any kind of torrid threesome with reality and falsity. At that moment, what I needed was a drink and a sit down.

Back in the kitchen, I poured a glass of water and drained it in two gulps. It was not very refreshing, room temperature and curiously un-watery. Just liquid, nothing else, with none of water's clarifying and revitalising properties. I did not feel like one of the flawless models in the adverts, blissfully receiving a bucketful of crystalline refreshment right in the chops.

Maybe what was needed was not water but a glass of wine. The thought provoked a sullen eddy of nausea from my innards and a dull throb from the polluted liquid in which my brain swam, but no real protest. I opened a bottle and prepared a glass. As I did this, one of the cats – that is, *the* cat, the remaining cat – pushed up against my legs, rubbing its back up and down on my calf and meowing persistently.

'You're still hungry, aren't you?' I asked it. 'I'm sorry, I'll get your food.'

I set the glass down on the kitchen counter – far from the edge, up against the wall – and went into the little utility room for the cat food.

The little room smelled wholesome and comforting. Nothing identifiable predominated in this subtle aroma, but it was so pleasing and homely that it enticed me to pause, testing the air to see if I could anatomise it. Dry food certainly contributed a large share, and so did cleaning products; unlikely conspirators, but here successful. They shared ground on the spectrum of the nose: there was a certain note that was just right, natural and savoury, with a hint of purifying astringency. It was all very domestic and reassuring, but there was also something about that space that strummed on my anxieties. It spoke clearly of a well-run household – supplies built up and maintained, shortages guarded against, needs anticipated and met. As Oskar's notes made clear, nearly all contingencies had been accounted for. I had no doubt that if, for instance, the power went out, I would find candles and matches. The air was pregnant with admirable qualities such as diligence, self-discipline, organisation, planning – in short, the sort of qualities that I lacked. I did not have a career to speak of, just a succession of freelance assignments. I was single. I had neglected to buy a flat or save anything. And here I was, in the realm of all the tedious self-satisfied animals that came out on top in the fables – assiduous ants, industrious squirrels, tenacious tortoises.

But ... the thought of Oskar's notes lingered with me. He had anticipated a large number of potential foul-ups on my part. Of everything that had gone wrong over the past few days, I thought only the death of the cat might surprise him. And he certainly saw the potential for a floor-related disaster. Wouldn't he have a supply of cleaning products suited to his floors? An insurance policy, a safety net, perhaps even something potent enough to undo epic damage of the kind that I had wrought?

Yes. That sounded like Oskar. That sounded *exactly* like Oskar. That was precisely the sort of precaution that Oskar would have made sure to take.

I surveyed the areas underneath the shelves on each side of the little room and saw, with a rush of hope, a corner of dusty yellow cloth hanging from a beige plastic basket between a box of light bulbs, a shrink-wrapped cube of washing-up sponges, and a jug of white spirit. This basket slid out with a waft of a pungent, spicy smell, laced with sweetness, complicated solvents and other chemicals. Chief in the bouquet was a strong, natural smell that was both sweet and savoury and it dominated the showier artificial scents of the modern products in a convincing blast of seniority. It was old, older than most household chemicals, and curiously like the ancient, indescribable smell that follows a sneeze. The smell was natural, unrefined honey, the beehive, and its source was clear: a dull, soft-edged moulded block, the shape of a gold ingot from a heist movie. A word was printed on it in recessed letters: *Bienenwachs.* It was a chunk of beeswax, as used for repairing scratches in wooden furniture and floors. It was anchoring a note.

> CLEANING PRODUCTS. These are cleaning products for the flat and for the floor. If something has dropped on the floor, or the floor is damaged, speed is important. There is a book, *Care of Wooden Floors*, on the shelf with the architecture. It is more detailed with instructions to put right minor damage to the floor. If there is damage to the floor, you must also call me! At any time! Let me know! – Oskar

He would want to know, of course. He would want all the details – the ruined floor, the torn sofa, the dead cat. He would be interested in the welfare of the surviving cat, as well. I picked up a can of cat food and returned to the kitchen.

The cat was clearly famished. It threaded itself through my legs, rose up against me, and kept up a monologue of insistent meowing. When I put the can down and took the tin-opener out of the drawer, it cottoned on to the imminent feeding and hopped up onto the counter. I shooed it back down, carefully. When there had been two cats, they had seemed as unbreakable as rubber balls. Now, this remnant seemed desperately fragile. The opener completed its circuit of the can and the top rose up, revealing a jellied gleam. One of these cans had fed both cats – would it be best to only fork out half a can, now there was only one cat left? And throw away the rest? Or keep it in the fridge, under a miserable, wrinkled square of bachelor cling film? If I gave it the full can, could it be harmed by over-eating? I would normally have thought it incapable of reckless overindulgence, but in the light of what had happened to its friend ... Was it aware of this change in circumstances? Was it grieving? What if I was misinterpreting shock and disbelief at bereavement as hunger? Would it be lonely?

As I forked the whole contents of the can onto a plate, my vision dissolved, and I realised that I was crying.

When I returned to our table with two fresh pints, I wondered again if Oskar might cry. Rather than contemplative, or irate, he now seemed wholly desolate. It was a risk, feeding him more beer – it could push him either way. My main concern was, however, that he might be lonely. I wondered how much support he was getting, how many friends he had.

'Where are you planning to stay in LA?' I asked. 'Do you know people out there?'

'A hotel,' Oskar said. 'Laura has a very large house, but it would not be appropriate. And the people I know there are her friends. It's not bad, I like hotels. There are some very good hotels in LA.'

'Look,' I said, trying to sound supportive, 'if you want to talk while you're out there, just call me, at any time. I want to help.'

'You will be helping just by looking after the flat,' Oskar said. He squeezed out a formal smile. 'All the talking is done, I think. It does not work, so we have to put an end to it. It is just a legal procedure now. You did not like her, did you?'

I paused. The road ahead was strewn with landmines. I would have to proceed very carefully. 'She was very different to you,' I said. 'Your relationship came as a surprise to me, and I was even more surprised when you got married. Sometimes those things work, and sometimes they don't.'

'But you did not like her.'

I edged forward with as much care as possible. 'I thought she was very rude to me.'

'Yes, she was,' Oskar said. 'It cannot be denied now. She did not often worry about what other people thought.'

This made me chuckle. 'Well, Oskar, you can be pretty direct yourself. Sometimes you're not very concerned with other people's feelings.'

Oskar stared into his pint. He did not look angry. 'I know,' he said. 'I like to be honest. There is too much bullshit. Maybe I am being a hypocrite. I set a very high standard for myself in my life, in my work. And I set high standards for other people. But not too high, I think.'

'Your standards are very high indeed, Oskar,' I said. 'About people, about life. That's not a bad thing in itself, I suppose, but it seems to make you so unhappy. Maybe you should consider lowering them a bit.' I paused to sip. Oskar was not looking at me. 'Anyway,' I continued, 'my offer stands. If you ever want to talk, just call me. You'll know where I am.'

A tide of misery washed across Oskar's face. It was as if its defining lines weakened and blurred. He looked so pale. Again, my stomach clenched and I silently pleaded with him, *Please don't cry.*

I was crying. Why cry? Well, what else was there to do? The cat was gone, and I could not relate to the mysterious, reduced thing of skin and fur and pendulum weight that I had dropped in the chute. But the other one was looking at me, eyes glinting with thought and enquiry. The idea that it might be lonely struck me as unbearably tragic. My eyes burned and my throat tightened. Tears brought with them the delicious, terrifying temptation to simply let go and see where emotion took me. But I kept hold of everything, and brought myself back.

The cat, which had not let grief affect its appetite, was biting chunks of food off the plate before it had reached the floor. I still felt shaky, so I filled up my glass with wine and went to the sofa. On the way, I saw that the floor had dried, and that the stain was as obvious and vivid as ever.

Through the windows, I could see the buildings across the street caught in the rich, side-on light of the afternoon's end. Windows looked back at me, all their greyish curtains hung in prehistory by an obscure and long-departed people. I tried to think what lay beyond the city – suede plains, mountains held up by rusting ski-lifts, creaking forests? – and I saw nothing. It would be morning on the West Coast. What was he doing? Was he considering calling? The flat's telephone quickly felt like a treacherous, explosive thing. I thought of Oskar drinking (and disliking) a black coffee over a plate of fruit in an American hotel breakfast buffet, the muscular, insistent, sweet smell of pancakes and waffles and maple syrup ... I tried to remember that smell, and found myself thinking of the beeswax again, the clatter of that bucket of cleaning goods, its promise.

As long as Oskar did not know about the cat, and the wine, I had a few more throws of the dice. The cat, in fact, was not dead until he learned it was dead, and that moment could be postponed until I had made an effort to put everything right with the floor. If the floor could be fixed, then I could focus on making amends (if amends were needed) for the death of the cat, which would seem more like an isolated tragedy, and not part of a campaign of wrecking. To fix the floor, there were products to try, strategies to adopt. To tell Oskar about the cat now would necessitate telling him about the piano, and maybe even the wine as well. Also, I did not see how I could tell him without revealing that I did not know which cat was which – something I could have asked about, without risk, days ago, but the opportunity had gone. If I waited, it would be easier to tell Oskar that the cat had simply disappeared. There was the complicating fact of the cleaner, of course. If she told Oskar what she had seen – what she *thought* she had seen – then things would get more complicated. But she had no proof, I had some elements of the truth on my side, and the most important thing was not to appear guilty. That meant not attempting to pre-empt her, and seeming calm and surprised at her allegations. After all, I had done nothing. I was guilty of nothing. The disposal of the corpse was a matter of hygiene. Oskar would surely understand a matter of hygiene. My hands were clean.

What made my position uncomfortable was the fact that my innocence was so slippery. I could not keep my grip on it. I would look, and it had oozed away, nowhere to be seen. All the facts were elastic.

A sound caught my attention, distinct, repeating. It was the soft smack, smack, smack of the cat eating in the kitchen, on its own.

DAY SIX

A door slammed. The front door; definitely the front door, with the jingle of the guard chain. My senses pulled back from saturation, the crackling fade to true colour after the burst of a magnesium photoflash bulb. A dying white-orange sun. Not dying, but morning, bright and sanctimonious.

The cat and I looked up, and then I looked at the cat. It was lying on the foot of the bed, now a watchful sphinx. The previous night, I had given it the option of going out on the roam, and rather than immediately disappearing it had lingered in a way that had left me deeply uneasy. Drunk and tired, I decided to let it stay. And here we both were.

And someone else. Someone was in the flat. Certainly the cleaner, I had no doubt, and the thought appalled me. Had there been a time when our interactions had been comfortable? No – every time I had seen her, I had felt the worse for it. I was frozen, waiting for some sequel sound to come, but none did. The bedroom door was open a crack. A sliver of silent, still hallway could be seen.

I threw off the duvet, walked softly on bare feet across to the door, and listened. The silence popped and tightened in my ears. Not perfect silence – there was the unending exhalation of the city. But no sounds from the flat. The stillness was surrounding, enveloping, seeping into the bedroom like dry ice.

On the bed, the cat closed its eyes in a meditative way. Then it opened them again, stood, jumped down to the floor and ran to the French windows that led out to the little balcony. There, it coiled around itself, rubbing against the window frame.

Feet cool against the floorboards, I tiptoed over to it.

'Don't you want breakfast?' I asked, keeping my voice down. 'Lovely tinned gubbins?'

It looked up at me in an insolent fashion. I twisted the cast-iron handles of the window, opening it a crack. Sticking slightly in its frame, the window vibrated in my hand. The cat jumped to the lip of the balcony and slipped over it – at first, I thought, to a two-storey plunge down to street level. I leaned out of the window to see that it had in fact landed on a generous concrete ledge between floors. Without pausing, it alighted from this foothold too, aiming at the balcony directly below Oskar's. From there, its route to the ground was clear, via the building's entrance, which protruded into the street a short distance away.

The fresh air on my bare legs made me aware of the fact that I was standing in a full-length window wearing nothing but boxer shorts, decency defended solely by the curve of the balcony. I quickly imagined a woman's scream, sirens. There was a pair of shoes on the balcony, the pair that had been soaked in the rain. I ducked back into the bedroom and put on the trousers that were in a crumpled heap on the floor, adding the socks that fell out of the trouser legs. Then I picked up the shoes and tried them on. They were dry.

Now, I had a clear recollection of the previous evening. I had been drinking, yes, but only a modest amount when set against the excess of recent nights. I had sat on the sofa, watching CNN, sipping wine and eating remains from the fridge. The cat had lain beside me, on its side, smiling a cat smile. Events in the past now rearranged themselves into a more legible narrative. There had been two cats. One had a white tip on its tail, the other did not. And one, I thought, was the hyperactive, inquisitive one that liked to play with corks, and drink; and the other was docile, lazier. It was only now that one was dead that I could see the difference between their personalities. It was only now, really, that I could see that they even had personalities, despite not being people: they were more than just automata. The way it, the surviving cat, had left just now – sudden, urgent, determined, at the wrong time of day – it was strange, and it had the undeniable stripe of personality.

Once the sun set yesterday, I realised that I was very tired. Without leaving the flat, I had exhausted myself. Before bedtime, however, I had remembered the pornography and the derangement of the bedroom. I spent a cathartic moment with one of the magazines, and then tidied them away, stacking them neatly, still in the date order I had arranged earlier. When I had heaved the bed back into place – guided by the indentations its feet had left in the floorboards – I was so tired that I wanted to fall immediately into it, into the escape of sleep. But the cat needed to go out, I thought, so I invited it to depart. It came with me to the door, but once there would not leave, backing from the exit in that perfect cat manner of total avoidance, the way magnets repel each other. I had little appetite for a struggle, and no energy to spend cajoling the animal, which threaded itself through my legs round and again, teasing and pandering. I let it stay.

I was still tired, I realised, now that the burst of adrenalin from the slammed door had worn off. My joints and muscles felt hollowed out, like compromised paper straws. There had been no noise of any kind from the kitchen or living room. Either the cleaner had left, and I had heard her parting shot, or she was still there and deliberately staying quiet, waiting for me.

I opened the bedroom door and stepped out into the hall. The flat was empty, I was sure of it. I walked towards the living room. Had she been here at all? There was no evidence of cleaning – my empty wine glass still sat on the coffee table in front of the sofa, next to a plate that held a litter of cheese rinds and little ribbons of pink plastic peeled from the edges of slices of salami, the debris of my supper last night.

But something was different – I had walked right past it, on the other side of the glass partition, in the kitchen. First, I registered sheets of grimy newspaper spread on and hanging over the edge of Oskar's steel counter. It made such a slight profile, I almost missed what had been laid on top of these sheets – the corpse of the cat. Risen, if not from the grave, then at least from the rubbish chute.

In something like a trance, I walked up to the counter, and the body. It had now been dead for at least 24 hours, and I was nervous of the air around it. How far had decomposition progressed? Obviously it wouldn't be falling to bits yet, but would it stink? I tested the air cautiously; a faint smell of garbage.

It wasn't falling apart, but it no longer looked as if it might at any moment spring awake. It was dirty, with a brown stain on the large white patch on its side, sprinkled with coffee grounds. No longer subject to continual preening and adjustment, the cat's fur was disordered, and the skin beneath was grey. One of its rear legs was bent up in an uncomfortable manner under its belly. Both its eyes and its mouth were a little open. The tail was a bedraggled mess. It looked smaller than I remembered, as if it had deflated. The bones of its shoulder were clear under thin skin, and the break in its spine was more obvious, a pronounced and sickeningly unnatural geometry. The blood around its nose and mouth had dried, and shattered into tiny black crystals caught in the cold hairs.

'Jesus,' I said. I thought of devotional paintings, with their pornographic attentiveness to the anatomy of the tortured Christ's emaciated frame, or the buckling body of a martyr, or the contortions of the residents of hell. With a dead thing in front of me, I could understand that sadistic pedantry. A clutter of grotesque details – the angularity of the shoulder, the contours around the eyes and the sudden inadequacy of the hair to conceal the papery skin, and of the skin to disguise the broken structures inside – crowded out a clear conception of the whole.

The cleaner must have gone down to the bins at the terminus of the rubbish chute and – my imagination recoiled from serving up a mental picture of this part – searched around for the cat. Then she had wrapped it in newspaper and brought it up here to leave for me. Why? To confront me? Or because this kind of refuse didn't belong in the chute? If she had wanted to confront me, why didn't she hang around and make a real scene of it? Instead, she had simply dumped the body and fled. Normally it was cats that left dead things for people to find and puzzle over. How would a cat feel about being treated this way? Maybe this was exactly what it would have wanted.

There didn't seem to be any way of interpreting this development as a benign act on the part of the cleaner. I did not believe that she felt she was doing me a favour ('you dropped this'). Clearly, this was a rebuke – either for the murder of puss, or for the callous handling of the last rites, or for some unlikely infraction of a local waste-disposal ordinance. But – this realisation appeared by fractions – these considerations were for the time being a distraction from the fact that a dead cat, dragged out of a dumpster, was laid out on Oskar's kitchen counter. And I had my doubts about the provenance and cleanliness of the newspaper it reclined on, let alone its effectiveness as a barrier. What if there was ... oozing? Oskar's steel surface had an autopsy feel to it, but whatever its aseptic air, you would not be happy preparing food on a morgue slab.

It (the cadaver was now clearly an *it*) had to go. Quickly. Processes, natural processes involving microbes and gases and fluids, were advancing inexorably. I had no doubt that these processes were fascinating, perhaps even beautiful, when filmed by a BBC crew and then broadcast to me in my living room, but they could not be permitted to perform their magic in Oskar's kitchen. For a brief moment, I pondered dumping the thing right back down the rubbish chute, a notion I quickly put from my mind. I could not tolerate the possibility, however slender, of the cat making another comeback tour. This second coming was irksome enough, a third coming could not be permitted. A more permanent solution, something outside the influence of the cleaner, would have to be arranged.

For the moment, the priority was getting the animal off the counter. I took a bin-bag from the cupboard and laid it out on the floor. Then, I picked up the sheet of newspaper by the sides, lifting the cat as if it was on a stretcher, and set it down on the bin-bag. It did not look much more at home there, diminished, wretched thing that it was, but I no longer feared seepage.

What to do? Some dark alley perhaps, a place already strewn with trash, where an extra bag would not look out of place. But this alley was abstract – I knew of only one actual place like that, the passage by the museum with the pockmarked walls. I did not fancy carrying the dead cat all the way into the centre. In fact, I had no desire to carry it anywhere at all, let alone to wander around with it, looking for a suitable spot to dump and run. And yet I realised that I knew pitiably little of this city; I had not yet fully seen its public face, let alone explored its hiding places.

My excursions now all felt like hurried affairs, without the leisure to observe and discover.

Except my walk to the canal. The thought of the canal was like lifting a latch, and a door swung open. *The canal.* How many dead cats had it consumed in its time? And dogs, and rats, and no doubt people. A splash, a lingering roll on the surface, and then down into the forgetful black water, with only ripples for a wave goodbye. Yes, the canal now seemed a pleasing prospect. I looked forward to seeing it again.

I took another bin-bag and used it to pick up the cat's body without touching the still fur and dead flesh. Its heavy coldness could be felt through the thin plastic. With what I thought to be an artful movement, I then turned the bag inside out around the chilly little corpse. Congratulating myself on this hygienic manoeuvre, I let my concentration slip, and without thinking squeezed the closed bag to push out any trapped air, receiving a blast of the dumpster smell directly in the face, a smell now augmented by the unmistakable taint of ... or was I imagining? Still, I retched, my face pinched in spasm and a whirlpool turned in my gut. When I opened my eyes again they filled with tears, and I quickly shut them.

The bag now clung close to the curve of the cat's spine – a curve kinked where the vertebrae had been shattered by the piano lid, a lid that should not have been left open. My fault, there. But Oskar had called – a little later, a little earlier, and the piano would have been left closed. I knotted the bin-bag three tight times. Then I took some spray cleaner from under the sink, squirted a generous amount onto the counter, and wiped it meticulously clean. I fancied that I could still taste the smell from the bag, that awful hint of something wrapped in it, and I welcomed the citrus-chemical assault of the cleaning liquid against the soft membranes of the sinuses. Acidic, astringent, potent. When I got back from the canal, I was going to unleash chemical hell on that floor. It was going to get everything in Oskar's arsenal. The thought of erasure was comforting. The cat slipping into the water; the stain effervescing and lifting from the wood, undone by some magical property of chemistry.

I looked down at the bag. Could a bystander tell what it contained? That curl of the spine and the body – did it clearly say 'cat'? Or, precisely, 'dead cat'? It looked, to me, like a cat, but I already knew what was in there. There was no obvious head ... and I saw that I had put the bag down by the stain, partly on it, so that the blue-red residue of the wine appeared to have sprayed outwards from the cat's head and neck. The scene resembled the halo of gore that accompanied a gangland killing in the films, complete with a victim in its black plastic institutional shroud, patiently waiting for its unhurried lift to the morgue while the experts appraised the splatter and talked of trajectories and trace evidence. Traces: they would rebuild the past, pull back the fleeing moments, reassemble the event by studying what it had left behind. The thought of wiping the slate was a fantasy, something was always left behind, some eloquent detail or blemish that would talk and talk until it revealed the truth. Or an ugly, blame-filled version of the truth. When people follow back these trajectories, they expect culprits to be standing at the other end of them. Even if there was no culprit.

This was crazy, I thought, spinning these ideas over and over. Perhaps I was crazy, grip loosened by solitude and the small, furry spectre of death. But that in itself was not a wholly sane thought – whoever went mad after less than a week alone? And not even entirely alone. The dead cat was here, and sharing my space with it was bringing on these thoughts. Its presence went far beyond that little wrapped form, filling the air with a sort of karmic radioactivity, permeating the flat to its corners and secret places. No wonder its friend had fled so dramatically when it got wind of what the cleaner had brought in.

I took a deep breath, but bungled it somehow, and it came out in a whimper, so I took another. Then I picked up the bag by its knotted black neck, feeling again its particular weight; not heaviness, but a certain gravity. With another deep breath, I walked briskly towards, and through, the front door of the flat, slamming it behind me and trotting down the stairs. I was not going to repeat the mistake I made last time, waiting too long and missing my opportunity. If I moved fast enough, I was sure I could make it out of the building before the cleaner was able to intercept me, and see the bag, which I now, only now, realised I could have concealed in my holdall – but I was out already, on the faded pavement, and the main door went *whump* behind me. I stopped, and the bag swung to knock sickeningly against my leg. There hadn't been the slightest sign or sound of the cleaner. She had missed me, or I had missed her. It was a bright day, and the sun gleamed on the dark varnished door and its bright brass fittings, even making the dull grey metal of the entryphone shine, its column of buttons like the front of a bell-boy's waistcoat.

The street was quiet, with few passing cars and no nearby pedestrians, but I felt a quick jab of paranoia. What was I doing just standing here? Once again, I had drifted into reverie when I should have been taking action. The sooner this sordid business was over with, the better. I set off towards the canal, the bag now and then bouncing against the side of my knee.

The canal had blackened in my memory, intensifying in the mind's eye into a flow of tar through a coal channel. Seeing it again, the water looked paler, but no fresher – a milky grey, unhealthily still, fringed with twists of hydrocarbon rainbow. Despite the pleasant weather, there was no one on the towpath – none of the joggers, cyclists or optimistic anglers who might enliven a British canal. I began to walk along the towpath, attempting to look like a man out for a relaxing stroll. Sweat prickled up my arms and down my back, and slimed my grasp on the black plastic. The only living things in sight were the thuggish weeds, some as developed as bushes, which pushed their way through the crumbling mortar of the retaining walls and the wounded slabs underfoot, and the incomprehensible algal scum that crusted the edge of the water. I scanned the ground ahead of me, wary of my footing, but also on the lookout for heavy objects that could weigh down the bag. When I imagined myself throwing the bag into the water, I saw its splash and its lazy turn as it settled into its new conditions, finding its weight and then diminishing, swallowed by ripples ... but sometimes I saw it turn and persist, pockets of air consolidating and inflating the plastic, giving it buoyancy ... and a new black islet being born, bobbing in the grey water, an outcropping of guilt drifting out of my control, a marker ... of course, the chances of anyone finding it, investigating it, would be minimal, infinitesimal, but I was not trusting my luck. It had to sink, it had to vanish. I wanted a weight.

I walked on. It was becoming clear that my memory had made all sorts of embellishments to the canal. The path, in my recollection, had been strewn with stones, bricks and rubble of all descriptions. In fact, it had a generous frosting of litter in the bushes and weeds at its edges, but little that was heavy enough to sink the bag. Splintered fragments of wooden pallets, small chunks of polystyrene packing rounded and browned with time, yoghurt pots, soft drink cans, used condoms. The arm of a shop mannequin, its hand lacking fingers. A coverless paperback book, laced with wormholes.

After a lengthy walk, I came across a short metal pipe, coated with rust, which seemed to suit my purposes. It was certainly heavy enough, and it was easy to tie the neck of the bag around it. With that done, I realised with a touch of surprise that the preparations were complete and that this spot was as good as any for the final act. I glanced left, right and up, checking for onlookers. The path was deserted in both directions and the few windows that watched over this site were empty, obviously industrial, large grids of glass with random panes smashed out like moves in a game of dereliction. I threw the pole, underarm, aiming for the middle of the canal. It and the bag struck the water with a clumsy splash, larger than I expected, and the bag twisted under. The loathsome black plastic bubble rose, as I had seen it in my mind, but was quickly pulled beneath the surface by the sinking pole. I watched the concentric rings spread out on the water, and thought of some hateful black frog with a bulging, subsiding, bulging goitre under its glum mouth. That bubble was a little scrap of atmosphere trapped in the canal. How long would it take for the plastic to degrade, for the air to leak out, and for the little submersible to complete its descent?

It occurred to me that I could have punctured the bag, allowing the air to exit and ensuring that it sank. But that would have meant risking odour, and I could not stomach that. Still, I now thought, it would be a long time before the water came in contact with the cat's body – would it decay properly? Would it, perhaps, mummify instead, like an Egyptian temple animal in a little household-hygiene sarcophagus? I was fairly certain that the water would get to it before that long ... but there was always the possibility that the canal was so polluted that it had the properties of embalming fluid, another way that the cat could be cheated of its opportunity to relax into microbial sludge.

These thoughts of the cat's onward journey were filling me with little worms of guilt. Best just to forget it now – it was gone, no longer a cat, no longer anything, an abstract, a memory. The palm of my right hand, slicked with sweat from holding the bag, was clammy despite the warmth of the day. The ripples had dispersed, radiated out to nothing, a lost broadcast, and the canal had resumed its stagnant stillness. It was impossible to identify the exact location where the bag had hit the water. All was quiet. Even the background buzz of the city was subdued.

I made a secret promise to myself: I would not return to the canal. This was my final moment with it. I would turn my back on it. Up ahead, I could see a flight of steps in a recess in the retaining wall, leading back up to street level. Although I would follow the canal back – through necessity, I had no other means of navigation – I would not return along the towpath.

There was no street at street level. The steps led up to a large expanse of open ground. Weeds sprouted extravagantly here and there. For a terrible moment I thought that the city had disappeared – that it had been scoured from the Earth by some catastrophe while I had been beside the canal. How long had I been down there? How far had I walked – was it possible that I had actually left the city, walked beyond its limits? But as I reached the top of the stairs, I saw buildings. Ahead, away from the canal, was a long, slab-like, brick industrial building, dark and broken, its roof sagging. Beyond it, further down the canal, was a collection of freight railcars. Apart from the crumbling mill structure there were further low buildings, indistinct in the summer haze. In the other direction, back the way I had come, was another large, stained brick complex, its windows shattered, greenery frothing out of its gutters. Stillness and dust filled the air.

I began my walk back, following the course of the canal. Underfoot was a patchwork of materials: heaving herringbone brick, swatches of cobble, listing, gritty concrete, bare packed earth. The fabric of the city had transformed as I walked along the unchanging canal, and I had not noticed. My eyes had been lowered, looking for debris to serve as ballast, and I had missed the change in skyline.

Nothing moved except me and the traces of brown dust kicked up by my feet. The sun was at its peak. On the other side of the canal were three short cranes, their delicate arms raised as if to shield their eyes from the yellow light. The building ahead, six storeys of evacuated factory, had brick walls braced by a crude concrete frame, like ribs on a Halloween skeleton. I saw that it extended to the canal's edge – there was no way around on the water side without returning to the steps and walking back along the towpath. The other route, the one I decided to take, was to turn away from the canal and walk deeper into this industrial zone. There was a passage or road parallel to the canal just a short distance away; my only concern was that I would lose sight of the canal for a long period, or be forced to move even further away from it and become disoriented as a prelude to getting properly lost. But the sun was bright and the silence of the zone seemed to be some protection – surely assailants would pick a place where there were people to assail. There was no one here.

The passage parallel to the canal was in fact wide enough to be a city street, but the word 'street' seemed wrong, implying a life or a sense of purpose that this dejected thoroughfare lacked. This was just a long space between buildings. A railway ran down its middle, set into the cobbles like a tramline. The metal tracks were silted with dirt, and had clearly not seen a train in decades. The broad utilitarian walls of the buildings were enlivened by messages just under their roof line, square capital letters the height of a man in flaking white paint. In Britain, these would have been the names of the company or its owners – here, I thought, they might be socialist slogans, stripped of meaning by the evaporation of workers and production. Rubbish of all descriptions was piled against the walls on either side – unidentifiable orange-scaled chunks of machinery, smashed wooden palettes, heaps of box files and green-lined paper liquescing under many rains. An office swivel chair, its fabric and padding ripped off by someone or something, stood in my path like a Dalek rape victim. Less than an hour ago I had been struggling to think of suitable places to dispose of the cat. And now, having ditched the bag, I had discovered this wasteland had been here all along, a corpse-throw away from Oskar's flat. Acres of land in which a dead cat would feel right at home.

'More than enough room to sling a cat,' I said to myself. And I laughed, loudly, an act that felt curiously deviant in its lack of inhibition, like leaving the door to the lavatory open when the house is empty.

Ahead, something large moved. I froze. A man in a plastic raincoat was rising out of one of the piles of rubbish – no, it was a large sheet of translucent plastic wrapping picked up by a breath of wind and folding over lazily. The breeze that propelled it reached me, and the moisture on my brow chilled.

At the end of the passage was another wide open area, mostly covered in aged concrete, broken as if dropped from a great height onto an uneven surface. Triassic weeds indulged themselves in the sun. On both sides were low metal sheds, ends towards me like empty wine racks, pitched roofs a sharp sawtooth line against the bright blue of the sky. Rust metastasised through the frames of these sheds so completely they seemed to hiss with decay. I thought of asbestos, toxins on the fly, and my throat tickled nervously. But my chest was filled with relief – in front of me, beyond this open space, was a brick row studded haphazardly with windows and strafed with black drainpipes. It was the back of a terrace of houses, the resumption of a cityscape that was at least a little familiar. Beyond that line, I thought, it would be a straightforward matter to find the street that led back to Oskar's building.

I stopped. The concrete had buckled like an ice floe being compacted by its own gathering mass. I stood atop a great sheet that had tilted through subsidence to form a geometric ridge. From this relative high point, I had an uninterrupted view of the terrain ahead.

It was alive with stray dogs. Perhaps there were fewer than a dozen of them, but they roamed in broad, speedy arabesques through the steroidal weeds, infesting the whole space. Their leanness, their nervy energy, and their rough hair told me in a glance that none of them had known an owner. But I was also drawing on another instinct. Some unknowably old circuit in my brain had made its calculation, and these animals clearly crawled with threat. A straight line across to where the houses met the canal bank would take me directly through their territory.

For a handful of seconds I stood on the ridge looking down at the dogs. I then realised that my clear view of them gave them a clear view of me and retreated down the concrete slope. Backtracking further, back to the canal, was a possibility; but perhaps the dogs infested the landscape I had just crossed, and I had simply been oblivious to them. The thought of being pinned in that industrial alley, with dogs to the front and rear, was scarcely very appealing. Retreating would also mean returning to the canalside spot where I had disposed of the cat, and possibly confronting it again in its black shroud. That would be to revisit a place I had told myself there was no need to see ever again. Ahead of me, though, was comparatively open country.

I started to walk towards the open line of sheds between me and the canal bank. It didn't seem to be possible to walk along the bank itself, but I could skirt the edge of the open space and hope that the dogs either did not notice me or at least did not take an interest in me. My pace, I hoped, resembled neither predator nor prey, while still covering the ground as fast as was seemly. The concrete underfoot was stained brown by rusty water dripping off the sheds; it flaked with age. Grit crackled under the soles of my shoes. Worried that I was making too much noise, I slowed down, and looked up. The roofs of the sheds had reduced to something notional, like the skeleton of a leaf striving to fill the same area with a fraction of the substance. My breathing seemed to involve more effort than usual. What I didn't want to do was to look towards the dogs – it was as if the strafe of my gaze would alert them, that eye contact was the thing that they locked on to. But there was surely no animal in history that evaded predators by not looking at them. So was that it, then, had I already cast myself in the role of prey? Couldn't I just be a passer-by, passing through? I tried to emulate a casual glance in the direction of the dogs.

They had seen me. They were watching. Their lazy circling prowl had been broken and the six to eight dogs I could see were all turned in my direction watching back. But I realised I was craning my neck to see them, they were already a little behind me – I was past the bulk of the pack. The ground was uneven underfoot, with sheets of oxidising corrugated iron and broken glass scattered over the heaving cobbles, and I had to look away to make sure I didn't stumble – stumbling, I was sure, would be bad. How would they signal an attack – by barking? All I could hear was my own rough breathing.

A flicker in my peripheral vision. I looked back. The dogs were moving. Three or four of them were trotting parallel to my path, heads all turned in my direction. Stumbling clearly didn't worry them. Their relaxed lope seemed insolent, a mockery of my mounting fear. I let my speed increase again, an acid taste in my dry mouth. They matched my new pace, and I saw that they were in fact not walking parallel to me, but instead closing the gap between us. There was no retreating now; I cursed myself for not returning to the canal when I had the chance, for letting a sentiment trump millions of years of instinct.

My escape route was clearly in view. Ahead, the line of houses was broken by a narrow alley, and through that alley was an enticing gleam, the sun bouncing off the bodywork of passing cars. It was an awesomely inviting and promising prospect, yet a great gulf seemed to separate me from it. The problem, my problem, was now not so much one of distance as it was a question of time and geometry. The dogs, four of them, black and brown, were describing an arc towards me. They were within ten feet, closer perhaps, a leash-length away, and if I stopped dead now, they could be upon me in half a second. At our present speeds, their route would intersect with mine at some point in the imminent future. My concern was that they would reach the alley before me, cutting off my exit. I continued to slowly accelerate, still walking, but moving faster and faster. They matched me. The alley was only thirty feet away, but the equation did not look promising. My gait was increasingly absurd, my legs stiff, each stride jarring, but I was still on the slower side of the line that separates walking from running. The line vexed me. If I threw my body past it, broke into a run, I knew that I could cover the remaining stretch in negligible time; but my muscles and limbs would be speaking a different language, the language of flight, a broadcast that easily transcended species boundaries in its meaning. The dogs would know the message, for sure: unambiguous fear, something I was certain already trailed from me like lines of signal flags. What cues were they picking up from me?

Were there traces of dead cat in my olfactory spectrum? Did that aura of death make me more or less tempting as a target?

The leading dog, an exotic alloy of breeds with wiry dark-brown hair, a blunt snout, round eyes and a tramp's stubble, was a pace and a half ahead of me. It turned and looked over its shoulder, and we made eye contact. The expression on its face was inquisitive, even sympathetic. Then it changed, its eyes narrowed, and it bared its teeth, bright white little sharp points against filthy hair. Its maw was wet.

I ran. The dogs did not hesitate to join me. My run was a hot, panicked, flailing thing, theirs a practised, bounding movement at the lower end of their possible speed. I was in the alley, hopping over the rubbish bags that were strewn across its floor, hoping that it would be too narrow for the pack to flank me, but the lead dog was at my side, eyes on fire, its mouth open and shining tongue out like a tropical flower's putrid, sticky lure. It had me, we both knew, the same vectors playing in our minds, and it lunged, head on one side like a mobster holding his weapon level with the horizon, and I felt the impact, a cleft blow, in my shin. Heavy jaws clamped on the muscled flesh at the top of my ankle, with a machine-like force. Gripping and ripping were implicit in the moment, they were in the flying air, and such was my surprise at the dog making contact that I almost stopped to see what had happened (*Don't stop!*). I threw myself forward in a renewed effort and felt the weight of the dog holding my leg back, and then that weight broke away and my leg was free but something yielded and tore as we parted. All this time I kept waiting for the pain to start in my leg, for the feel of the hot blood on my shin, pushed by my racing heart through a ragged hole and out onto the filthy asphalt, but none of that happened, and when the bitten leg hit the ground again, it felt fine, whole, unhurt. I twisted my head to see the stray break its step and fall back, fall into retreat in a majestic, grudging half-circle that reversed its direction while making it look as if its target hadn't shifted. The rest of the pack had broken off their pursuit, turned back. I was on the street now, with traffic and passers-by in sight. They had missed their chance. Only a few feet separated a realm where it was possible for a man to be attacked by a pack of stray dogs from a world of human activity where it was unthinkable – in daylight, at least. Or did I exude a particular vulnerability, something that made me a target or a threat, whereas someone else, a native of this city, could have walked through that space without any trouble?

The dark hunched forms of the dogs moved together down the alley, shapes blending into one bowed thing, boundaries obliterated by the bright blue sky in its tall frame of walls.

The run caught up with me. My thighs twitched and buzzed, my lungs and throat burned. I was quivering, muscles ticking with the flood and withdrawal of adrenalin, sweat soaked under my arms and between my shoulder blades and trickled past the small of my back. Dark patches spread on my shirt. I felt shame – it is somehow shameful to exhibit the signs of effort and exertion, we are supposed to make everything look so effortless. Leaning against a lamp post, I fought with my breathing until it was back under control. A couple of pedestrians looked at me through narrowed eyes – I was not dressed for jogging. My trouser leg was torn at the cuff around my left ankle, where the dog had got a bite on me. A ribbon of cloth trailed along the ground. I bent down, gripped this strip, and tore it sharply off. The fragment of blue fabric felt damp in my hand, either from the dog's spittle or my own sweat. I threw it back into the alley.

Nearby, the street bridged the canal, intersecting with a road that followed the water. I took this cross road. The canal, and the tall, narrow houses that looked down on it, gave the street a Dutch feel, and it was planted with trees, providing some welcome shade. It seemed a world away from the industrial trench I had dropped the cat into, but it was the same body of water. The distance of the memory of throwing that black bag, of watching it swirl into the water, shocked me; it already seemed so remote an act, maybe I could extract myself from this situation after all. In the meantime, my head thumped with dehydration and my legs had not regained their steadiness. I needed water.

Tramlines ran over the next bridge – this one returned to Oskar's building. On the corner was a small supermarket, an aberrant wedge of white glass and light in the monotonous grey stone and stucco, spangled with fluorescent paper stars bearing felt-tipped prices. I wanted water, and the fridge in the flat was empty.

Behind the store's sliding doors, an air conditioner was blasting, drying my sweat and chilling me. The fluorescent lights were on, sizzling like the radio trace of the Big Bang. I picked up a wire basket and filled it – bottled water, cheese, tomatoes, a salami sausage, a suspicious loaf of dark, dense bread. Two bottles of wine – I hesitated, put one back on the shelf, and then returned it to my basket. The supermarket had a provisional, temporary feel – laminate-covered fibreboard shelves bracketed to utilitarian frames, hand-written signs – but it groaned with food. I took spaghetti and a jar of what looked like pasta sauce. My purchases filled two carrier bags. Again, I felt that plastic tug on my fingers. I thought of the cat, quiet and cool on the canal bed, sediment settling in the black folds of its shroud.

It was a short walk from the canal to Oskar's flat – it felt even shorter now, the second time I went that way. This slender slice of the city now seemed to be in a slightly higher resolution than the rest. Little details on the street were fixing in my memory – a painted shop sign, a balcony frothing with climbing and hanging plants. A place of blocks and routes was showing signs of becoming a place of memories. How long was it before a place became familiar? I wondered how much longer I would be staying here, how familiar the city would become. Certainly, it could never feel like home. The cleaner knew about the stain, and knew about the cat – did she have the means or authority to call Oskar and tell him? Had she done so already? What would Oskar do? Call, or return? I felt certain that he would want a face-to-face confrontation, precisely because that was what I wanted desperately to avoid. But now there was no cat, and shortly there would be no stain.

With both hands full of shopping, I pushed through the front door of Oskar's building with my shoulder, head down, and almost collided with the cleaner. The tiled floor of the hallway shone with water, and she was prodding this mirrored surface with a mop. She saw me, her face a mask of obstinate displeasure. I smiled, a helpless automatic reflex, and my muscles tightened to dash past her and up the stairs, but I realised that my shoes were filthy after my excursion – not wanting to further worsen relations by leaving a trail of muddy footprints across the wet floor, I wiped my feet on the mat, conscious of my ragged trouser-leg.

'——!' she addressed me, making it clear she was confronting me with something. '——!'

'Look,' I said, in what I hoped was a bridge-building tone, still moonwalking on the mat, 'you know I only speak English. I saw you found the cat ... I had nothing to do with ... I have, er, laid it to rest, and I'll explain everything to Oskar, so if you wait ...'

It was senseless – not only could she not understand me, she wasn't even listening. Instead, she was looking at the bags I was carrying, and her expression and the note of her harangue had shifted from contempt to horror. Unsure as to what had caught her attention, I raised one of the bags. There did not appear to be anything unusual about it, apart from the fact that it was anonymous white plastic, lacking in the proud display of branding that it might have worn in the UK. But the combined curves of the bread and the sausage, pressing outwards against the pale skin – did she think that the cat was in there? The act of raising the bag only increased her agitation.

'It's shopping!' I said, too quickly, my voice a squeak. 'Look!'

I set one bag down on the floor – bottles chinked – and reached into the other, disrupting the cat-like formation and pulling out the sausage. 'Look! Look!'

She recoiled, the expression on her face beyond description. In a lurching moment of self-awareness, I realised that, far from being reassuring, brandishing this sausage was making me look like some kind of sex fiend.

'It's just shopping,' I mumbled, shoving the sausage back into the bag. The cleaner had recovered from her shock and resumed what displayed all the signs of being an accusatory tirade. I picked up the second bag and scurried towards the stairs, her angry words ringing off the clean tiles behind me.

Back in Oskar's flat, I secured the door with the guard chain. Enough interruptions. My patience with this city, this building, this flat, was wearing thin. I left the shopping in the kitchen and fetched the plastic box of cleaning supplies from the utility room. Oskar's note was still where I had left it, anchored by the ingot of beeswax.

These are cleaning products for the flat and for the floor, Oskar had written. Yes, Oskar, that was obvious. There is a book, *Care of Wooden Floors*, on the shelf with the architecture. That was a little more helpful.

The book was at the far end of the lowest shelf, almost invisible next to the fat, heavy monographs of European and American architects. It was a slender brown hardback. On the front cover was a line drawing of a man easing a floorboard into place with an expression of Zen passivity. Already the book was putting me at ease. It looked like an artefact from the fatherly world of Haynes car manuals and *Protect and Survive* leaflets. It would know what to do. I opened the book. There was a note from Oskar inside the front cover – more than a note, a decent-sized letter, filling at least one side of A4 paper with writing that was more expansive, less controlled, than his usual style. At the top was a heading or caveat written in small capitals, perhaps fitted in as an afterthought:

> IF NOTHING HAS HAPPENED TO THE FLOORS, KINDLY DISREGARD THIS NOTE.

Underneath that:

> My Dear Friend,
>
> IF YOU HAVE JUST SPILLED SOMETHING, WIPE IT UP WITH A WET CLOTH IMMEDIATELY! DO NOT DELAY! DO NOT LET A STAIN SET!
>
> But if you have found this note you have found this book, and so it is probably too late. You tried water, and it did not work. The floor is stained. Maybe this book can help, but I do not think you will be capable of repairing the damage.

My bowel clenched, and my face heated. I bit my lip. I do not think you will be capable of repairing the damage? How dare he? I knew Oskar's arrogance, his casual dismissiveness, but fresh instances of it never lost much of their sting. Now I wanted to smash a couple of bottles of red on the floor and use their jagged necks to score my name on the boards.

But I wasn't going to do that. I was going to fix the damage, without a trace, and get away with it. It would be a silent, secret victory, but I would always know. Then I was going to lie through my teeth about the cat. It went out and never came back. Perhaps it was Oskar's prolonged absence that did it, a little twist of guilt. If the cleaner contradicted me, I would call her crazy. My story was far easier to believe. No body, no crime. Habeas Bagpuss.

The note went on:

> The floor was expensive. The best way to care for something like that is not to damage it. If anything has happened to the floor, please call me and let me know.

Why? Why, if the damage was irreparable, if caution had failed and the opportunity to make good the situation had passed, why did Oskar wish to be told? What could he advise that had not been expressed in his many notes? What did he propose to do? Return home immediately to inspect the disaster site and exact retribution? It wasn't impossible. More likely the request was an expression of his desire to micro-manage everything. Plus I was sure he would not want to miss an opportunity to do some judging and blaming.

I continued to read, fuming and marvelling at the length of the note:

> If there is an answer, it may be in this book, but you may be doing more harm than good. It is essential that you call me before attempting anything, I may be able to help.

Now he was just repeating himself.

> The floor is important to me in many ways. When I got this flat, the first thing I decided to do was put in a new floor. It meant a total remodelling. Everything was changed: new floor, new kitchen, new furniture, all redesigned according to my wishes. There were old floorboards. They were worn and battered. Many people like that. I think you would like that. But I preferred new. Everything had to be perfect. I could make an island of perfection, and from there the rest of life could be perfect too. There are complacent sayings: 'Nothing's perfect.' This is not true. The floor is, was, perfect. So was the flat. So was life. It takes a little effort to start things perfect, and then some effort to keep them that way. I remember our conversation in the pub – that the standards I expect of people are too high. It was like an arrow in me. I am used to being disappointed, and I believed that eventually I would meet people who would not disappoint, and those around me could be cultivated so that they did not disappoint. You told me to lower my opinion of humanity. You told me to think less of humanity! It is so simple to prevent damage to the floors. Maybe you will. But I write this note because I

think it is a real possibility that you will somehow damage them anyway, so perhaps I am already lowering my expectations. Maybe this is a test.

There are instructions in the book, but I urge you to call me.

Your friend, Oskar

Was Oskar cracking up? But the note had been written at least a week ago, so: had Oskar cracked up? I tried to imagine him in the flat, a day or two before going to California to be humiliated and possibly ruined by legal specialists, obliged to leave his beautiful flat, his perfect sanctuary, in the hands of someone he did not have faith in, mapping out disaster scenarios in his mind and writing notes to cover the possibilities. Trying to maintain control. How long had it taken him to get it all on paper? I had found dozens of notes, and there were certainly more to find. A day of writing? Two?

I flipped the note over, meaning to get started on the book, and found yet more written on its back:

When something goes wrong, you can trace back to a moment when it could have happened differently, a moment when a word, or silence, or an act, or a stillness, could have changed everything.

I am thinking now of the floors, and this book.

This book is full of ways to 'correct' things that have gone wrong, but it is all false. It can all be described in the words 'do not do the wrong thing in the first place'. When the wrong note is struck on the piano, you cannot

> later 'correct' it, make it look like it was never struck – it cannot be un-struck. You will always know.

That was it – no salutation, no signature. After pouring a glass of water from the bottle I had bought, I took the book to the sofa. Next to me were the claw-marks of the deceased cat. Was it the dead cat, or the living one? I suspected the dead one. The other had not yet reappeared – surely it was hungry by now? The day was arching overhead, and the patches of light cast by the tall windows had narrowed from kites to sharp, long slivers.

I opened the book again, taking out Oskar's note and laying it on the coffee table. The introduction had large, friendly type and a colour photograph of the author, a large, friendly type squatting on a floor of glowing boards that matched his golden hair. There was a pristine paint-brush in his hand.

Wood, the text read, is a magical material. It continued, in a jaunty fashion:

> Unlike other flooring materials, real wood has a life of its own. Literally! It had a life as a tree before it became your floor. When you choose a wooden floor, you bring a bit of that life into your home. As a craftsman, I can tell you that no other material is so flexible to work with, and so pleasurable to handle, as wood. Every tree, and every piece of wood, is unique. And every wooden floor tells its own story. Properly cared for, your wooden floor will be yours to enjoy for decades – and a treasure to pass on to the next generation.

That's the key to getting the best from your wooden floor: Care. You should care for your wooden floor as you would care for a fine piece of furniture – maybe the most important piece of furniture that you own. Treat it with love, and it will glow with love.

Oskar's floor was a beautiful thing, certainly. But did it glow with love? Fighting my instinct to look at the wine-blemish near the sofa, I took in an immaculate expanse of board near the bookshelves. It was pale and clean. The slightest blush of wax or finish made the surface shine with reflected light, which picked out the minimal texture of the grain. If it was broadcasting love of any kind, it was on a higher frequency, only perceptible to a more advanced human being. An atavistic impulse swept through me, again. How destructive could I be? How much ink was there in the house? There was plenty of wine, but I would be needing some of that. If the wood was not well guarded against stains, was it very fire-resistant? Or I could just leave. I thought of the airport, its myriad possibilities, the freedom it offered me. There was bound to be a late flight to London that I could catch. I thought of the airport's metric hectares of hardwearing terrazzo, designed to withstand the footfall of millions without changing. Lock the door and drop the keys through the letterbox. But there was the cat to consider – even if I had exhausted my sense of duty towards the apartment, I still felt responsible for the surviving cat. Wherever it was – surviving, I hoped.

Any wooden floor will, over time, show some signs of use. This gentle wear and patina is part of its vital character – part of the spirit of the wood.

Yes, wood has a spirit! Before the coming of Christ some primitive Europeans believed that trees were inhabited by spirits. The belief can also be found in many tribal societies in the world today. And traces of it can be found in our own, modern, culture. Have you ever heard someone say 'knock on wood' or 'touch wood' to ward off bad luck? That's belief in the spiritual power of wood. Pagans believed that tree spirits, or dryads ...

The book sagged in my hands. This spiritual mumbo-jumbo was very far from what I expected. I had expected, I *wanted,* a hard-edged practical manual, not this wafty New Age nonsense. My stomach sinking, I skimmed through the next dozen pages.

... Judaism and Christianity share the 'tree of knowledge', and Buddhism has its 'Bodhi' tree, the fig tree under which Siddhartha Gautama attained enlightenment ...

...Yggdrasil, the Norse 'world tree' ...

... the cedar totem poles used by the Native American peoples of the Pacific Northwest ...

... healing properties. Acetylsalicylic acid, better known as aspirin, is derived from willow bark ...

... druids used mistletoe ...

... the Golden Bough, which Aeneas and the Sybil gave to the gatekeeper of Hades ...

... shard of the True Cross.

Someone was clearly out of his tree. I turned back to that author photograph – the idealised blond hair, a mystic glimmer in the eyes, smiling mouth neatly filled with perfect white teeth. It was unlike Oskar to have looked to this particular nutcase for guidance about his floors. Very unlike Oskar. And there was something about the author, about the writing, about the flavour of his dementia, about those teeth. That cloying folksiness, the inane, chatty style, the mix-and-match philosophy. On the back cover:

> ABOUT THE AUTHOR: Chandler Novack is a craftsman, educator, writer and life coach. He is the author of 20 books, including *Care of Wives, Care of Husbands, Care of Children, Care of the Inner You, Care of Paintings, Care of Vintage Cars, Care of Antique Furniture* and *Care of Swimming Pools.* Through his books and his teaching, he has brought his unique lifeview of holistic self-care to more than 10 million people worldwide. Chandler lives in California with his wife and five children.

California. Also on the back cover: '$21.95'. No price in pounds or euros. This book had been bought in the United States and I was prepared to bet everything I owned that it had not been bought by Oskar. There was not a hint of this kind of sickly hocus-pocus in Oskar's nature, not so much as a wind-chime or joss stick. He was an empiricist – he dealt in what could be seen and measured. No, this book bore the stamp of Laura, that unknown quantity. A gift, then, one that betrayed a breathtaking lack of insight into her husband's personality. The lines and angles of the divorce resolved into clearer focus – well-meaning efforts to reach out to Oskar's chakras met with that A-lip sneer, a tide of yoga and yoghurt crashing against a flinty cliff-face. But, based on my limited experience of her, that didn't really feel like Laura either. Was it a fleeting, unconsidered gift, seized without inspection from an airport bookstore as a flight was called? An unknowable in-joke, with passages that had been read out between gasps of laughter in dimmed light over empty wine glasses? Perhaps Laura had consulted Mr Novack on another matter – *Care of Paintings*? *Care of Husbands*? *Care of Anal-Retentive Euro Pianists*? – and found some help or solace. But, in the long run, not enough.

No wonder Oskar's note had been discouraging. Feeling a little better about myself, I referred to the contents and turned to the chapter that dealt with stains:

> Accidents do happen! We're human, all of us.

Part of me, the part closest to Oskar, clenched.

> I remember when I was building my first home with Allegra ...

There was another tsunami of fluff. In its wake, there were admonitions, delivered in the form of homely proverbs and anecdotes, about prevention being the best remedy. Novack's self-deprecating mode of storytelling mysteriously failed to conceal his Olympian self-regard. But further on, the focus clearly shifted to practical matters –

there were bullet-pointed instructions, line drawings, boxed-out tips.

> If the stain has had time to set, then you'll need to remove it with an abrasive. The best is called 'rottenstone', or 'tripoli', a fine powder that's used for polishing rocks. Mix some rottenstone with linseed oil to make a fine paste, and then use it to rub away the stain, always following the direction of the grain of the wood.

Book in hand, I walked to the kitchen, where I had left the box of cleaning products.

'Rottenstone,' I murmured to myself. 'Rottenstone or tripoli.'

I did a quick inventory of the box – some cloths and dusters, an aerosol of wood polish, sheets of fine-grain sandpaper, three dusters (one of which was scarred by use and chemicals), a pair of washing-up gloves, a couple of clean paintbrushes, a tin of polish or varnish of some sort and a small, sinister brown glass jar filled with a fine white crystalline powder and covered in warning triangles and hazard signs. Before I had finished looking, I knew there would be no rottenstone. It even sounded invented, made up, a cleaning product favoured by magic elves. I had no confidence in it. Novack would have to do better than that.

> If you have no rottenstone, then ground pumice will do, or even a sheet of fine sandpaper.

Sandpaper – that was more like it. A treatment that came from the hardware store, not the Body Shop. I selected a clean sheet of sandpaper from the plastic box and examined the stain. What I needed was a test area where a fix could be tried out before risking it over a larger expanse of floor. There was an outlying splash the size of a five-pence piece that would do nicely.

> Sand the floor gently but firmly, in smooth strokes that travel in the direction of the grain.

This almost immediately made a difference to the satellite stain, but also to the floor around it. The stain receded to a stubborn blush, a shadow of what it had been. But this ghost floated in a frighteningly pale oval of naked wood. This snowy patch jumped out at even a passing glance – its interruption of the floor's quiet shine with a matt interval would be enough to catch the eye even without the colour difference. I was also now painfully aware of how vulnerable this patch was – stripped of even the most cursory protective finish, it was a magnet for dust and defenceless against further spills. And the stain might be seriously diminished, but it was not gone. I sanded for as long as I dared, conscious that I was eating into the substance of the floor, but still a rosy trace lingered. The light from the windows, slashing low and deep into the room, fell across the kitchen floor. In its brightness, sometimes I thought I had finally eliminated that last blush, only to see it again – and blink it away, to find that what I had actually seen was a reddish blob floating behind my eyes, the retinal impression of staring at a shining spot for too long.

My head throbbed. The litre bottle of water I had bought was now empty. Employing the sort of care that nuclear technicians call upon when handling unstable fissile materials, I opened a bottle of wine and poured a glass. It was most welcome. Leaving the glass on the shaped steel draining board by the sink – I didn't want to risk it anywhere else – I consulted Novack again.

> You might not be able to remove a really deep stain through abrasion alone. But don't panic. Make up a solution of oxalic acid crystals in water, soak a clean white cloth in it, and apply it to the stain for about an hour. EXERCISE EXTREME CAUTION – oxalic acid is very hazardous to skin. Wear protective gloves throughout preparation and application of the solution. When you're done, neutralise the acid with household vinegar.

Novack, you magnificent Californian loony, you've pulled it off. This proposal didn't necessitate a trip to Homebase, it needed a trip to the periodic table. Oxalic acid – that was the kind of plain-speaking substance I could have faith in. My confidence surged as I immediately thought of that medicinal brown jar in Oskar's box, its festive display of hazard icons, and the crystalline matter inside. I looked at its label again, and my trust was redeemed – oxalic acid crystals.

In a past life, I might have paused at this point and given a thought to the environment. The ocean or the aquifers might have selfishly competed for my attention. Not now. At that moment, if there had been a button I could have pressed that would simultaneously obliterate every stain on the floor and every living panda, I would have pressed it without hesitation. I was very serious about cleaning this floor.

Wearing the rubber gloves, I made up a small glass of the acid solution and poured it onto a clean, new dishcloth from the cupboard. Then I placed this cloth on the bare patch of floor, coiled into a tight mound to expose as little undamaged wood as possible to the acid. There was no satisfying hiss or burst of flames, no acrid odour – the floor looked as it had done before, only with a blue washing-up cloth balled up on it. I took a careful sip of wine and looked at the clock. It was more evening now than afternoon. An hour seemed like a long time; dead time, too, the time between trips to the oven when preparing a complicated supermarket curry in many plastic trays.

I ran the gloves under the tap, took them off, and went into the utility cupboard to find a bottle of vinegar. When I came back a couple of minutes later, carrying a suitable bottle, something didn't look right.

Kneeling, I examined the cloth on the floor. It was covered in a simple pattern, a grid of blue lines, just like every dishcloth I had known. But the pattern had changed. The lines had lost much of their definition – they were blurring into one another. And the shadow at the edge of the cloth wasn't a shadow. It was a ring of blue dye, leeching out of the cloth and into the floorboard underneath.

'Shit!' I cried. 'Shit, shit! Shit!' My arm tensed to snatch the cloth from the floor, but I remembered the acid. I pulled on the gloves with flailing fingers, grabbed the cloth and dropped it into the sink, turning on the tap above it.

There was a mottled blue circle on the floor, seeped into the wood, darker at the edges than at its centre, where the bastard remainder of the wine stain could still be seen. I ran my hands under the tap again and pulled off the gloves. Vinegar, vinegar, neutralise the acid with vinegar. The cap of the vinegar bottle was stiff between my fingers, which seemed to have lost all power to grip. The bottle slipped, almost fell. Holding it with white knuckles, I sloshed its contents over the blue lagoon. Pale bluish liquid flowed freely over the floorboards. Cursing, I passed a new cloth under the still-running tap and started to mop up the spreading spill.

What remained on the wet floor was a varied bruise the size of a coaster in place of a near-defeated blush smaller than my thumbnail. With numb interest, I noticed the many qualities of this new blue presence – its slightly darker outer edge, where it had interacted with the finished floorboard, the paler, dappled blue where it had enjoyed free access to the sanded wood, and the violet birthmark at the centre, where it lay over the wine without having the time to dissolve it. In a couple of places, I noted, it was possible to make out the grid-pattern of the cloth, transferred onto the floor.

Novack, I thought, you son of a bitch, why didn't you warn me? He had, of course – he had specified a white cloth, un-dyed, without making the importance of that instruction clear. The floor would have to be scrubbed again, left to dry, sanded again – a larger area than last time – treated with the acid again, and then, maybe, barring further mishaps, polished. It was going to be a long evening. Thank heavens I had bought that second bottle of wine, I reflected as I reached for my glass.

Later, I would carefully replay earlier events in my mind to identify the point when I had picked up the wine glass while wearing rubber gloves that had oxalic acid on them. The glass was barely a third of the way between the sink and my mouth when my thumb and forefinger prickled with intense heat. I had barely a fraction of a second to register this oddity when the heat was replaced with scorching pain.

My lower brain instantly took control and did what, in its estimation, was the sensible thing to do. I dropped the glass. In fact, it wasn't so much dropped as flung away like a venomous snake. Its contents arced in the air; it smashed against the boards. It had been almost full.

But that wasn't the most important thing in my life at the moment. At three points on my left hand, the skin had turned scarlet and was puckering up. I let out a low sound, two parts moan to one part scream, and threw myself at the sink.

Of course – as the later mental replays made plain – in order to wash acid off one's gloved hands, one must first turn on a tap with a hand in a glove that is covered in acid. And that acid, unless one was thoughtful and diligent, will be left on the tap. Once the water had soothed my left hand, this was the tap I reached for with my unburned right hand.

Meanwhile, in a hundred places, red wine trickled and dripped over broken glass.

DAY SEVEN

It had been a restless night. What little sleep I managed to get was broken at 4 a.m. by the banging of the French window. When the time had finally come to call it a night, after an evening of disaster relief, the cat had not returned. I laid out a fresh plate of food and left the bedroom window ajar, in case it reappeared on the balcony in the night. But a modest summer storm had struck in the small hours and gusts of wind had thrown the window back with a crash. I was obliged to bolt it to prevent rain blowing in. Of the cat, there was no sign.

The living cat, I mean. Its late colleague did make an appearance, in a dream, whiskers dripping with muddy water, coat matted with filth. It loomed over me accusingly like Banquo's ghost. Then it was gone. Some rain did penetrate the room – I barely cared. I considered letting it stay there, on the floor, not concerned that it could degrade the finish and warp the wood. But the vestiges of my sense of responsibility stirred themselves, and I mopped up with the hand towel from the bathroom.

Despite my exhaustion, when I returned to bed, sleep did not come. The pain from my burned fingers had subsided to mild stinging – but this was enough to keep my mind on the situation in the kitchen. The glass I had dropped – thrown, almost – had exploded on the floor, and the wine inside had spread over a barely believable area. After I washed the acid off my hands – blisters were rising on three fingers and both thumbs – I was shocked by the extent of the splashing, and alarmed to see that it had reached as far as the bookcase. Fat drops of purple-red were rolling down the spines of half a dozen of Oskar's large hard-cover art books. These became my highest priority. Their susceptibility to stains made the floors look like Teflon-coated PVC.

Getting the wine off the books was a delicate task, made agony by the knowledge that everywhere the floor was under attack. A damp cloth, wrung out as hard as possible; tiny, feathery motions. A couple of the books had glossy dust covers that resisted the stain; another couple had dark covers that made any remaining traces near impossible to see. But on two books, purple spots persisted, and could not be budged without wearing a hole in the pale, creamy paper of their jackets. They were small marks – but on otherwise perfect books, they seemed a vast and tragic violation.

I then set about the rest of the floor with many cloths. The wine had not been on the boards long, only minutes, and in some places came away immediately without leaving a trace. But elsewhere it remained, and quick removal was complicated by the scattered shards of glass. I worked from the outlying, suburban splashes inwards towards the metropolitan core, an eyebrow-shaped streak of red a foot long. There was certainly less damage than from the spill that had been left overnight; but nevertheless, that original darker jellyfish had now been joined by the burst of a rosy firework.

Despite this new turn of events, I was not ready to despair. Excluding the outer drips and splatter, the bulk of the damage was concentrated on only five or six boards. This was extensive, but not beyond control. Novack's instructions had not yet been followed through and, I saw, he had more to say beyond oxalic acid. I selected a new test area – a short streak near one of the kitchen cabinets – and again set to work with the sandpaper and the corrosive crystals. There were no suitable white cloths, so I had to sacrifice one of Oskar's linen napkins to the greater good, figuring that he was unlikely to miss one. And it worked – in the first and only positive development of that whole day, the acid did what it was supposed to do. The stain had gone.

After waiting another hour for the cleaned patch to dry, I applied a layer of the wood finish from the tin that was among the items in the box. The result, wet, looked pretty good, but it had to dry before I could be sure. It was late by then, past eleven, and there was nothing left to do but go to bed.

My first waking thought was of the vengeful dream-cat, whiskers bent under the weight of polluted water-drops. My second thought was of the floor. It would be dry by now – how did it look? I rose from the bed and pulled on my trousers. The bedroom was stuffy, with light filtered through a thick milkshake of cloud. There was no cat on the balcony, but I opened the window anyway, trying to stir a breeze. The skin of the soles of my feet clung a little to the polished floorboards like the grip of an insect.

Seeing the kitchen floor again with more objective eyes, separated from the panic of the previous day, was a reminder of exactly how serious the situation was. A constellation of stains, a new and unfriendly landscape I had given birth to in Oskar's paradise. It had advanced beyond the kitchen with that last smashed glass, into the living room, stretching to the bookcase. The inner variety of this sprawling system made it far worse. If it had all been brought about by a single accident, then it could be explained and understood in isolation – a one-off, a quirk of fate, an outlying mischance, something from the thin parts of the bell curve of the human experience. But here were two or three incidents to explain, a great shipyard of rusty chains of cause and effect. It looked too much for mere misadventure – it looked like a storied history of neglect, or even vandalism. Drunken rages. Botched parties. Paralytic pratfalls.

I searched for the patch that I had tried to fix, and found it far too easily. If all the sanding, scouring and re-finishing had worked, the repaired area would be imperceptible, a memory, its location only guessable from the relative position of its surroundings. Instead, there was a yellow blot on the floor, another colour in a spectrum that also included the blue of the dishcloth and the pink, red, purple and grey of the dried wine. It was as if I had tried to polish the floor with orange juice. The tin was useless, the wrong stuff. There was no other likely-looking substance in the flat, and I had zero chance of finding any in the city. And all this could be determined from a distance. As I got closer—

—something happened, pricked and cut and flesh yielded. I stopped and pain started, a jabbing telegram from the sole of my left foot. I winced and steadied myself with a hand against the counter top, raising my foot to see what had hurt it.

A shard of thin glass was sticking out of the wrinkled skin of the arch of my foot. A small dark bead of blood winked at its point of entry. Awkwardly, I gripped this glinting blade with my free hand and pulled. Imagining it breaking off inside me, or scraping against bone, I felt my stomach lunge. But the splinter freed itself without argument – an inch-long stiletto of curved glass, clearly formerly part of the bowl of a wine glass. At the point of puncture, the bead of blood began to grow rapidly, swelling to become a black pearl and breaking loose of its anchor, sliding across the bottom of my foot at the head of a scarlet trail – sliding down towards the floor. A red drop filled and fell before I could move my hand to intercept it. It hit the wood, a perfect little sunburst.

My foot was bleeding freely – more drops were crowding to join the pioneer that had escaped. I clamped my right hand against the injured sole, feeling the pain. But I couldn't form a good seal over the wound, as I was still holding the fragment of wine glass between thumb and forefinger. Blood lubricated my fingers. It crept along the lines and creases of my hand.

I had to get off the floor. The thought struck an absurd note, and I almost laughed – in fact, I made a strangled noise, an abrupt little *huh.* How does one get off a floor? I couldn't even move – putting my foot down would tread blood onto the boards. Instead, I was stranded on one leg, in the world's least relaxing yoga position.

The bathroom. The tiled floor of the bathroom. I had to get to the bathroom. There would be plasters and running water and no risk of stains. But it meant a return down the corridor, through the bedroom – an impossible trek, given that I could not make a single step. I remembered the cats' wall-mounting run down the corridor and into the kitchen, how easily they seemed to taunt gravity and dispense with the floor. For me, the only option was to hop.

Three hops later, I had reached the corridor, but the drawbacks of this form of travel had multiplied. Gripping my foot with my hand as I was, it was impossible to keep balance. And every hop threatened to dislodge the blood that was collecting under and around my clasped fingers. On that third hop, a drop fell; on the fourth, I almost fell. Both my arms shot out to try to regain balance, and I dropped my foot. My bloody hand, still delicately holding the glass, left a smeared print on the white paint of Oskar's wall, and my injured foot slipped wetly on the floor. The pain made me gasp.

Speed, I decided, was more important than care. I hobbled clumsily towards the bathroom, using the heel of my injured foot. Once in the bathroom, I stepped freely, grateful for the cold tiles, not caring about my gory trail. The little wound looked pathetic, trivial, under the fluorescent light – it was a wonder that so much could pour from so small an aperture. Oskar, to my total lack of surprise, was well equipped with antiseptics and sticking plasters. I quickly applied both and limped back through the flat, damp flannel in hand, to deal with the blood.

There were a couple of minor streaks on the bedroom floor, fresh and minimal, which lifted easily with a single swipe of the flannel. The hallway was more troublesome – crime-scene troublesome. Both the footprint on the floor and the half-handprint on the wall left subtle yellow-brown traces after a dose of the flannel. The footprint was insignificant enough to be forgotten, or at least excused – it almost disappeared into the grain of the wood. But the handprint was against the icily pure white paint of Oskar's wall, and not far off eye level. It was also expressive, anatomical, a clear impression of most of the little and ring fingers over the broad curve of part of my palm. Recognition snares the eye, and this was recognisably part of a hand. The two drops that had oozed out in the kitchen also left spots.

Rinsing out the flannel in the bathroom, I looked again at the shard of glass sitting in the soapdish. It was still smeared with blood – with my blood. I was puzzled as to how it could have embedded itself so deeply into my foot. If it had been simply lying on the floor, it could have given me a nasty cut or scratch, but there was no way that it could have impaled me in the way that it did. Had it been stood up on end somehow, perhaps caught in a crack between floorboards? A paranoid shadow fell across me, the thought of the floor angry, vengeful, wanting blood. I wrapped the glass fragment in toilet tissue and threw it in the bin. Returning through the bedroom, I put on my socks and shoes.

Back in the kitchen, I trod lightly, expecting at every step to hear the *crunch* of another fragment of glass. I remembered a story I had seen in a horror comic – a reprint of some 1950s American pulp crime series. After committing a murder a man realises that his fingerprints are all over the scene. He sets about wiping every surface he thinks he has touched, a laborious and time-consuming job. In frustration, he smashes a cup – and realises, horrified, that his prints could now be on any one of a thousand scattered shards. So he tries to find, and clean, every last splinter, unable to accept the risk of leaving even part of an identifying print behind. In the morning, the police find him, buffing the toys, frames and coins in the attic, quite mad. I was beginning to sympathise with that man.

Close up, the patch of re-finished floor looked worse than it did from afar. Not only was it clearly a different shade from the rest of the floor – too yellow, and too brown – specks of dust and hair had adhered to it during the night. Cat hairs. And in the centre of the test, there was a small area where its silky smooth surface was broken and rough. I studied this aberration – it was approximately circular, as if someone had pressed their thumb into the polish before it dried, but its edge was far too rough and uneven for a thumbprint ...

It was a paw print; a cat's paw print. I stood up rapidly, making myself dizzy. The quietness of the flat suddenly seemed unsympathetic, watchful. There was nothing on the sofa – the study door was ajar, with stillness beyond.

'Here, puss,' I said, self-consciously. 'Here, Shossy ... Stravvy.' I clicked my tongue and made a succession of the little nonsense noises that people make when trying to catch a cat's attention – clucks, whistles, kiss-kiss sounds. There was no response. Was it possible that the cat had returned in the night? Where was it? Had it slipped out again before I woke to close the window, or was it still here – somewhere?

I felt compelled to check the piano. It was as I had left it: closed, silent. Unable to relax, I lifted its lid. Nothing was out of place, save for the single drop of the dead cat's blood, now dried black. How different the study seemed against the rest of the flat – the same minimalist décor, the same white walls and wooden floors, but with none of the anxious sterility that pervaded the kitchen and living room. It was restful, personal. This difference, I saw, did extend to the floor. A broad area near the desk was visibly worn, beaten by the rollers of the swivel chair. Now that I had become a connoisseur of floor conditions, I could see it. It did not surprise me – I too would spend most of my time in the study if this were my flat. That had been my plan at first, I now remembered – to sit in this room and write, to create something. The memory seemed to originate from another age, another season of my life. There might yet be time, I thought, but I would need to be calm and undistracted, and that would be impossible until I had exhausted every possible option with the floors.

For now, there was the question of the cat. It must have returned in the night – *a* cat had left its mark, even if it wasn't *the* cat. A superstitious reflex caused the word *ghost* to manifest itself in my frame of thought – I shook it away like I was clearing an Etch-a-Sketch. Nevertheless, there was a moral symmetry to a spectral cat helping ruin my effort to repair the floor, even if it was doomed anyway. The flat now seemed tilted against me, perhaps even vengeful – certainly, no longer neutral.

But it had never been neutral. It had always been subtly against me. I saw it now, every little gemlike detail. I had been intimidated the moment I had walked in the door. Maybe that was the purpose of the flat. Perfection is aggressive. It is a rebuke.

The cat. Did ghosts eat? Cats ate, for sure, and after twenty-four hours in the wild, Oskar's would be hungry. If it had made a visit in the night, perhaps it had eaten some of the food I had left out for it.

I turned to leave the study but, before going through the door, I felt compelled to turn again and check that the piano lid was closed. It was. The black-lacquer S-curve of its side turned reflected sunlight into shining vertical lines, helplessly orderly.

It was hard to tell if the cat food had been raided in the night. There was a lot left on the plate, but I was still leaving out a whole tin of the stuff, enough for two. The only way to be sure that some had gone would be to take the empty can out of the bin and scoop the plate's contents back into it. I was not going to do that.

On the kitchen table was a third-full bottle of wine, a used wine glass, and the dirty plate I had eaten a light supper from the previous evening. *Care of Wooden Floors* lay beside the plate, Chandler Novack's face grinning up at me from the back cover.

I looked back at the failed patch of re-finished floor. It was no less noticeable. If anything, it appeared to be getting more yellow. Its surface was too shiny, a trashy splash of glare against the silky sheen of the undamaged boards. What else did Novack have to say? He had not written a short book – it couldn't all be about rugs and Yggdrasil and inner oneness. I knew there was more.

> In cases of severe or extensive damage, it might be necessary to re-sand the whole floor with an industrial sander ...

No, not possible. I scanned ahead, through paragraphs and pages about sanders and dust and facemasks and all the things I would not be doing. Then:

> Alternatively, depending on the quality of the floor, it may be possible to simply lift a damaged board and flip it over, hiding the problem area.

That sounded possible. It sounded better than possible – it had the shape of the perfect solution, effective and elegant. The stains did not have to disappear – Oskar could live with them unaware. They might never be discovered.

But how to lift the floorboards? Oskar had the tools, but the boards were beautifully laid, without space between them for a sheet of cigarette paper. The small nails that held down the boards were more like surgical pins than construction equipment – their dull silver heads were microdots flush with the surface of the wood. It was immediately obvious that the boards could not simply be levered up, nor could the nails be prised out, without gouging, denting or cracking the skin of the wood.

The problem perplexed me for a time. It was a question of finding an angle, some chink or flaw that would accept the claw of a hammer or the sharp end of a screwdriver or chisel. Before long, my eye fell upon the step that separated the kitchen from the living area. At the edge of this step was a simple protective wooden moulding held in place by unguarded cross-head screws – if these screws and the strip of moulding were removed, the end of the kitchen floorboards would be exposed and they could be safely prised up. I could then flip them over to reveal their undamaged undersides. Of course it was possible that the undersides might not have the same high-quality finish as the top of the boards. More than possible – however good the floor, surely it wouldn't be sanded and polished on both sides of each board. But it was worth a try.

I gathered the tools I thought I might need on a sheet of paper on the floor next to the step and paused. Why I paused, I don't know, but I stopped. Perhaps it was the fact that I was kneeling, but for a moment, I felt like praying. I wanted to ask for good fortune – I wanted this to work. If the boards could not be flipped, or the job fouled up somehow and could not be put right, I had exhausted the possibility of fixing the floor. I would have to surrender and either be honest with Oskar or flee the country. The first of those options was not very appealing, but the second did have a certain allure. I had never fled a country before; I suppose few people of my background have. There was a glamour to it. The thought gave me the same thrill that sometimes came to me when I looked for my flight on the departure board of an international airport. Reading that endlessly refreshing list of names – La Paz, Riga, Lagos, Jakarta – I am filled with a sense of equidistance from every point in the world. The straight line of my planned journey scatters like a narrow beam of light shot through a prism, revealing its spectrum. I could go anywhere.

But I would not be going anywhere – I would be fleeing home, back to London, back to the off-white walls and hairline cracks I had left behind, with a fresh pile of bills on the mat. Strange how little choice we have over the rooms in which we live our lives – I was shunted into a barely satisfactory flat, with a toilet by the front door, by the clumsy mechanics of the market, and I spent my time toiling in that flat, or equally unappealing offices, in order to pay the rent. Oskar had had the – what? Talent? Skill? Cunning? Discipline? Dumb luck? – *good fortune* to exercise total control over his environment, to build this personal paradise. And when he had offered me the chance to look after it for him, it had looked like a chance to break free of the old patterns of my inadequate world. And now a week had passed and all I had to show for it was a trail of devastation. In spoiling Oskar's flat, I had spoiled my own chance to use it as a springboard to self-improvement. If there was a chance that the situation could still be put right, I had to take it. And I wanted to know right away if the plan could work. By the end of today, I vowed to myself, either the floor would be fixed or I would tell Oskar the truth. And I would not just tell him about the floor: I would tell him about the sofa, the cleaner, the cat ... the cats, plural, if the other had not yet returned.

I set to work. The cross-head screws that held the strip of moulding in place came out cleanly and a two-foot length was easy to remove. I tried to put it back in place – it fitted perfectly, and the screws seemed to spin back into their holes without a fuss. Returning it to its old position would not be a problem.

Now the ends of the kitchen floorboards were exposed. I examined them. It was impossible to get the grip that would let me pull one up with my fingers alone – I would have to slip something between the floorboard and the joist it was nailed to in order to lever it up. It was a very close fit, with not the slightest gap between the two pieces of wood, pushed down by the weight of everyone who had walked in Oskar's kitchen. I was not convinced that the heads of Oskar's screwdrivers were slender enough to worm in between board and joist without damaging the wood, and he had no suitable chisels.

On the plate on the kitchen table was the little paring knife I had used the previous night to cut slices of cheese and salami. It had a slender blade culminating in a sharp point. But it also had traces of food on it, and I was concerned about bending or even snapping it, or dulling its ferocious edge. I opened the drawbridge door of the dishwasher, pulled out the white wire tray on wheels, and put in the knife and the other dirty things from the table

– with the exception of the wine glass. Then I resumed my hunt for a suitable prising implement, finding after a short time a springy palette knife in a drawer.

To my surprise, this knife slipped sweetly between the floorboard and the joist, and the board rose a millimetre out of place with only the slightest effort. A small push created a large enough gap for me to slip in my fingers and pull up the board. Its underside felt smooth and cool, just like the top. My fingertips thrilled at the sensation – it felt the same! It was the same!

There was a noise from the direction of the bedroom – a muffled rattle. It could have been a feline knocking something over. I listened – nothing.

'Puss?' I said.

An un-catlike metallic jingling was followed by the unmistakable rasp of a key being pushed into a lock.

My heart dropped into a bucket of ice water.

'Oskar?'

No answer. The lock turned and the door opened, and I heard a shuffle of feet. In a terrible moment of vertigo, I saw myself, I saw what I was doing, I saw how it *looked*. The stains, the removed moulding, the floorboard lifted out of place. Panic lurched through me – I wanted to put everything right or cover everything up in an instant, but it was impossible, there was no time, literally, zero time. I stood up, acting mostly on instinct, without any plan. My knees complained and my foot remembered its wound, making me wince.

Through the glass partition, I saw the cleaner advancing down the corridor. And she saw me, fixing me with a sulphurous scowl. She was carrying a mop, its lank grey end up like the shrunken head of one of her victims on a pike. In an unpractised rush that must have reeked of wrongdoing, I leapt to the end of the hallway, attempting to halt her before she saw the kitchen floor. In her mopless hand was a bucket full of cleaning supplies.

'Hi!' I said, trying to sound bright and cheerful, but instead just squeaking. 'Hi. This isn't a good time, actually – do you think you could come back tomorrow?'

She didn't even slow down and, death-ray eyes locked on target, marched right into my space. I had to flatten myself against the wall to avoid a collision. The bedroom door was nearby – it was so tempting to slip through it, barricade it behind me, pack, and see if I could exit through the window like the cats. But the cleaner had reached the kitchen already. I heard a gasp of theatrical horror, followed by a monosyllabic exclamation and a metallic clash as she slammed a heavy bunch of keys down on the counter. She had seen the floor.

I scuttled after her, into the kitchen. Hearing me approach, she turned around and put down the bucket. Black fury blazed in her eyes. Her upturned bat nose flared like a shotgun's twin snout.

'——!' she yelled, thrusting the end of her mop in the direction of the most recent wine stains. '——!' she added, this time giving special emphasis to the floorboard I had lifted out of place.

Negotiation was clearly pointless, and I was a long way past trying to smooth things over. I wanted her out of my flat.

'Look,' I said, walking up to her, 'this isn't a good time. I want you to go, now.' I stretched out my arm and pointed as firmly as I could in the direction of the flat's front door. 'Go, now!' I said, willing my voice to develop a hard edge.

There was little space between us, but she advanced on me anyway, eyes very wide, speaking to me in a way that put – equal – weight – on – every – word. She was holding the mop like a weapon, *brandishing* it at me.

'I'm not joking,' I said, but in spite of my intention of making a stand, I was forced to take a step back. Nevertheless, I continued to point. 'Get out. Get out of my flat!'

Wait, I thought, *what do I mean by* my *flat?*

I was interrupted by the bedraggled grey head of the mop, which jabbed me in the solar plexus with unexpected force. It was wet, and smelled faintly of disinfectant and stagnant water. Batface was repeating her staccato speech, and on this recital prodded me in the chest with the mop on every word. Again, I had to retreat a step, with care as I sensed the raised floorboard and step behind me. It would be easy to trip. Still she advanced, and each time she prodded with the mop, she did so with a little more strength. The mop head was attached to the handle with an angular metal fixing. It hurt.

This was insane. She was hurting me. What was she going to do, beat me? Drive me into the bedroom or out of the flat altogether? This was *assault*!

Blood roared in my ears. All my muscles frosted with energy.

'Stop that!' I said – I shouted. 'Just – stop!' I shot out my right hand and grabbed the mop just below its head, stopping her thrusting at me. The glare she had focused on me broke and she looked down, puzzled, momentum lost. With a monosyllable that was certainly a curse, she shook the mop, hard. My grip almost broke, so I seized the mop with my left hand as well, taking hold of the stretch of shaft between her hands.

'Give-me-that!' I said, intending to yank the mop from her grasp, but she was a good deal stronger than I expected and barely budged. We stared at each other. Taking back the momentum, she thrust out her arms, trying to push me back and perhaps even push me over. I staggered, and she turned the push into a pull, clearly meaning to jerk the mop from my hands while I was off balance. But I was not off balance, and instead of letting go I surged forwards, pushing her back.

This surprised her. She let out a gasp and stumbled back, her hands flying off the mop. It was mine. Trying to regain her balance, the cleaner took a big step back, windmilling her arms. Behind her, just above floor level, was the open drawbridge of the dishwasher. I opened my mouth to shout a warning, but it was already too late. She tried to take another step back and struck the side of the door with her thick ankle. Although her feet were stopped, the considerable weight of the rest of her body continued to travel back, and she half-fell, half-sat on the white wire drawer of the washer with a sickening, jangling crash.

'My God, are you all right?' I asked, taking a step forwards, mop still in my hands.

She did not answer, of course, but stared back at me, eyes and mouth wide open with shock, not anger. The colour had drained from her face, leaving it like newsprint. Arms waving in the air, she replanted her feet on the ground before slowly and with obvious effort and pain raising herself up. I wanted to drop the mop and rush over to help her up, but I remained motionless. My feelings were briefly a mystery to me – then I realised that I was terrified.

The cleaner was back on her feet, but unsteady. Unknowable emotion gathered in her face. All the rage in the room had dissipated and was replaced by grey fear. There was something odd about the way the cleaner was standing. She seemed to acknowledge this, lifting her arms away from her bulk and looking down at her right leg. It was trunk-like and strained under artificial fabric, but I could see nothing wrong with it, and apparently neither could she. Still looking, she started to turn around.

I believe that I saw it before she did; in any case, we both saw it within a second of each other. Sticking out of the back of the cleaner's right leg was the silver handle of Oskar's sharp little paring knife. It had been in the drawer of the dishwasher, point up – its effective little blade was now buried in the fibrous rolls of muscle and fat at the top of the cleaner's leg.

Neither of us moved for a moment, and nothing was said, though both our mouths were open now. This handle, this protuberance, was an absurdity, a stray switch from a cyborg appliance – it took a moment to get used to it. I blinked and marvelled at myself – *get used* to it? She had a knife sticking out of her, it wasn't something that I should be assimilating into the normal pattern of my day. The damn thing was jutting out of her *leg*.

Guilt surged up inside me, writhing black ropes of it squeezing my innards. Had I stabbed her, somehow, by proxy? By an elaborate Wile E. Coyote contrivance that had somehow come right? I ran backwards through events, like leafing through a flick-book the wrong way, scanning each frame for culpability.

'Jesus,' I said. 'Are you all right?'

That was stupid, obviously wrong. What I meant was: *How wrong are you? Do I have to call 999?* Was it even 999?

The cleaner moved. Maybe only a couple of seconds had passed since we both saw the silver knife, but it could have been weeks. Colour and animation had returned to her face. She shut her mouth and closed her hand around the silver handle. Without any hesitation, she pulled the blade out of her leg. We both winced. There was no noise. Blood covered the metal, flag-red, and ran off its pointed end – a couple of drops fell towards the floor.

She looked at the red blade. I looked at the two drops on the floor, a vampire's bite, thinking of how quickly the other blood, my blood, had formed a permanent mark.

This thought, of staining, broke me out of the strange, shared reverie. I had to act. I took a step forward and lowered the mop, meaning to use it to remove the blood. But the cleaner also moved, quickly, making me jump. She had tensed, and the anger had re-ignited in her eyes. There was a difference in the way she was holding the knife – no longer as a dumb object she had picked up, but as a weapon. She was furious, and she was armed.

My mind a blur, I tried to get a barometer reading on the level of crazy in the room. High? Low? Rising? Falling? There was a blood-slicked knife pointed at me, wielded by someone now watching me with unabashed hatred. But the possibility of actually being slashed or stabbed by this knife, this person, seemed supremely abstract, an outlying scenario on the thin edge of likelihood.

'The blood,' I said, appealing to her as a cleaner. 'I just want to catch the blood ...' I stuck out the mop, reached the red drops on the floor, and she lunged at me.

It was a clunky attack, one that showed she was as unfamiliar with knife fights as I was – starting as a stunted sweep through the air, it ended with a twitchy jab in my direction. Practised or not, it was dangerous, and I leapt back like an electrocuted frog. The cleaner, scything only air, raised the blade above her head and charged at me like a dumpy ninja. Either she screamed or I did – it could have been both of us. I raised the mop to parry the blow – not thinking, arms working on their own initiative – and met success; the blade hit the wood between my white-knuckled hands with a loud, hollow *thonk*. Another drop of blood was shaken from the knife and hurtled towards the floor.

The cleaner withdrew her weapon and I backed up slightly, wanting to give both of us more space but also to see where the last blood drop had flown. It had travelled a good few feet, propelled by the force of the blow, and I turned to swab it from the floor. Again, she came at me, moving the instant I lowered my guard. But her approach was slow, and I had a moment to form a response. What, however, was there to do? Hit her? Try to force the knife from her hand or incapacitate her? I had nothing, I was a blank. Crazy she might be, but she was still an old woman – an *injured* old woman. Splitting her skull with the mop did not seem to be a reasonable approach to the situation.

She was on me, this time stabbing upwards, and again I parried with the mop, blocking her with the middle of the handle. Our eyes met – I expected animal savagery, but instead found angry puzzlement, as if my refusal to passively accept a frenzied knifing was a cause of dismay and disappointment for her. A dark-red flower was blooming at the back of her thigh – I saw its creeping edge, and imagined blood trickling downwards, lured by gravity towards the floor. We circled each other, eyes locked, her expression not even flickering. Surely, I thought, there would be pain – she could not be that well padded.

A noise, vast and astonishing, broke into the space, and repeated. As one, we started, and turned to its source: the telephone, ringing. Oskar? It seemed unlikely – it would be midnight, or the tiniest hours of the morning, in California. It continued to ring, an insistent electronic baby yelling for attention.

In that moment of distraction, the cleaner disengaged from me and arced the knife around, aiming for the left side of my ribcage. I struck out with the mop head, intercepting the blow, making it easy to avoid. She yelled, not a word, just a cry of frustration. I tried to manoeuvre the mop so that I could repel my adversary with one end and clean the blood scattered by the flailing blade with the other. But it was impossible, there was no way of reaching the floor without lowering my defences. The cleaner also changed tactics, this time targeting my hand with the knife. Surprised, I squealed, and tried to step back. My retreating feet met the kitchen step, and I toppled over backwards, hitting the floor hard.

I was sprawled on my back on the kitchen floor, arms and legs flailing. My pelvis felt like it had dislocated. For once in my life I wished I were fatter. My head must have missed the still-open door of the dishwasher by inches. Blood rushed into my mouth from a bit lip.

The cleaner, despite her modest height, somehow managed to loom over me. She was breathing heavily and muttered at me. My eyes flicked from her face to the sliver of metal in her hand. As if following my gaze, she too examined the knife, holding it as if she had just found it on the floor. Muttering again, she walked towards me, stepping up into the kitchen. Still on the floor, I flinched to one side, pressing up against the cold steel doors of Oskar's cabinets. This was it – she was moving in for the kill. But instead of plunging the knife into me like an Aztec priest, she walked past and dropped it into the dishwasher, point down. I eased myself back onto my feet. The cleaner was still mumbling to herself between hard, uneven breaths. As if in a trance, she moved to the sink and washed her bloodied right hand. Then she turned back in my direction, looking down at her feet, at the stained floor.

'I can fix it,' I said. 'I can make it like it never happened.'

Shaking her head, keeping up the monologue that only she could hear or understand, the cleaner sank to her knees and spread her hands flat against the wooden boards. Her face was very red, and her breathing was faster now.

'Seriously,' I said, my voice high in my ears, 'it's really nothing to worry about. I can fix it. It's not worth getting upset about.'

The muttering stopped, and so did the rapid, whistling breathing. The bent-over figure of the cleaner appeared to relax. It sagged like an inflatable losing its air. She slipped forwards slowly and kept moving until she was face-down on the floor, arms outstretched.

There was silence. The cleaner was very still. I could hear my own breathing, my own heartbeat, but nothing from her.

With great care – my muscles cracked as if they had not moved in years – I reached out with my foot and nudged the cleaner's shoulder with my toe. Nothing happened. The roundel of blood on her thigh was already drying. With relief, I saw that it was off the floor – there wouldn't be any more damage as a result of the fight. But – I stopped myself. That was hardly the most important thing at the moment. Enough damage had already been done.

Crouching, I picked up the cleaner's right hand by the wrist. The skin was pale and wet. I could not find a pulse.

'Shit,' I said to myself, a sudden, hissing exclamation – I had been holding my breath without thinking. My lungs burned.

'Shit,' I said again. The cleaner's face, pressed against the floor, was turned slightly away from me. I walked around her to see it. Her eyes were open and glassily stared at nothing.

Beside the phone was one of the sheets of Oskar's welcome note, the sheet that gave the numbers for his hotel and emergencies. Was this an emergency? Was there anything to be gained by acting quickly?

There was a number for the police. I let time drift by.

My pelvis ached from the fall onto the floor, and my legs were weak. I sat on Oskar's sofa, which sighed under me. Sitting down, I could no longer see the body in the kitchen. That was good.

Was it a body, then? Had I killed someone?

I had killed someone.

These words meandered through my mind in a disconnected way. It was like watching an advert on television – a random little claim on my attention. Wrong, of course. Impossible. I had killed no one. It was an accident. She was old. It was natural causes. I had tried to be reasonable. It was bad luck, as much my bad luck as hers. A mistake. No – not a mistake. An accident. If she had put the cork more firmly in the bottle ... and now look what had happened.

But I didn't look at what had happened. Instead, scenarios played in my mind. In one, I call the police, and explain ... and then it gets hazy. They understand, or I go to prison. Even if I am spared prison – and I was not confident that my explanation had the clear complexion of truth – I would be in an uncomfortable position for some time.

Oskar would know. How much did I have to tell the police? An explanation of the fight would be needed, but would they want to know about the floor? How did it look? Hours would be spent talking patiently with people, or waiting, staring at the worn surfaces of institutional desks or tiled floors under unkind fluorescent lights – hospitals, morgues, police stations, embassies, who knew?

If I called Oskar now, what would he say? What could he say? Perhaps it had been him on the phone earlier, during my grappling match with the cleaner. He was still innocent of all this – in his universe, nothing had happened to the floor, both the cats were alive, the cleaner was alive. I wanted very much to be back in that universe. Calling Oskar would not help me. The only person who could help me was me.

For some minutes I had been sat on the sofa, elbows on knees, thinking and listening to the sounds coming from beyond the window. I wanted to hear a sound behind me, from the cleaner – a groan or a sudden cough of breath. Even some kind of cry would have been welcome. I closed my eyes, pinched the bridge of my nose, tried to focus. The hum of the city mingled with the seething disorder in my mind, a chaos that parted here and there to reveal a frozen, irreversible moment of violence. My memory of what had happened was a burst of nonsense, a fumbling multi-limbed anarchy rather than a clear order of events. I wanted a coherent picture of what had taken place, laid out like dance instructions – but I was getting a frame of film exposed many times, many slices of time layered into one meaningless image. She pushed, I pushed, an instant like a thread breaking, and I was here. Behind me in the kitchen was the problem, the problem that raved and crashed around in my head, demanding my attention, threatening to destroy everything. The fact of the cleaner's death was growing in my mind. It was as if her body was swelling, inflating like the bag of an antiquated hoover, wrapped in that same taut, waxy fabric. I thought of what happens when we die, the bacterial banquet and the gases it creates, gases that blow up our bodies like balloons ... and the cat in its black sack at the bottom of the canal, and everything that had happened and could not be undone, thirty years of life spooling out uselessly up to this dismal moment in another man's flat with a dead body that had nothing to do with me – it was none of my business! I wasn't responsible for her death, and I wasn't responsible for her now! I hadn't done anything!

A noise escaped my mouth, something between a sob and a cry of frustration and anger. The sound, loud and shapeless, and its roughness in my throat, startled me, and I opened my eyes. Taking a deep breath, I tried to clear my mind. The problem, the question of what to do, had tangled itself into a knot of abstractions in my racing mind. I had to see it for what it was, which was a dead body on Oskar's kitchen floor.

I got up and went to have a look at this body. It was still there, I noted with a little disappointment. So this was a dead body. It was the first I had seen. My family favoured closed caskets and cremations. It – the body – seemed smaller than I remembered, but its appalling stillness gave it an air of solemnity. Very, very still. I squatted and placed a hand on the cleaner's shoulder. It was warm – or, at least, it was not cold, not the chilly, creepy thing I expected. I pushed, shook her, trying again to rouse her.

'Wake up,' I said, and immediately I felt foolish, childish, for failing to face facts. Not cold, then, yet; there was a person there, or their remains. Dying warmth.

I stood. 'Shit,' I said again, and the word ended in a choke, the cracking of something inside. The possibility of tears, a sudden hot emergency around the eyes. I blinked furiously, inhaled hard and held the breath in, thinking over and over *Don't think about it, don't think about it.* The crisis passed. It was fine – everything was fine.

Nevertheless, it didn't look good. This question of appearances gnawed at me. I fretted over the possible reaction of hypothetical observers – their imagined train of thought always took an ugly turn towards blame, wrongdoing, crime, murder. The cleaner lay face-down on the floor, arms splayed out. Her body was orbited by wine stains, which inevitably suggested a spectacular eruption of gore, although the only actual blood that could be seen was on the knife, point down in the dishwasher tray, and the dark patch on one of the cleaner's thighs. But the wine, the knife, the dead body – it did not look good.

Maybe it could be improved a little. I edged around the body to the dishwasher and rolled the wire tray into the machine. A couple of drops of blood had fallen onto the inside of the dishwasher's steel door. Thinking of the single black drop the cat had left inside the piano, I shut the door and started the machine. It clicked and whooshed. I smiled. A self-cleaning crime scene. So convenient. Just a couple of simple movements and the evidence was gone, blasted away in a secret, lightless world of powerful detergents and above-boiling water. The television criminalists would be baffled.

If only everything else were that simple. The body was still there, unavoidable. I wanted to wipe it away too, obliterate it at the touch of a button.

Maybe that wasn't so unrealistic. The knife had been dealt with. I had been quick enough with the mop, so there was no visible blood on the floor. What other traces had she left in the flat? Besides the body, there was the bucket of cleaning products, the mop, and the bunch of keys on the worktop. These items, at least, could be removed without a problem.

Which, of course, left the body, the elemental problem. I had to get rid of it. She had died of natural causes – it was just a matter of removing her corpse from Oskar's flat, where it had the unfortunate effect of implicating me in her demise. What crime had been committed? There might be laws against failing to report a death, or something similar – but removing her would prevent a miscarriage of justice that might tragically entangle an innocent man.

A chaos of ideas, from the unpromising to the disastrous, fought for my attention. Just dumping the body somewhere was not feasible. She was short but stout, and moving her any distance – such as beyond the building – would be impossible. She would not be joining the cat in the canal. I thought of the garbage chute and winced – a dumpster burial seemed grotesquely cold and I hated myself for the idea. Besides, I doubted she would fit, and the lithe body of the cat had been problematic enough. Similarly, destroying the body – fire, dismemberment, an acid bath – was altogether too grisly and too difficult. Whatever I did, I vowed, I would do it with some respect.

My eyes turned to the cleaner's keys, a hedgehog of grimy metal on the mirror-clean steel counter. There were a lot of them – enough to open every door in the building, I imagined. And, of course, they would include the keys to her own flat, on the first floor, directly below Oskar. If I moved her there, her death would look like an accident.

It was already an accident – it just had to look like one, one that didn't involve me.

I took the washing-up gloves from their clip above the sink and stepped back over the cleaner's body. The more time I spent in the company of the corpse, the more comfortable I felt around it. To my relief, it was easier and easier to think of it as a thing – easier, in fact, to not think about it too hard at all. As I put on the gloves, I thought again of the murderer in the horror comic, obsessively polishing pottery shards and attic junk because he cannot rid himself of the fear that his fingerprints have been left somewhere – that could not be allowed to happen to me. I had to be careful from the start. There had been no murder, but I was committing a crime for sure – I just had to make it an invisible, unnoticed crime. I had to prevent traces.

Oskar's front door opened with a soft click and I peered out onto the landing. It was deserted. How many apartments were there in this building? A dozen, as many as twenty? And yet the cleaner was the only other inhabitant

I had seen. Still, there was an undeniable risk that one of Oskar's neighbours might make a surprise appearance while I was shifting the body.

The cleaner's flat seemed tantalisingly close – indeed it was close, only one or two feet away, straight down. The floor's solidity taunted me. Even if I removed more boards in the kitchen, enough to lower a body through, there would be some other layer to breach. I looked up. The ceiling was plain white plaster. It would be necessary to hack through that, then clear away the dust and debris, re-plaster and re-paint the ceiling – impossible. A better man, an Oskar or Novack among men, would have trouble with that job, and I was thwarted by floor maintenance they found simple.

Back inside the flat, I paused by the bedroom door. Perhaps the body could be wrapped in a sheet, like a shroud, somehow disguised ... but a corpse has a distinctive profile, weight and awkward bulk, and cinema and television have trained us well to identify them. If I transported her as she was, it would look less suspicious in the event of being surprised – of course there would still be an unpleasant scene, and many questions to answer, but I would look less like a man attempting to avoid detection, and I could perhaps claim that I was dragging her to the street in order to seek help. It was better to remain undetected, though. If I was put in the position of having to explain anything, it was already too late. The point of the exercise was to avoid explaining anything.

I scooped the keys from the counter and put them in the bucket with the sponges and the bottles of bleach.

Then I carried this bucket down the two flights of stairs to leave it outside the cleaner's flat. It looked unimpeachably innocent there, left momentarily in the hall outside its owner's home while she attended to something. There was nobody to be seen. It was time to move the body. There would be no better time.

The etiquette of corpse-handling is not widely known, but some of its basics were obvious. It was more seemly to take the cleaner by the shoulders than by the ankles. She was heavy, but slid easily on the smooth wood of the floor, and I had her out of Oskar's flat and onto the landing quicker than I had hoped. Descending the stairs was more difficult and I proceeded slowly. The cleaner was still face-down, the same way she had slumped to the floor, and her feet turned and twisted on their toes as we bumped down each step. Her head hung horribly from her shoulders, swinging loosely from side to side with each jolt. For a moment I feared the rough ride might wake her, that she might suddenly lift her head and look at me, but she did not. I was glad that I could not see her face.

On the cleaner's floor, the sounds of the street were louder and clearer. Car brakes squealed at the junction and a tram rumbled by. The footsteps of passers-by rang clearly on the pavement. I took the keys from the bucket and froze. There were maybe three dozen keys on a series of linked rings, with no apparent hierarchy or organisation. Some were marked with twists of wool, blobs of paint, numbers scratched into the metal or written in fading marker pen. I looked at the door – shut, locked, robust. The keyhole was almost identical to Oskar's, highly polished brass, but here years of polish had blackened the wood around it and worked grey-green residue into its cracks. There were numerous keys that resembled Oskar's in the bunch. I tried one at random. It slid neatly into the hole, but refused to turn. The second I tried would only go in halfway.

I felt a vein throbbing in my neck and swallowed. Sweat moistened my fingers inside the gloves. The passing footsteps in the street seemed louder and louder and as each set ascended my throat constricted, waiting for the moment when the walker would pause and I would hear the building's heavy door being pushed open. I hunted for a third key to try and my fingers slipped – the bunch fell to the tiled floor with a crash. The sound went straight through me and resounded against the hard edges of the stairs. And as I bent to retrieve the keys, clumsy and ridiculous in the yellow gloves, I saw with fresh revelation what lay on the floor at my feet – the body, a dead thing, a great indivisible final fact. Its reality and unreality struck me. An actual human corpse – a silent tumulus with extraordinary power to overturn my life and evaporate my freedom if I was discovered in its presence, or an investigation even associated me with it. And yet it was so little, barely more trouble than a heavy trunk or more awkward than a double mattress. Maybe that was its awful secret, the thing that we all turn from: that time in the company of the corpse of a stranger isn't a ceaseless nightmare; it could even feel normal. Just don't think about it too much, I told myself. *I won't think about it.*

The fourth key did not turn. The fifth key turned smoothly and the door opened, revealing a slice of crimson carpet, yellow-green wallpaper and a thick crowd of faded winter coats and plastic macs supported by a buried row of pegs. I opened the door wide and pulled the cleaner into the flat as quickly as I could, bringing in the bucket of bottles and sponges too, and then shutting myself in.

With the door closed, I leaned against the wall, breathing deeply, trying to get oxygen back into my body. Sweat broke everywhere against my skin; I felt I could still hear footsteps on the street, on the stairs, ready to push through the door or round the corner and see me with the body, and I told myself over and over that it was OK, the danger had passed. The cleaner's flat shared a plan with Oskar's, but it was much darker. Where Oskar had inserted a glass partition between the hall and the kitchen, here the wall was still solid brick, creating a gloomy corridor hung with pictures and terminated by a bead curtain.

Pressing myself against the wall, I listened intently. Nothing. The thick pile of the carpet made it easy to advance down the corridor without making a sound, but the bead curtain rattled as I parted it. The sea of swirling crimson underfoot flowed through to the living room, where a plastic-covered sofa faced a television, metal folding chairs were stacked against a small dining table and dressers and cabinets supported a large population of china and knick-knacks. It was cluttered, but there was no sign of any other inhabitants.

I returned to the body – an indistinct shape in the under-lit hall, perhaps a coat fallen from the mass on the pegs. It was surprisingly difficult to drag it down the corridor – the deep carpet put up more resistance than tiles or polished wood. The added effort triggered a deep weariness in me, a desire to be finished with the corpse, and with the floors, and with Oskar's flat – but the weight, the effort, also seemed appropriate, worthy of respect, a reminder that I was dealing with something substantial.

In the living room I faced an unanticipated question: Where to leave the body? Face-down on the floor did not seem natural. It had to look as if it had not been moved – that she had simply dropped on the spot and stayed there. I pulled her into the centre of the room and turned her over. Her head, blank eyes still open, rolled as if she could not stand to look at me. Her arm, where I held it to flip her, was cool, and the flesh of her face was losing its colour, highlighting the little hairs on her cheeks and blue-tinged lips. As she turned over, the dark rosette of blood on her thigh was hidden, and I remembered my unfinished job upstairs, reversing the floorboards. There was all the more reason to do it now, with the possibility of rogue corpuscles of the cleaner's blood somewhere in their grain, waiting to slander me to forensic investigators. Would it come to that? Not if I could leave her in the right condition down here.

I sat on the cleaner's sofa. Its clear plastic covering squeaked under me. Before this week I might have thought the plastic a fussy, unnecessary precaution; now it seemed very sensible indeed. And that crimson carpet looked very good for concealing stains. My initial impression of the cleaner's apartment was gloomy disorder. Looking more closely, I saw how well kept it was. The kitschy china statues of shepherdesses were all carefully arranged. There was not a speck of dust on the lacquered surface of the low table beside the sofa. Next to the television remote control – the numbers rubbed off half its buttons by years of use – was a framed black-and-white photograph of a man in an anachronistic military uniform, three small medals on his breast. A husband? Father? Brother? Lost love? The portrait could have come from any year between 1930 and 1970, but something made me certain the man was dead. He looked away from the camera, lost in time. She would have relatives, of course, friends, acquaintances, neighbours here in the building – a personal cosmos orbiting around her, now gone. She would be missed, like this man in the uniform – and would anyone remember him, now? A desperate sadness mounted inside me, and I swallowed it, thinking hard about my breathing, thinking *I'm not going to think about that.*

An arch, hung with another bead curtain, led to the kitchen, where pine-fronted cabinets skulked. Another thing swept away in Oskar's remodelling, with all its structural solidity replaced by glass, openness, natural light and, presumably, somewhere, some heavy-duty steel taking the load. The side wall of the living room, where Oskar built his bookcases, was here entirely covered by a full-colour photograph of a waterfall in a forest, blown up to life size. This decoration had faded with time, taking on a bluish hue. A stag looked out nobly from the scene, peering over a sideboard loaded with ceramic animals.

Care, and time, and work had gone into this apartment – the same sort of devotion that Oskar expended on his own. It demanded that I leave the cleaner in some kind of respectful state, even after the monstrous disrespect I had so far piled upon her. Again, I had to fight with myself, to stop myself being overwhelmed with melancholy and what I supposed was guilt. I looked down at my hands, still in their stupid Tweetie Pie yellow rubber gloves, their insane, inappropriate jollity, and across at the corpse. She still didn't look as if she had just fallen down – she was too straight, and her legs were awkwardly crossed at the ankle. But I had no idea how she might look if she had simply dropped on the floor from a heart attack – even the swan-dive that she had actually fallen into when she died up in Oskar's kitchen didn't look natural. The best I could think of was to sit her on the sofa, as if she had felt unwell and sat down, only to die.

It was worth a try. I rose and tried to pick the body up, my hands under her armpits. But my arms were already tired after dragging her all the way down from Oskar's flat; the muscles in my forearms ached and my bones were shadows. Although I could move the body to the foot of the sofa, there was no way I could lift it onto the cushions.

Not with my arms outstretched, anyway. Taking a deep breath, I stood astride the cleaner's body, hooked my arms under hers and put my remaining strength into lifting her off the ground. We were brought together into a kind of embrace, her cooling weight against me, her face dangerously near mine; a wrong move and her head could turn, her cold cheek could brush against mine ...

Her rump slid onto the squeaking cushions and I let her go, stepping back and brushing off my chest and forearms reflexively. She was on the sofa; her pose was all right, head against the cushions, one arm hanging limply over the side, legs apart but not obscenely so. A spasm of nausea gripped me, but I swiftly had it back under control – everything was fine, she was on the sofa, I could leave now.

I returned to the front door to move the bucket of cleaning products from where I had left it to the kitchen. There had been something else, too – the mop, which would have to be fetched from upstairs.

Turning to take the bucket back to the kitchen, something caught my eye. The clouds that filled the sky had parted enough to briefly reveal the sun, which was rising towards its peak. Light was spilling across the floor. Carved into the thick pile of the carpet were two clear grooves, parallel tracks leading into the living room and curving round to the foot of the sofa, where the cleaner was slumped. It was a trail, left by the cleaner's feet dragging along the floor. And it was unmissable.

Still holding the bucket, I rubbed the toe of my shoe against this groove. It was possible to obscure it, but only by replacing it with a scuffed, disordered patch that looked just a little more natural. I looked, slightly desperately, for an undisturbed area of carpet, to see how it should appear. It was ... not exactly orderly, but its disorder had an unforced rightness about it. I worked my way down the corridor, trying to smooth out the grooves with the sole of my shoe. After leaving the bucket in the kitchen, I examined the results.

It didn't look quite right. The grooves were gone, but in their place was a pattern of strokes left by my foot. I walked up and down the corridor, toeing the carpet here and there to even out some patch or tuft that looked suspicious, feeling like a gardener tending to a prize lawn, but without the pleasure or pride. By the time I had finished, any pattern had gone, but I still felt the texture of the path from door to sofa looked irregular, that aberrant activity could be detected in it. Was that really true, though? Wasn't that just my mind, knowing what it knew, seeing signs that no one else would pick up – signs that might not even be there?

Nothing could be done about it, in any case. I grabbed the keys and headed for the door. Again, the stairwell was clear; I locked the cleaner's front door and affected nonchalance as I ascended the stairs.

The keys, clutched in my gloved hand, gave me another nagging source of concern. They would have to be left in the cleaner's flat, and ideally, to complete the illusion I wanted to create, her door should be locked from the inside. But then how would I get out?

Standing once again in Oskar's flat, wiping the mop handle with a tea towel to remove any prints my fingers might have left on it, I mused on the problem of the door. Successfully moving the body downstairs without being seen had given me a surge of confidence. Finessing the job by locking the door from the inside would satisfy me, and reassure me that I had thwarted any possible investigation. As ever, the floor was the obstacle – the direct route without using the door or the stairs would be straight up, through all the plaster, joists and boards. If I were more familiar with the building I might have known of secret passages, servants' stairs, dumb waiters – but for all my intimacy with Oskar's possessions and floors, I barely knew anything of the rest of the structure he inhabited. No doubt the cleaner had known it best.

The air had thickened with moisture and the flat was warmer; I was paying in sweat for my fight with the cleaner and the effort of moving her remains. I took off the gloves, went into the bathroom, washed my hands under the cold tap, and splashed water on my face. The mirror was in front of me, and I examined what I saw. Those eyes had seen a dead body now, up close. Did they look any different? Was something added, or gone?

In the living room, the light had diminished, squeezed out by the gathering weight of purple-grey clouds. A stray gust of wind thumped the windows, hurling a few fat drops of rain against the glass. Thunder sounded, like furniture being moved in a flat above. I had to leave, I had to get home, if not today then tomorrow. There was nothing more to stay for, not after what had happened. I telephoned the airline and asked about flights; there was nothing today, but seats were available tomorrow afternoon. I gave my card numbers, having barely listened to the substantial price the operator gave me. Then I dialled the number of Oskar's hotel room from the note on the table. It would be very late in Los Angeles, but maybe not too late. But the phone rang unanswered; seven rings, eight, nine ... I killed the connection and dialled the second number, for the hotel reception. The calm American voice announcing the name of the international chain was so welcome it seemed almost angelic.

Was Oskar in his room? The receptionist rang up; there was no answer. I left a message, asking Oskar to call me, thanked her, and put down the phone.

Oskar didn't strike me as a heavy sleeper – unless he had taken a pill or was drunk, I was prepared to believe that he was not in the room. Terror washed through my gut: maybe he had left, checked out of the hotel, was already in a Lufthansa jet headed for Frankfurt. No – wait. Surely the hotel would have told me if he had checked out. But shadows of the fear still lingered. I had been thinking of Oskar as connected to his location; checking there and finding him gone was unnerving.

Steady, heavy rain began to fall. I could not remember if I had left the bedroom window open or closed, and hurried through to check. It was closed, bolted, and the cat had not reappeared on the balcony.

The balcony. The cat. That was how to leave the cleaner's front door locked. I slid back the bolt on the window and stepped out. The street was loud with drumming, running, splashing water and the occasional whoosh of a car. Another balcony was directly below Oskar's – attached to the cleaner's bedroom, I imagined – and beneath that was the drenched street.

Now or never, while it was raining and there were few people out. After putting the marigolds back on – an act that now seemed horribly associated with criminality – I grabbed the mop and the keys and left Oskar's flat. The hallway was of course empty; by now I expected it to be empty. It rang with a sound of rain hitting skylights and windows. Drainpipes concealed somewhere in the building's fabric gurgled.

I let myself into the cleaner's flat in a rush – too quickly, in fact, without any preparation for what I would find in there. As soon as I was through the door, I saw the corpse where I had left it on the sofa, outlined in the grey light from the windows. It made me jump, like seeing a mannequin or a dressmaker's dummy at the wrong moment in the wrong circumstances. The rain filled the flat with sounds and for a dumbstruck, nervy few seconds I stared at the body, its head at an uncanny angle, trying to tell if it had been moved or not since I had been here last.

But the plan was the plan. I hunted through the keys and, finding the right one, double-locked the front door. Now locked in, I took the mop through to the kitchen and left it leaning on the wall. The keys I put on the counter above the bucket of cleaning supplies. Passing back through the living room took me near the corpse again, and I found myself compelled to look at it. Its attitude, the position it took on the sofa, sickened me somehow – there was something foully unnatural about it, as if it were a caricature of something that had been alive. And its deadness, the fact that the life it was once home to was irretrievable, could never return to this vessel, seemed to mock me. There was no going back now, its inner renewal had ceased, it was on the path to decay and dispersal.

My mouth was dry; I swallowed. Outside, it was still raining, and although the body had not started to corrupt the air in the room, it felt distinctly unhealthy. Entering the cleaner's bedroom gave me a searing dose of guilt – an uninvited stranger, I felt I was perpetrating a further profanation. Moving the corpse was one thing – I knew the body, I had met it when it was alive, I had been involved (however indirectly and innocently) in its demise, and my transporting of it could be interpreted as an act of respect. But I had no business in this intimate space; I was an even greater intruder here. I hurried through the room, deliberately paying as little attention as possible to its contents, registering only details – the sheets on the bed tucked in hotel-tight, a cross on the wall, a dressing table, coats and dressing gowns on hangers on the wardrobe door. The window onto the balcony was not bolted, a good omen. Once on the balcony itself, I quickly shut it behind me to prevent rain getting into the bedroom.

As I had hoped, the rain meant that few people were on the streets. As I stepped out someone walked briskly underneath, umbrella up, oblivious to everything above eye level. I crouched down all the same, trying to be as inconspicuous as possible. The street was clear. I stood and lifted a leg over the curved wall, resting it on a slender decorative ridge around the bottom of the balcony; then I brought over the other leg. Without anything protecting me from a fall, the street now seemed further down. My shirt was quickly soaked through. The cats had made it look so easy, so graceful, but there was no easy halfway stage for me between where I was and the ground.

I started to lower myself into a crouching position, still clutching the lip of the wall. For the first time, I was grateful for the rubber gloves – without them, it would have been difficult to maintain a grip with cold, wet hands. I took one of my feet off the balcony and let it dangle free in space. I lowered my centre of gravity as far as possible, before letting the other foot slip, hanging, all my weight on my arms. My upper arms burned, taut; my shoulders strained and I expected for a sick moment the popping pain of dislocation. Swollen drops of water fell from the balconies above and splashed distractingly on me, trickling down my neck. The shining flagstones still seemed a long way beneath my feet. But every second I delayed was another chance to be discovered. I let go.

The landing jarred my ankles, winded me, and cracked my jaws together painfully. Water splashed my ankles and into my shoes. As I tried to recapture my breath, a tram passed by the crossroads on the perpendicular street. Inside it, the lights were on – a row of pale, blank faces stared out through condensation-streaked glass like baguettes behind a sneezeguard in a café. They stared at me, but I don't know if they saw me in the moment they whisked by, a sodden figure in inadequate clothes and washing-up gloves, hair plastered to his head, standing dazed on a cross street. There was nothing to connect me with the balcony above my head, no way of knowing what was behind that window, and they would have no explanation for the grin of victory spread across my face.

The low throb of the dishwasher, steadily disposing of evidence, still permeated Oskar's flat. Its gargling rhythm was a comforting domestic sound, and I thought of home, my own home. Restlessly, I turned the Earth in my mind, watching its dark and light halves, conjuring flight times. If Oskar had departed in the Californian morning ... if I left now ...

Time passed and I fretted, fearing that at any moment I might hear a policeman's gloved hand hammering on the door. My legs and arms shivered and twitched in the dry clothes I had put on, a delayed reaction to the earlier heavy lifting and my drop from the balcony – and, no doubt to the adrenalin leaving my system. I poured wine into a dirty glass, the same glass I had drunk from last night after clearing away the fragments of its shattered brother.

The floorboard in the kitchen was still loose, lifted out of its place. It was as if a secret switch had been found somewhere, pushed, and pop, up came the board, revealing a secret stash of gems or a hidden warren of forgotten rooms. A loose board like that exerted a powerful and mysterious appeal – the lure of an excavated road or a peephole in a featureless fence. And if there really was a simple way of just hiding the stains, of reversing all that had happened, I realised I could not let it pass by before I left. Fooling Oskar, leaving the damage almost in plain sight, but where he would never find it, was too tempting to resist.

It was easy to prise the remaining nails out of the joists they were lodged in, freeing the floorboard. Disappointment lay beneath – a thick layer of insulating material, and a wire stapled to the joist. It wasn't even pleasingly filthy – the insulation looked new.

I turned my attention to the lifted board, wondering if it could be flipped over, regarding its streaks of red wine with dismay. It was puzzling – they were in the wrong place, not where I remembered. The streaks appeared on the side of the board that had nails sticking out of it – the underside. I turned it to check the topside. It too was stained with wine.

This was alarming. Could the wine have penetrated the floor, seeping through the cracks like groundwater into a lightless cavern? The boards were tightly fitted together – it didn't seem possible that any more than a tiny amount could drip through, if that. It looked as if the boards were the same on both sides, meaning that they could be flipped – unless they were ruined on both sides.

After a gulp of wine, I set to work on the next board, gently working the palette knife under it and levering it up. Again, the nails relinquished their grip with surprising ease, and the board lifted out of place. If this one couldn't be flipped, then it was time to give up. I pulled the other end of the board free with my bare hands and turned it over.

It was over. The underside of the board was, if anything, worse than the top, branded with a great slick of a stain. Beyond the stain, there also seemed to be physical damage, a scar that looked like the result of impact by a heavy, hard object. I sighed, put down the board, and sat cross-legged on the floor. No longer nervous, I placed the open wine bottle and glass on the stains beside me. The removed board was laid across my lap and I inspected it closely.

The damage didn't make any sense. How did so much wine infiltrate the boards? And why did it spread across the bottom of the board, rather than just dripping down onto the insulation? I knew of little miracles like surface tension and capillary action, and even if I didn't understand them, I had some idea of their capabilities. But this seemed totally beyond such miracles.

Something else had been troubling me, something that seemed vaster even as I struggled to get a clear view of it. Then I saw it in a moment of total revelation that made it seem bizarre to me that I had not seen it earlier. The stains had identical qualities on both sides of the boards.

Someone had tried to clean the other side of the floorboard.

Just as I had wiped, they had wiped, and just as I had scrubbed, they had scrubbed. No doubt they had cursed. My despair had been their despair. They had been here before.

And I knew that they had a name: they were called Oskar.

Oskar had ruined his own floor.

I pulled up a third board and it told the same story: a spectacular red-wine disaster. The familiar patterns of splash and slick, and variations: a footprint from a man's shoe. On the fourth board I lifted, there was an area that bore the rough signs of sandpapering and an attempt at re-finishing. It had been badly botched. My own efforts, for all their failure, and been more successful. A smile formed on my face and powerful feelings rose within me – not elation, but a kind of mania, a dizzy gleeful sense of upset. These boards had really been messed up – the fourth one also showed signs of bungled acid treatment, which had bleached the wood and caused the grain to rise like an allergic reaction. Of course Oskar had feared damage to the floor. He knew first-hand how difficult it was to clean, and he knew that some of the boards had already been flipped over once, using their get-out-of-jail-free card. Something inside me writhed in delight, and I wanted to laugh.

A wide trench had now been opened in the floor, shattering its insolent, seamless beauty. Its mystique was gone. I leaned over to pull up a fifth board – and stopped.

Under the floorboards, resting on the puffy insulation, I could see a sheet of paper. Oskar's handwriting covered it. I reached in and retrieved it.

My dear friend,

The book, *Care of Wooden Floors*, says that very damaged floorboards can be simply turned over. Very easy – like a second chance. But there is no third chance. If you damage those same boards, then the floor is destroyed. So if you find this letter – it will be clear now. You see the damage.

Maybe it gives you pleasure. I remember how you used to roll your eyes when I asked you to remove your shoes or to use a coaster – all of you did it, everyone. You thought I was being unreasonable. It all seemed quite reasonable to me – to keep everything perfect.

I must now disappoint you: I did not break the wine bottle, I was not the one who damaged the floor. It was Laura. There was a terrible fight. One time when she visited she spilled a small amount of wine. I was unable to clean it, and I think maybe I talked about it too much.

This was easy to imagine: Oskar endlessly moaning about the damage to the floor, bringing up the subject again and again, sighing and tutting.

> When she returned, she brought the book, *Care of Wooden Floors*. It was the cause of a huge fight. I believed that she was mocking me, and she swore that it was an honest act. We were both very angry, and she smashed a bottle of red wine on the floor at my feet.
>
> She left the same day, back to America.

What was it like to be with Oskar at his most angry, and to be the focus of that passion? All this time I had feared Oskar's ire, and yet I realised that I had rarely seen him openly angry. His anger had always been directed at other people, and it had been terrible, but hidden, like the fires that can burn in deep coal seams. Was it so bad to be exposed to it? I had never seen the kind of fight that involved thrown wine bottles, something I reflected on as I sipped my own drink. The noise, the concussion of it against the wood, the radiating blast of wine and shattered glass.

> The floor could not be fixed, of course, and the boards had to be reversed. She refused to come back to the flat. We had argued often over this flat – my orderliness. She did not feel it was welcoming. Her home in Los Angeles is beautiful, but much larger, and they have people for everything. Our cleaner here is not very cooperative.

My elation dissipated.

> People say that it is difficult, disorderly, to live with cats. I have never found them troublesome. People are the source of all chaos in life.
>
> I insisted to Laura that it was not difficult to keep the place perfect, if people just took certain precautions, and did everything the correct way. I said that no one could find it difficult if they followed the correct procedures, and lived with care. She did not agree. She laughed at me. She said it was impossible to keep everything perfect. She said that it was inevitable that the floors would be damaged.
>
> Did you find it difficult? If you are reading this, you are under the floorboards now. You should call me.
>
> You are my dear friend.
>
> Oskar

I looked across at the uprooted and disarranged floorboards. It was difficult at a glance to tell who had caused what stain, and when. The wine and the blood all looked the same. The hole in the floor caused my thoughts to drift to the Telltale Heart, the secret beating away beneath the boards – of course, there is no sound, just guilt. And the pulp comic tale, the murderer obsessively cleaning the tiny shards of broken china, fearful of the smallest fragment of a fingerprint. I knew that killer, but now I saw it could equally be Oskar, seeing a wholeness shatter into a thousand possible outcomes, trying to hunt down and control every last piece of life as it continued to splinter and subdivide in his hands.

You should call me.

With a little trouble, I stood up. Red wine on an empty stomach. What time was it there? Past two in the morning? Three?

They sounded hourlessly breezy at the hotel reception. It would be dark over the Pacific. I told them I wanted to leave a message.

There was still a little wine left in the bottle. I opened a second one anyway.

DAY EIGHT

A concussion. A burst of noise in my head, doubled up, blood pressure in the ears surging, heart starting or stopping in a single moment. I had been falling, and then I landed, on the floor.

The floor.

The floor stretched out in front of me, a vast expanse of plain, the lines of floorboards converging, the surface dappled with stains like the shadows of clouds passing over razed fields. It was all at an angle and I was pressed up against it. My head throbbed with wine and dehydration, and when I raised it, I found that my cheek was stuck to the floor. It peeled off like the free CD attached to the cover of a magazine. Levering myself further up, I found most of the feeling had gone from the arm I had slept on, and my neck and shoulder hurt, yanked tight by my sudden waking. The clock on the kitchen wall said it was a few minutes before 9 a.m.

A double concussion, bang-bang, incredibly loud to me, heard by the ears but felt as ice in the jaw, the chest. A man's voice, raised to carry through the thick polished wood of Oskar's front door, saying something I didn't understand.

Again, fist heavy on wood, vibrations in the doorframe, through the walls, the floor, me. Three, four times. I jerked like a kite string, scrambling to my feet. Around me were the loose boards levered up from the kitchen floor, splashed with red. The cleaner! It was the cleaner. No – I remembered the weight of her, moving that bulk, our unexpected, unwelcome, intimacy. She was dead. She is dead. The past, present and future had all flattened out into that unchanging fact. The world's possibilities diminished. I remembered details, circumstances.

A man's voice behind the door.

Police.

I imagined a gloved fist on the door, a cap, creased trousers, no smiles, the squawk and burble of a radio. A clattering gurney and pulsing blue lights. Neighbours standing in their front doors, arms crossed, grim, fascinated. Questions.

As softly as possible, I stepped across the living room to the window. I had slept in my shoes and the floor creaked under me. Another volley of banging from the front door.

There were no police cars in the street. But this was the street to the side of Oskar's building – they would surely have parked at the front, by the main door, beneath the bedroom window.

The man's voice again, gruff, serious. None of the words meant anything, but it was clear that he wanted to come in.

Trying to be catlike, I went through to the study, opened the window, and looked out. A couple of cars and a van were parked outside – no police cars. Detectives? Unmarked cars? The cleaner's bedroom window was closed and nothing stirred beyond.

I could climb down. Escape. Go out onto Oskar's balcony, climb down to the cleaner's below, then drop to the street, just as I had done yesterday. But if they had found the cleaner's body, they would be in her flat – I would have to go right past them. If it wasn't the police, who could it be? Angry relatives? Oskar? No, not Oskar, it wasn't Oskar's voice, and he had a key.

Bang. Bang. The jingle of the door chain, disturbed by the impacts. Another loud enquiry from the far side of the door. Maybe not angry, but certainly determined. He was – they were? – not going away. I speculated about the strength of the door chain – enough to protect me if I relied on it? What kind of muscle mass went with that voice?

'Wait,' I called out, trying to make it loud but finding my voice crack under the sudden exercise. Then, with more confidence: 'Wait! I'm coming, wait a moment.'

Back in the living room, I looked down at the floor where I had spent the night. It bore no signs of my presence, no extra stains or marks. For some reason I had expected at least some impression from me, as if it could crease and rumple like bed sheets. Two bottles on the floor, one empty, one mostly empty. A glass with an inch of wine left in it stood by the note I had found under the floorboards and some other sheets of paper with my handwriting on them. The floorboards were still up, still stained liberally on both sides. It didn't look good, but there was no quick way of making it all go away. I ran my fingers through my hair, tentatively sniffed an armpit. Old sweat.

With the chain firmly secured, I opened the front door.

Two men in brown overalls stood in the hall. One was short, bulky and had been in charge of the knocking. He carried a clipboard and raised his hands in a what-kept-you gesture when he saw my face behind the chain. His colleague, younger, slimmer and taller, with a pointy nose and steel-framed glasses, hung back in the hall, holding a toolbox.

Clipboard man said something that sounded like the set-up of a joke and looked at me expectantly, waiting for the punchline, eyes mischievous. Then he repeated the line, slower, waiting with mouth open for me to reply.

The tall man stepped forward. 'He want ... know ... if you have good sleep,' he said. 'You have good sleep.' His colleague smiled, an action that vanished his eyes behind a concertina of lines pushed up by chubby, unshaven cheeks.

'Sure,' I said vaguely. 'Can I, er, help?'

Clipboard man nodded in the direction of the chain and said something, a question. He raised the clipboard meaningfully, patting it with his free hand. The clipboard was important. This was all about the clipboard. I didn't say anything; instead I examined the men as closely as my sleep-slowed mind would allow, looking for clues to their purpose. Their overalls were clean, but worn. Each had a green logo on the breast pocket, a stylised house. It seemed very unfair to have to put in all this mental effort first thing in the morning. I wanted the men to go, to leave me alone.

'We go in?' the tall man with the tools and the developed language skills asked. Clipboard man glanced back at his colleague and flashed a smile at me.

'I don't know,' I said. I really didn't. The end of the door's guard chain was taking more and more of my attention, this little metal knob in its slot. It was an absurdly small thing, such a tiny ally, no obstacle. A hard charge with a shoulder could break the chain, surely. Maybe not my shoulder, but clipboard man looked like he could have broken a few doors in his career.

'Does Oskar know about this?' I asked.

A fractional turn of the planet, then much nodding, affirmative noises, 'Oskar, Oskar'. Clipboard man reached into his breast pocket and pulled out a gnawed biro, which he tapped against the forms on the clipboard. He looked at me, wide-eyed, still expectant, and mimed a flourishing signature in the air between us.

Was Oskar being evicted? I was sure that he owned this flat – he had redecorated, and replaced the floors. But I wasn't really familiar with the workings of property law in my own country, let alone this place. I could imagine Byzantine apartment block covenants that restricted leaseholders' natural rights to dispose of dead cats and engage in knife fights with the concierge ... I could imagine that easily. For now, the workmen seemed benign, even sympathetic, but I was sure they could quickly become impatient.

I released the chain and opened the door. The clipboard was immediately thrust at me. Yellow sheets of flimsy copy-paper, covered in smudged fields and boxes. Most of the areas had been ticked or filled in by another hand and a large X indicated the empty dotted line at the bottom. None of it was remotely comprehensible. The only part I came close to understanding was the logo, the same as the insignia on the overalls, a house simplified down to the most basic house-ness.

'Wait,' I said, 'what's this?'

The two men in overalls looked at each other uncomfortably and then shrugged as one.

'I can't sign this,' I said. 'I don't know what I'm signing. I need to speak to Oskar. He owns the flat.' Clipboard man gave no indication that he had understood any of this. He was still holding out the biro. 'One moment, one minute,' I said, raising a finger. 'I am going to make a phone call.' I mimed 'telephone', holding a fist to my ear with thumb and little finger outstretched.

When I returned to the living room, the sight of the stained, pried-up floorboards hit me as if I was seeing it for the first time. It was as if someone else had done it, and I was now discovering the disaster. But for someone else, this shock and amazement at the damage done to the flat might turn into anger; for me it had nowhere to go but remorse and self-loathing.

Standing amid Oskar's designer furniture, I closed my eyes and held them closed. Perhaps, I thought, all this might recede and I would wake up elsewhere. But my sense of my situation remained like the lingering blotches of light left on the eyes by a camera flash. I could get no more conscious – this was it, awakeness. When I opened my eyes again, the men had followed me into the living room. They had seen the floor and were talking quietly, seriously, to each other. Together, they shot a glance at me – no anger or judgement, but a curiosity that could have been wariness. Did they know I was dangerous? Did they know I had killed someone?

And it occurred to me that I could kill them. Then I would be left alone to deal with the floor.

But I hadn't killed anyone.

'There was an accident,' I said, acknowledging the floor.

The taller, bespectacled man nodded wisely. 'Accident,' he repeated, carefully, trying out the word.

I tried to do the mental arithmetic that would give me the time in Los Angeles, but it came apart in my mind like wet tissue paper. The number of Oskar's hotel was a row of nonsense when I first looked at it, and I had to blink to make it legible. Time felt stretchy and sticky; I wondered if I was still drunk. It seemed like a safe bet.

A Californian accent said the name of the hotel. At that moment, that voice seemed like the only real thing in the world. She connected me to Oskar's room; there was a harsh beep and a sequence of electronic clicks and chatters before recorded music took over; solo piano. I tried to clear my head, to arrange the words I wanted to say, to picture Oskar's face. But all I could see, all I could think about, was his flat, the precise picture of what Oskar wanted to be, which I had ruined, and which was now invaded, compromised. For a moment I wanted to cry, but the music cut out with a dead star crackle.

'Yes?' Oskar said.

'Oskar, it's me,' I said.

'I know.'

'Oskar, there are some men here – they look like workmen,' I said. 'I don't know what they want, but they're asking me to sign something.'

'They're early,' Oskar said. 'I did not think they would be this quick.'

'What?' I said. 'Who are they?'

'I called yesterday,' Oskar answered, 'but you did not pick up. They are removal men. They are here to estimate how much it will cost for me to move out of the flat.'

I swallowed. It was like gulping down a rusty ballbearing. My lips were dry. Oskar sounded very calm.

'You're leaving the flat?'

'Yes.'

'Because of me?'

'Yes.'

There were tiny noises on the line, perhaps the sound of Oskar switching the phone receiver from one hand to another.

'I got your message,' he said. I realised that I hadn't spoken in a while. Wine-blurred memories shuffled around. I remembered leaving the message; I remembered asking the receptionist to be precise. But the details of its contents escaped me.

'About the floors?' I asked, partly a guess.

'Yes,' Oskar said. 'I already knew. Michael mentioned it. So did Ada.'

'Ada?'

'The cleaning woman. I spoke with her yesterday evening.' Yesterday evening? How was that possible? Perhaps she wasn't dead after all. Hope and terror rose in me, a jolt like the final moment of a horror film when the killer is shown to have survived. Then I remembered the time zones.

'Right, yesterday morning?' I felt pinned to the spot, surrounded by tripwires.

'Yes,' Oskar said with a hint of impatience. 'I wanted to tell her that the workmen were coming, so she would let them in.'

'Right,' I said, my mind spinning. The knife, the blood. 'She was, uh, quite upset about the floor,' I added cautiously.

'Yes,' Oskar said, his voice plain, hard to read. 'I don't suppose it matters now. Since I am going.' I willed him to elaborate, to say more, to give some sign of what he knew about the floor, the cat, the knife. 'Are the men still there?' was all he asked.

They were still there, silently watching me on the phone from across the room, both wearing the same expression of guarded affability, as if I were a potentially dangerous mental patient. I wondered how I looked; not good, surely, after a night on the floor.

'Yes, they're here,' I said.

'Sign the form. Let them work while we talk. There are things I must tell you.'

I walked over to the workmen, took the clipboard, and signed. The after-effects of last night's drinking – of the week's drinking – made my hand tremble, and I made a messy job of it. The unnatural scrawl was hard to recognise as my name, but it would do. The men smiled and started to discuss something between them, like statues coming to life. Removal men – Oskar was moving, because of me. I sat on one of the soft leather chairs in the living room and picked up the phone again.

'Oskar,' I began, wanting the initiative in the conversation, 'why are you moving out? What do you mean, it's because of me?'

'Because of you, yes,' Oskar said. 'There is a lot of damage to the floors, yes?'

'Yes, but I'm sure they can be fixed,' I said, hurriedly. 'I can pay, if you want a professional ...'

'No, no,' Oskar said. 'I will have them sanded, but it's not important. There was some damage already, I think you saw.'

I decided to play one of my cards. 'I took up a board,' I said, 'to see if it could be reversed, to hide some damage. In the kitchen. I saw that the underside was damaged, too.' As we talked, I was trying to analyse Oskar's tone. It was a difficult job – there was a strange, suppressed quality to his voice, as if he was holding back from something. But it wasn't the anger that I had expected, it was something else.

One the other side of the flat, the workmen were in the study, measuring the piano.

'So you saw the note, then,' Oskar said. 'Laura threw a bottle at me ...' There was an unidentifiable noise on the line. It was not electronic – was Oskar crying?

No. He was chuckling.

'I am sorry,' he said, containing himself. 'It is funny ... You see, Laura and I have decided to make another try. We have stopped the divorce. I am moving because I am coming here, to America. We will try again here. I will finish my symphony and live with Laura. There is a great deal of space here.' His tone was unmistakable now – he was happy. He was excited. It had been some time since I had heard him in this state.

But it was hard to believe. 'Wow, Oskar, wow,' I mumbled inanely. 'What about the flat? Your job? The cats?' I bit off the *s* at the end of cats.

'The flat will be sold. The men will ship me some of my things, the rest can go into storage for now. The Philharmonic will have to find someone else. They will survive, I am quite replaceable.' Modesty – he was in a rare mood indeed. 'The cats ...'

'Oskar –' I broke in. 'The cats – one of the cats died. I'm sorry.'

Silence. And then: 'Which one?'

'I don't know. I was never really clear which was which. Its tail had a white tip.'

'Stravinsky,' Oskar said solemnly. 'That's very sad. I'm sorry you had to deal with that.'

'It was ... no trouble,' I said. Sympathy was not what I expected.

'How did he die?'

'Just an accident, I think,' I said. 'I left the piano up, and the lid somehow fell on him. I think. I didn't see what happened. I found him dead.' Another silence yawned open in the conversation. I couldn't help myself. 'It wasn't my fault. Just an accident.'

Oskar laughed. 'Of course, of course. Was the piano damaged?'

'No.'

A contemplative pause. 'It's very sad. Poor Stravvy. He was a good cat. How is Shossy?'

'He was fine the last time I saw him,' I said carefully, wishing against follow-up questions. 'I'm very sorry about Stravvy – it was an accident, you know, I found him dead, I couldn't do anything ...' Stop talking, stop talking, fool.

'Yes, I know,' Oskar said. 'It's OK, really. I suppose it does simplify things – the cats will go to stay with Michael and now there is just one for him.'

'What about me?' I asked. 'Do you need me to stay any longer?'

'No, no,' Oskar said. 'The building is quite secure, Ada can look after the flat until it is cleared and sold. Michael will come later today to take Shossy. You can leave now if you want. Did Ada come up with the workmen? Can I talk with her?'

I froze. Of course he could not talk with Ada. Ada was not here. Maybe this was the moment to tell the truth. Every time I had lied, or concealed the truth, the misfortune around me had intensified. Candour had worked, though: I had told Oskar about the floors, about the cat, and had emerged unscathed.

'Oskar ...'

A fusillade of sound cut me short, making me jump, a cascading jangle that took a long half-second to process, to understand – 'Chopsticks' played loudly and without finesse in the study. One of the workmen was playing the piano with impressive gusto, if not much talent.

'What, what's that?' Oskar said sharply. 'Is someone playing the piano?'

'Uh, yeah, one of the men,' I said.

'Well, *tell them to stop*!' It was still the old Oskar.

'Hey! Hey! Stop that!' I shouted in the direction of the study. The impromptu recital terminated and clipboard man poked his head around the study door, a stagey expression of regret on his face.

Oskar tutted, a sound so crisp that for a moment I thought it was the click of the call being ended. 'Do you see? Whenever there is a stranger in the flat, there is trouble. Maybe the flat is the problem.'

'Oskar ...' I paused, trying to formulate my question. When I shifted in the seat, my shirt clung to my back. I needed a shower. 'Oskar, if you don't need someone in the flat, if Michael can take care of the cats, the cat, why did you need me to come here at all?'

A sigh was transmitted across the Atlantic. It would be getting late there, I thought. 'A little of it is like I told you – I did not feel comfortable leaving the flat unoccupied for such a long time. But you are right, there was another consideration. After I had that final fight with Laura, when she threw that bottle of wine at me, at the floor ... Much of that fight was about the flat, and the flat was a big subject in the talks we had before deciding to divorce. I had been very angry with Laura because she had damaged the floors, but she believed that I was being unreasonable. Accidents happen, she said ... She felt it was wrong to devote so much effort to keeping the flat perfect. I told her that I did not feel it was too much to ask, and that she was being very careless about my wishes and my property. The disagreement was a barrier between us. Laura said that I had made my flat inhospitable, and it was a sign that I was not ready to share anything with anyone.'

He trailed off. The taller workman had joined me in the living room and was measuring the sofa with a metal tape. It added its hard little noises to the muted sounds of the street, closing at the push of a button with a hiss and a snap. The bell of a tram sounded below us, and I heard its juddering approach.

'Faced with these problems, we formed a plan, an idea,' Oskar continued. 'A test. We knew that I would have to come to California to arrange things ... rather than leave the flat empty, I would invite someone to stay. A third party.

'If this third party damaged the flat – in particular the floors – then Laura was right, no reasonable person could live there and be expected to keep everything perfect. I believed that, with proper instruction, it was a simple matter to live in the flat without damage. Laura said I could leave whatever instructions I wanted. We had to agree on the right person, and you were perfect. She had met you, you see. You were perfect.'

'A test?' I didn't know what else to say.

'If something happened to the floor, to the flat, then Laura was right – the situation was too fragile, damage is inevitable, it's not the fault of the culprit, the fault lies with me, with the flat,' Oskar said. 'If nothing happened, then I was right – it is possible for anyone to live in the flat and stick to the proper way of doing things and keep everything perfect. I could show her that even you could manage it, and you, my friend, are chaos.'

'I don't understand,' I said, although I understood perfectly. 'I'm not a ... *rat* in a maze. I don't like to be tested to see if I *measure up*.' Anger had risen inside me, but I wasn't feeling it – it was an abstract, separated thing for me to contemplate. It was as if I felt I should be angry, and here it was, to be deployed if needed.

'It wasn't a test with a right or wrong answer, something that you could fail,' Oskar said. 'It just had two outcomes, A or B, and we wanted to see which it was.' And I could see that this was a perfect joint venture between Oskar and Laura – his prissy pedantry combined neatly with her passive-aggressive non-judgemental therapy-speak.

'Fucking hell,' I said. I had felt myself coiling up with tension, but now that was passing – on an ocean of stress, the tide was going out. 'Were you ever really planning to divorce? Was that just a ruse?'

'No, that was real,' Oskar said kindly. Earlier I had detected a note of triumph in his voice which had bordered on smugness or mockery – now it was gone. 'We both thought it would happen, the papers are prepared ... but when Michael told me about the stain, we started to talk properly again, and after I spoke with Ada it was clear that Laura had been right. Maybe it will not work, but we will try again.'

'Wouldn't you feel used,' I said, 'in my situation?'

'I don't think I would be in that situation,' Oskar replied with total assurance. 'I am grateful to you, anyway.'

'Right,' I said. 'Well, you're welcome.' I wanted very much to be enraged with Oskar, to shout and call him names. But I was not certain how I had been injured by him, other than the general insult of his behaviour. And he had absolved me of responsibility for the floors, the cat, everything – he did not seem to care. That, I felt, was fuelling my desire to be angry: I wanted us both to be furious, to scream at each other, to nuke the friendship and be done with it. Some sort of settling-up was needed – but I did not know where I stood or, really, what I thought about any of this.

'It is a hostile environment,' I said. 'Your flat – it's not relaxing. It made me very uncomfortable, from the beginning. In a way, I hate it.'

'The flat, or me?' Oskar asked. 'I know that I am sometimes not the easiest person to know. This is something I will have to work on.'

'In LA?'

'In LA. This is not a bad place, I have decided. There is culture, after all. There is the ocean. It is good to be near the ocean.' I heard a yawn being stifled on the Pacific coast.

'Will you come back at all?' I asked. However relaxed Oskar might sound now, it seemed inconceivable that he would let his flat be emptied by strangers without supervision. I hoped this was merely a new lease of life, not a nervous breakdown.

'Sure,' Oskar answered. 'I'll come back in a week or two to take care of things. There's no need for you to wait for that.'

'So what now?' I asked.

'What now?' I heard Oskar exhale wearily. 'Now, you can go home if you want.'

I remembered calling the airline, but only now did I feel as if I might actually be going to the airport.

'There's a flight this afternoon,' I said. 'I'm pretty sure I'll still be able to get on it.'

'I can arrange for a taxi if you want,' Oskar said. 'I know a number. Is noon good?'

That gave me more than two hours to pack. 'Fine,' I said. 'Thanks.'

'I'll call them after we finish,' Oskar said, back to a familiar, businesslike tone. 'Leave the keys on the table in the kitchen. Give me a call when you get back. You should come out here some time and visit us.'

'I'd like that,' I said, finding such a trip hard to imagine.

'Thanks again for looking after the flat.'

'No problem,' I said weakly. 'OK then. Noon. I'll give you a call.'

'See you soon, then,' Oskar said.

'See you soon, Oskar,' I replied, thinking that it was unlikely to be true. A moment of silence passed across continents, the last instant of the life of something, and there was a rattle and click.

I packed my clothes and toiletries on top of unread, unopened books. My passport was still in the inside pocket of my jacket, with the boarding-pass stub from my last flight. It took very little time to pack – I had brought little and picked up few souvenirs. Ticket stubs from the concert and strip club, a tram timetable.

After some thought, I collected up a handful of Oskar's notes – from the kitchen table, from Novack's book, from under the bed and under the floor – and slipped them into my bag.

There was food in the fridge – it would rot if I left it, so I ate a large, unusual breakfast and threw the rest away. On top of the discarded food, I put the balled-up half-finished notes I had written to Oskar the previous night. They were obsolete, there was nothing more to say. I had not been able to put down on paper what had happened with the cleaner. With Ada. It was all useless explanations of the state of the floor – but even those seemed empty without talking about everything else that had happened. The cat food was scraped on top of them, and I put a fresh can-load on the dish. Then I pulled the bag out of the bin, knotted it, took it from the flat, and dropped it down the rubbish chute. There was no one in the hall. The silence was patient, understanding.

The workmen completed their measuring and departed, with a near-mute charade of smiles and bows to indicate goodbye. Oskar's flat had been reduced to a set of dimensions and estimated weights, jotted by stubby pencil into black-bound notebooks. The place felt larger without them, but also finite, exhausted. With time enough to spare, I slotted the stained floorboards back into their place. The nails needed only the slightest tap-tap-tap with the hammer and they were driven home, back into their old holes. It was satisfying work, constructive and simple, and the result was no worse than it was before I took up the boards.

It was after eleven. I showered, and moved my bag into the hall. Then I roamed the quiet flat, looking at every room, making tiny adjustments – replacing CDs on their shelves, making the bed, cleaning my plate and glass, emptying the dishwasher, picking up the little steel paring knife with a napkin and returning it to its drawer. The courtesy seemed utterly futile, and was certainly more than I wanted to do for Oskar, but the little jobs needed to be done and I felt compelled to do them. In the light of what Oskar had said, returning things to the way that they were on the day that I arrived took on an unpleasant complexion. Everything had been in place for a precise reason. Oskar had built a machine – a device for proving his superiority over other people. He – and maybe only he – could move through this space without touching the sides, while lower forms blundered and thrashed about, leaving our shameful signature. It was like a sieve through which only Oskar's higher sort of human being could pass.

But for the floors, and the sofa, and the porn, and the dead and missing, the flat was restored to order. I took down one of Oskar's architecture books and sat in the living room. Pages of new museums flicked past, empty white spaces in expressive boxes scattered across the world. The light outside surged and failed as the high sun was repeatedly interrupted by clouds. Trams passed, their rhythm the same as it was every day, enlivened sometimes by the ringing of the bell.

The door buzzer sounded, making me jump. At the other end of the intercom, a hoarse voice said 'Taxi'. I told him I would be right down.

For the last time, I ran through a mental checklist of things I might have forgotten. It occurred to me that I had left the bedroom window open, so I went through to close it.

In the bedroom, the cat was lying on the bed. Hearing me come in, it looked up, and rolled onto its back, wriggling comfortably. I smiled at it and moved to stroke its stomach. It purred happily.

'Hello again,' I said to it. 'Thanks for coming back.'

I closed the bedroom window and addressed the cat again. It regarded me with complacent semi-interest.

'I'm leaving now,' I said. 'Michael will be here later. I'm sorry about your friend. There's food in the kitchen, if you want it.'

It blinked and hopped off the bed as I left the room, and followed me through to the kitchen. Shossy, I thought, watching it – him – tuck into the heaped dish of food, once again oblivious to me. 'Goodbye, Shossy,' I said. I dropped the keys on the kitchen table, took a last look at the living room and walked out, shutting the front door firmly behind me.

The old fabric of the city gave way quickly, and the taxi rocked along a rough-skinned expressway flanked by fading yellow blocks of flats. The bodywork of the cab rattled and squeaked, and Jesus dangled nervously from the rear-view mirror, swinging and twisting. In the sky were huge, unlikely, weightless clouds.

I watched the blocks of flats pass one after the other, like pages turning in a book. As each moved by, it revealed a new random selection of life inside: washing hung out, satellite dishes, flags in windows, children's toys on balconies. The reflected sun raced across the façade of each block, flashing from many windows, and the block was gone, maybe never to be seen again. I thought about how I left Oskar's flat, empty and quiet, tidy but ruined, and wondered how many people would glimpse it today from the rolling trams and traffic. Tidying the flat in those last moments had been like re-setting a trap, I now realised. Oskar's psychological experiment, which would establish whether dumb, chaotic humanity could rise to his expectations. Conclusion: no. It was like a complicated mousetrap, with one-way doors and buttons to press and electrified floors.

But I wasn't the only one trapped. My flat, with the black freckles of mould on the ceiling above the bath and the grey marks on the walls around the light switches, did not feel all that bad now. It was at least absent from my mind. It made few demands on me. What had obsessed me, sitting in its magnolia spaces, staring at the smudges on its window panes, was not the actual flat, it was another, imaginary flat, the possible flat, the ideal flat. It was the idea of perfection – that if I had a better place, I could be a better person. And I was similar to Oskar in that; he thought that way, and he had built his place. Laura had been right – in making a home for himself, Oskar had excluded everyone else. The trap snared him more fiercely than anyone. He had been obliged to find someone to cut him loose. But I, I was free. I had always been free, but in love with the idea of bars. I was at peace with being in chaos.

Beyond the window, the city had undergone another change, almost disappearing. We were on a newer stretch of expressway which hissed contentedly under the wheels of the taxi. Around us were the quasi-urban shed territories, giant grey distribution warehouses and container farms behind quivering razor wire; outposts of American fast-food franchises, with twenty-four-hour neon and low-pitched roofs barely distinguishable from the beetle-backed cars sunning themselves around them; giant plots of dead land, vacant but for litter and Martian plant-life, billboards at their side promising thousands upon thousands of square metres of new space, to open one year, two years hence. New space, a world made over. Brown mountains piled up against the horizon. Jets pointed themselves at the sun. The world was unlimited.

ACKNOWLEDGEMENTS

This book would never have been completed without the advice and encouragement of my agent, Antony Topping. Clare Smith, my editor at HarperPress, has been a passionate champion of the book. Fatima Fernandes' sympathetic ear kept me going. Peter Smith made perceptive remarks on an early draft. Hazel Tsoi-Wiles helped me in innumerable ways.